"A fast-moving ... series."
—Sheila ...

"Perfect timing! In her charming ... ...nes creates the perfect contemporary cozy—with a smart and engaging heroine, a quirky and mysterious Berkshires town, and a cast of characters to rival any who live in Cabot Cove. Don't waste another minute—this is your new favorite series!"
—Hank Phillippi Ryan, Agatha, Anthony, and Mary Higgins Clark award–winning author of the Jane Ryland series

"The clock ticks ever faster in this delightful debut mystery . . . The story, with a hunky barber, Ruth's childhood friends, and conflicts between the new town manager and the 'old' Orchard, winds up to a suspenseful and satisfying end."
—Edith Maxwell, Agatha Award–nominated and national bestselling author of the Local Foods Mysteries

"Take one tightly wound plot, a charming clock shop in the Berkshires, a woman you want to be your best friend, and you have *Just Killing Time*. Don't waste any time, read this book."
—Sherry Harris, Agatha Award–nominated author of the Sarah Winston Garage Sale Mysteries

"With its bucolic setting, engaging characters, and clever plotting, Julianne Holmes has crafted a mystery to stand the test of time."
—Jessie Crockett, national bestselling author of the Sugar Grove Mysteries

"The Clock Shop Mystery series has zoomed to the top of my must-purchase-on-release-day list. *Just Killing Time* offers an intriguing premise, a fun mystery, and a town and heroine with heart."
—Barbara Ross, author of the Maine Clambake Mysteries

just
killing
time

JULIANNE HOLMES

BERKLEY PRIME CRIME, NEW YORK

BERKLEY PRIME CRIME

An imprint of Penguin Random House LLC
375 Hudson Street, New York, New York 10014

JUST KILLING TIME

A Berkley Prime Crime Book / published by arrangement with the author

ISBN: 978-0-425-27552-8

PUBLISHING HISTORY
Berkley Prime Crime mass-market edition / October 2015

PRINTED IN THE UNITED STATES OF AMERICA

10 9 8 7 6 5 4 3 2 1

Cover illustration by Cathy Gendron; *Clock Face* © by harlowbutler.
Cover design by Danielle Abbiate.
Interior text design by Laura K. Corless.

Penguin
Random
House

To Paul and Cynthia Hennrikus.
They passed on their love of mysteries.
And they made me believe anything was possible.
Thank you for being wonderful parents.

acknowledgments

That you are holding this book in your hand is a dream come true. I'd like to thank two people who played a critical role in this effort, Allison Janice, my editor; and John Talbot, my agent. Thank you both for your support, your attention to detail, and your belief in me.

I would not be on this journey were it not for Sisters in Crime, especially the New England chapter. This wonderful organization has provided me mentors, friends, and a cheerleading section over the years. I am a proud board member. I am also a member of Mystery Writers of America, another wonderful organization for crime writers.

In 2013, Sherry Harris wrote to a few of us and asked about starting a blog. The Wicked Cozy Authors (wickedcozyauthors .com) were born. Being a part of this group has made such a difference in my life. All of these women forged the path I am now on and have been instrumental in helping me navigate it. Thank you to Jessie Crockett, Liz Mugavero, Barbara Ross, and Edith Maxwell for friendship and support. And a special thank-you to Sherry Harris for her editor's eye.

Thank you to Jason Allen-Forrest, my first reader. To Sergeant Patrick Towle of the Bedford Police Department. To David and James Roberts of the Clockfolk of New England. To Liz Bolton, for her guidance on real estate matters. To my blogmates at Live to Write/Write to Live (nhwn.wordpress .com): Lisa J. Jackson, Diane MacKinnon, Lee Laughlin, Jamie Wallace, Susan Nye, and Wendy Thomas. And to everyone else who gave me guidance and advice while I was working on this book. Your help was invaluable, and any mistakes are my own.

And finally, a huge thank-you to my friends and family. Where would I be without parents like Paul and Cindy Hennrikus? Sisters like Kristen Spence and Caroline Lentz? Brothers-in-law like Bryan Spence and Glenn Lentz? Nieces and nephews like Chase, Mallory, Harrison, Becca, Tori, Emma, and Evan? My amazing friends? I am one of the luckiest women in the world. None of this would be as much fun without all of you in my life.

chapter 1

The brochure lied. A week in the mountains of Vermont had not, in fact, helped me achieve a peaceful Zen that would pervade my life for the coming weeks, helping me approach old challenges with fresh energy. Instead it had made me aware of two things. First, much as I hated to admit it, I was addicted to technology. Not being allowed to have my cell phone for seven days was an interesting experiment at first, but an exercise in frustration toward the end. Never mind that the battery was completely drained of power by the time I got it back.

The second realization? Coffee and I couldn't break up. I did wonder, briefly, if a week of no coffee had crushed the addiction. The green tea I'd drunk by the bucketful had enough caffeine to keep the headaches mostly at bay. And I knew that any addiction was a vice. But honestly, aside from the occasional glass of wine or beer, coffee was it. Coffee and baked goods. I walked into the first coffee shop I found on my way back to civilization. I ordered the French roast but hesitated before I ordered the scone. It looked dry and a little anemic. Not worth it, I decided. Maybe that was progress? I did grab a protein bar and filled up my water bottle at the water station in the store.

I took the coffee back out to the car and sat inside with the key turned and the windows cracked. I plugged in my phone, but it didn't come back to life right away. I took a deep breath and looked out the window at the view. October was a stunning time to live in New England. The leaves were turning and the mountains were smeared with splashes of orange, red, yellow, and brown in between the deep green of the pines. The air was crisp, but not cold. Layers were necessary. The sky was a stunning crystal clear blue with white puffy clouds. Even I had to admit the scenery was beautiful. Especially with a cup of coffee. I closed my eyes and took a sip. Heaven.

I unwrapped the protein bar and grabbed my black bound notebook from my bag. I'd taken to carrying one notebook and using it as a combination journal, to-do list, sketchbook, and message pad. I took a bite of the protein bar, which tasted like chemicals. I should have tried the scone. I'd inherited the notebook habit from my grandfather, and he'd inherited it from his father. There were boxes of notebooks from all the Clagan clockmakers in my grandfather's attic. Or at least the past four generations, since the first generation had emigrated from Europe.

I wondered if the notebooks were still there, or if G.T.'s wife had tossed them. What was her name, anyway? I honestly couldn't remember. I'd nicknamed my grandfather G.T., Grandpa Thom, when I was a little girl, during one of my summer-long visits to my grandparents' house in Orchard,

Massachusetts. It wasn't that he was ashamed of being my grandfather, my grandmother had explained. It was that *Grandpa* wasn't professional in the shop. So G.T. it was. If that was the rule for working in the shop, I was more than happy to comply. Because my summer visits hadn't just been a welcome reprieve from my parents' benign neglect, they had been my introduction to clocks and time and how humans could work with both. G.T. was a master clockmaker, and he had passed on his passion, and some of his skill, to me.

I turned on my phone, which finally booted up. I checked the time and smiled. There was great accuracy to the clock on my cell phone, but little art. Time could be so much more. I flexed my shoulders back and mentally prepared myself to check my voice mail. I had been in a vulnerable place during a "Healing" workshop at my yoga retreat last week, and I'd sent G.T. a postcard asking him if I could stop by on my way back to Boston. My grandmother's death six years ago had broken both of our hearts. G.T. and I had a falling-out when I brought my then husband (now ex) to meet him and they didn't hit it off. The falling-out became a full-out rift when he called me a couple of months later to tell me he had gotten remarried. I'd sent him Christmas and birthday cards, and he'd sent them to me, but we hadn't seen each other in five years. It was time to change that.

When the phone rang, I almost spilled my coffee. I didn't recognize the number, but the 413 area code identified it as western Massachusetts. Maybe G.T. had a cell phone?

"Ruth Clagan here." I sounded so officious, even to myself.

"Miss Clagan, this is Kristen Gauger. I'm a lawyer here in Marytown. And a friend of your grandfather's. I'm afraid I have some very bad news."

chapter 2

G.T. was dead. Kristen Gauger was not only G.T.'s friend and a lawyer, she was *his* lawyer. They'd found the postcard I sent him at his shop, the Cog & Sprocket, and had been trying to reach me all week. The reading of the will was today. Would I possibly be able to make it?

"Reading of the will?"

"There are some issues that need to be addressed in the next few days. We decided to do the reading this afternoon so we could start getting the will processed through probate. At one o'clock. Might you possibly make it?"

"What time is it now?" I looked down at my watch. "Eleven o'clock. I can try, but it will be tough. I'm up in Vermont."

"We could reschedule, but there's a preliminary meeting

with the Board of Selectmen at three, and the contents of the will may have some impact on the meeting."

"Really?" My grandfather had always been a concerned citizen. The Clagans were one of the oldest families in Orchard. But still, impacting a town meeting?

"Ruth, I'll tell you what. Write down this address and come to my office when you get to town. We'll delay as long as we can." She gave me her address in Marytown, which I wrote down in a shaky scrawl and then programmed into my GPS.

"I've got it," I said. "I'll be there as soon as possible. I don't even, I mean, wow, this is starting to sink in. What happened? Had G.T. been sick? We've been out of touch. I'd hate to think I wasn't there to say good-bye." There was a long pause on the phone. For a second, I thought we'd been disconnected.

"Oh, Ruth, there's no easy way to say this. I'd rather tell you in person, but you should hear it from me. They think that Thom died of a heart attack. But he was being robbed at the time. The police are treating it as a murder."

I was riding an emotional roller coaster as I drove toward Orchard. Sadness and grief overwhelmed me. The ride down took almost five hours. Tears caused some of the delays. And there were a couple of times when I just needed to pull over and scream, trying to get rid of some of the emotions. Anger that I'd been robbed of the chance to see G.T. once more. Guilt that we'd been estranged. Overwhelming sadness. And a slow burn building up inside me.

Screaming in the car had been very cathartic for me over the past year as I tried to move past my divorce, and it helped this time as well. A little. Not enough. But some.

Even under the best of circumstances, chances were good I would have been late. I could build timepieces, but I couldn't keep time. An irony in my life—one of many.

But seeing the Berkshires again brought forth a flood of happy memories as I recognized old stomping grounds. I felt some pride in seeing how spruced up Main Street was. Of course, Main Street was always the center of attention, since it was in Marytown, the closest thing to a city in these parts. Six years ago I'd driven away from a region full of hardworking people trying to figure it all out. Some new businesses had brought economic vibrancy back, but the town was still a pale imitation of what it had once been, at least according to my grandparents. But now? Storefronts were open. The street itself was newly paved, with freshly painted lines. Streetlights had been replaced by gas lanterns. Marytown looked good. I wondered if Orchard had fared as well.

Had the town finally come into its own? After the last great flood wiped the town out in the 1920s, the townspeople of Orchard worked hard to bring the apple orchards back and to embrace the possibilities of the future, but true prosperity always passed the small town by. I used to refer to Orchard as the town that almost was. Almost was the site of a railroad station, until another community won the bid. Almost saw a new mill built after the flood, but the aforementioned railroad station took that off the table. Almost was the site of a huge private college in the early 1900s, but that honor also went to another town, five miles south.

Maybe Orchard's luck had changed, even if G.T.'s hadn't.

• • •

Kristen Gauger had directed me to the offices of Gauger, Spence, Colfer, and Lentz in Marytown. A lot of names for a tiny office that consisted of two desks, three chairs, and a couch.

"Ruth? I'm Kristen Gauger." She walked around her desk and held out her hand. I shook it and walked toward the desk. Kristen Gauger was shorter than I was, but the high heels she'd kicked off would have made us eye to eye. She had brown hair streaked with gray and pulled back into a ponytail. Her makeup was a little smudged and there were dark circles under her brown eyes. Her shirt was untucked from her suit skirt.

"Let's sit over here." She motioned me toward the couch. "Can I get you anything? You sure? Well, sit down while I pull the file. Forgive the office clutter. A bunch of us share the space. We have 'offices' all over the Berkshires, but most of them involve our dining room tables and home visits with clients. You made decent time getting here."

"Not good enough. I missed the reading. And I must have missed the funeral," I said. I sounded pitiful, but she didn't seem to notice.

"There hasn't been a funeral. Thom didn't want one, according to his will. Caroline would still like to have a service, but wanted to talk to you."

That was her name, Caroline. G.T's wife.

"Your folks already told Caroline they aren't planning on coming back," she continued.

I'd long ago given up making excuses for my world-traveling parents, and so I didn't respond. We e-mailed and talked on occasion, but I hadn't seen them in a couple of years. Again, Kristen didn't respond to my silence, but instead moved on.

"I'm sorry you had to hear the news from me that way. But I know you have a few voice mails and I thought you should hear it from a human being."

"Thank you, I barely listened to my messages. I just wanted to get here."

"Well, you should know, he didn't suffer. He got hit in the head and then he had a heart attack. It was pretty quick."

"Where was he?"

"Out in back of the shop, getting into his car. There had been a robbery a couple of weeks before, and the police are assuming that the robbers came back for a second round and ran into Thom."

"A robbery? What did they steal?"

"The first time? Five clocks. I don't have the descriptions handy, but Caroline says they were worth about a thousand dollars each."

"Wow. What was he doing with that kind of inventory?"

"He had bought out a couple of estate sales recently. Including the Winters' house. Do you remember Grover Winter? He passed three months ago, and his son, Jonah, has been selling off the estate. Apparently he and his late wife were clock fanatics."

"I remember him. Wasn't his nickname the Chairman?"

Kristen nodded.

"I don't remember her that well."

"Harriet," Kristen supplied. "She passed last fall. She'd been sick for a long while. But the Chairman, his death took everyone by surprise. Anyway, Thom has a full shop."

"He always did," I said, sadness overwhelming me.

My life with my grandparents had been filled with clocks. Both real and imagined. We used to spend hours designing clocks that would do all sorts of things. And dream of building them together once I finished my education. I thought about the drawings I'd made while I was on retreat and realized I'd give anything to show them to my grandfather and talk to him about what I'd been working on lately. But that was never going to happen.

Kristen handed me a box of tissues, and I wiped my eyes.

"He'd actually cut back on the inventory last winter, but then he bought a couple of estates of collectors lately. He called them his swan song before retirement. Not sure if it helps or not, but he was making noise about offering to let you buy him out. I offered to help him find you, but he wanted to get things cleaned up first. His words, not mine."

"I'm not sure if that helps or not either. Makes me sadder."

"Well, then, this isn't going to help at all." She handed me a thick envelope. "His will was pretty straightforward. Caroline gets the house and everything in it. You get the Cog & Sprocket and everything in it. According to the will, you need to come to terms regarding the contents of the workshop at the house. There are some other bequests, but they can be taken care of easily. Right now his estate is tied up in inventory, so there isn't any cash to speak of. But he owned the shop; taxes are paid. If you want to sell, it should get a fair amount."

"The shop? I don't know what to say."

"Well, I have a couple of things to say. First, you should know that Jeff Paisley—he's the chief of police in Orchard— he's working on this case morning, noon, and night. Second,

Caroline Adler has an alibi, just in case you were wondering. She was also in Vermont, visiting her son."

Again, I didn't respond directly. "Anything else?"

Kristen shook her head slightly and smiled. "You remind me of your grandfather. There are a couple of codicils to the will. Not binding, but Thom's wishes. He made Caroline promise to give you first dibs if and when she sells the house. And he asked that you consider keeping Caroline and Pat Reed on in the shop, if you chose to run it. She's been helping Thom run it for the past few years, keeping the books. And Pat has been working there part-time for a while."

"Forever. When I was young I never understood what Pat did. G.T. called him a handyman and the most important part of the operation."

"Pat and Nancy Reed are part of the backbone of Orchard. They helped see the town through some hard times. Now that things are turning around, I hope they benefit. But times are still tough for a lot of folks. Your grandfather kept Pat on the payroll even when he was slowing down. Pat's taking his death very hard."

"I haven't seen Pat in a while, since my grandmother's funeral."

"Well, he's looking forward to seeing you. Ruth, I know you are processing a lot right now, and I don't want to overwhelm you. But there's a lot going on in Orchard, mostly having to do with rezoning the historic district."

"Historic district?" I couldn't help but smile. "Since when does Orchard have a historic district?"

"Since the new town administrator decided to make Orchard a Berkshires destination town. The Cog & Sprocket is central to the district in more ways than one. Anyway, I know you're going to have questions, so take this packet with you and go through it when you have a moment. I put all my contact information on the envelope. Call me day or night with any questions or concerns. Anything.

"The key to the shop is in the envelope. Pat Reed has the other one. There are new locks on the doors, and a security system is being installed. Despite everything, being there is perfectly safe, so don't worry about that. Let me know when you are going there, and I'll let Pat and Caroline know. I don't know when the last time you visited was, but there's still a place to stay upstairs."

"I remember. My grandparents lived up in that apartment before they bought the cottage, and I spent a lot of time there in the summers as a child."

"Sounds perfect then. Though I have to warn you: there are a lot of clocks. A lot of clocks."

"There can never be too many clocks as far as I'm concerned. Don't worry about calling Pat or Caroline. I'll touch base with them tomorrow. I'll head over now. The Cog & Sprocket was my favorite place in the world. I can't imagine that will have changed. But I don't want to get there in the dark. It's closer than Boston, and I'm done in."

And so I made two brief calls, one to leave a voice mail for my boss at the museum, who I had been waiting to hear from about funding for my position, and the second to my friends Steve and Rick to let them know what was going on so they didn't call the police and start trawling the Charles River for my body. Then I got back in the car for the very short trip to the Cog & Sprocket. My shop.

chapter 3

I backtracked to Washington Street, deciding to go to the shop down the main thoroughfare of Orchard. I slowed down when I approached the official town line, where Main Street in Marytown became Washington Street in Orchard. We didn't make things easy for the tourists in the Berkshires. The faded old wooden sign from my childhood had been replaced, but the new, fancy, hand-painted sign still had the same image of the apple tree bearing fruit. I rolled my shoulders and let go of the steering wheel as I crossed into Orchard. I had a couple of miles to go before I hit the town center.

The fading October sunlight allowed me a full view of what I considered my hometown as I drove on. My happiest memories of my childhood were from Orchard. The library looming on my left marked the unofficial beginning of downtown, which I guess was the new historic district. I loved that library and had spent hours discovering new worlds while hiding in its stacks.

The Corner Market nestled next to the library, set back a bit from the street, with the coveted half-dozen parking spots in the front of the store. I noticed signs that said ORGANIC and LOCALLY GROWN in the windows. That couldn't be old Mr. Clark's doing, since he hadn't ever spent money on things like signage, shoveling in the winter, or sprucing up the outside in the spring. G.T. had always said Matthew Clark could squeeze blood from a stone, and I'd believed him. There must be new owners.

The old diner was across the street from the Corner Market, as out of place as always. I'd never understood how the Board of Selectmen talked the town into letting a '50s diner get approved, especially downtown. Chrome and polished steel had its charms, but here it just stood out like a sore thumb, especially since the chrome was only a façade, pasted onto a boring angular building to make it look more hip. The wooden building had a single story in the front, but rose to a second story in the back. The vaulted ceilings always made the insides look like a '50s diner and a hunting lodge had an illicit love child. My grandfather had tried to explain the backroom politics behind the approval of the building, but I couldn't remember the details. Just that it was meant as a slight to the chairman of the Board of Selectmen that term, one of the most ineffective selectmen in town history. I sighed. Orchard politics at its best: a permanent eyesore to upset a temporary politician. Or, on the other side of the coin, where dreams were thwarted when the dreamers got on the wrong side of the board.

The diner looked better though, its back half painted blue-gray and its trim painted black and white. Last time I'd been in town it was teal with bright pink trim. The red window boxes also softened it. But the neon teal, gray, and pink coffee cup still lit up the outside, with the new name in red cursive. The Sleeping Latte? Lattes? In Orchard? I could only imagine what my grandfather thought of that name. But if it meant coffee, that worked for me.

I saw the white siding of Parker's Emporium peeking over the top of the diner. I always loved that name—it elicited a much grander establishment than the assemblage of family businesses that all existed under one ad hoc roof. A drugstore took up the right half of the building. On the left side, the beauty parlor that sat at the front of the building was always a town center, where people went as much for gossip as for haircuts or blowouts. As an afterthought, there was a barbershop tacked on the back of the building. Flo Parker and her family had lived upstairs for as long as I remembered. I slowed down a bit. The drugstore still sat on the right-hand side, also with a face-lift, but the left-hand side had a large plate glass window replacing the paned bowfront window of the past. I saw a barber pole outside the shop. Was the beauty parlor gone? I slowed down to a crawl and peered to my right, looking for a name.

A bang on my hood jolted me. I'd been creeping so slowly the car barely registered stopping. I looked around and saw a tall, scruffy blond man on my left come into view just as I tapped the brakes. Worn jeans, old-school Levi's. A hoodie worn under a brown leather bomber jacket. Reddish blond hair worn a little long. A couple of days' growth of beard. Aviator sunglasses hid the eyes, but I'd bet they were blue.

Blue eyes would fit with the rest of the look. I rolled down my window to hear what he was yelling.

"Don't you have crosswalks back where you come from? Pay attention, lady. You almost hit my dog."

"Wow. Sorry, I didn't see the crosswalk. Is it new?" It may or may not have been new. I never used crosswalks in Orchard.

"New? What are you talking about?"

"Never mind. Sorry." I rolled the window back up, and the scruffy man just stood in front of my car, staring at me. I stared back, which wasn't hard. Sure, he needed a shave and a haircut. But the jeans fit well. Really well, from what I could see over the hood of my car. I stopped staring and looked back at his eyes. I smiled as sweetly as I could and waved him on.

I watched as he crossed the street, meeting the large Australian shepherd who sat on the corner, tail thumping behind him. The dog seemed none the worse for the near-death experience, and his owner went into Ben's Barbershop. That's what it was called, according to the paper taped to the front door. Ben's Barbershop. I wondered if Mr. Scruffy was the owner or, more likely, a client in need of services.

The street curved a bit and then there it was, a half block away on my right. The Cog & Sprocket. My love. Now, the Cog & Sprocket wasn't the biggest building on Washington Street. That honor belonged to the bank across the street. But it did anchor the end of Washington Street before it forked out into two separate smaller roads, one of which led over a small bridge. There was a small service road right before the bridge that ran along the back of the shops, along the river. When I was a little girl visiting my grandparents in the summer, I'd spend time down at the river, poking at rocks and throwing stones. But most of the time I'd stay inside the shop, falling more and more in love with clocks. My destiny had been preordained when I was born a Clagan.

I looked toward the middle of the fork, looking at the town cemetery with a pang. Not that I knew anyone in there, at least not well. My grandmother's ashes had been buried out at the cottage, where a tree was planted in her memory. I'd always known we would do the same thing for my grandfather. I just hadn't expected it to be so soon. Or under such awful circumstances.

I pulled up and parked in one of the four spaces outside the shop. I turned the car off and sat for a moment, soaking her in. The butter yellow paint looked fresh, and the white trim wasn't only fresh, the trim itself looked new. I loved the symmetry of the wood-framed building. The twelve-pane front door sat in the center, framed with a wide door-frame and black lanterns on either side. There was a shade pulled down on the front door, and a CLOSED sign hanging in the middle. I looked at the two-story porch that ran along the front of the building, noting that the rocking chairs were still out on the first floor. I wondered if Caroline made G.T. go outside to smoke his pipe, like my grandmother had? Or did he still smoke his pipe?

On either side of the front door there was a large double-hung window. Honestly, they looked more like doors, since they ran almost floor to ceiling. They could also be completely removed, which helped when large pieces came in and out of the shop. These windows were closed off with a film that didn't let in light. They also had shutters inside that were meant to be closed during storms. They looked like they were closed now. "No need to be in a fishbowl" was how G.T. explained his dislike of open windows. The sun's rays weren't much good for the clocks either.

I looked up at the second floor, noting that the shutters around the two windows had been painted black. There was a center door in between the upstairs windows and a small porch ran along the second story. I could never remember actually using that door to go out to the porch. Instead, we'd open it for a cross breeze in the summer.

There were flower boxes on the railings of both the upper and lower porches, with mums peeking over the top. My grandfather's wife had kept the space up well; I had to give that to her. I knew it wasn't my grandfather, unless he'd really changed since my grandmother died and developed a green thumb. But then again, I wouldn't know, would I? What a stubborn fool I'd been.

I looked across the street to the old bank, the largest building by far on the street. Wait—what? The bank sign was gone. I noticed a number of shades of green painted on the siding, and the old porch had been ripped out. The big bowfront window was blacked out with a large BOOKSTORE COMING SOON: BEEN THERE, READ THAT sign in the window. A bookstore? Interesting.

The only building that didn't look like it had been refreshed was the old Town Hall to the left of the bookstore. It was set back from the street, with a large front area that had been lovely gardens while I was growing up. Now I noticed a bike rack and some overgrown flower beds. I could see the peeling paint even from this distance, but I'd explore the changes in the Town Hall later. Right now, I needed to get reacquainted with the Cog & Sprocket.

chapter 4

I stretched as I got out of the car, moving my hips around to get them less stiff. I pulled my fleece back down and looked down at my yoga pants. Luckily I'd brought some wrap dresses and tunics with me, so I could dress it up a bit. The retreat was already becoming a distant memory. Now it was time to get back to life.

I walked around to grab my bag from the passenger seat. It was so heavy that it registered as a person, so I had taken to buckling it in so that the car would stop beeping. I hauled it up and was pulling the strap across me when I felt a tap on my shoulder. I screamed and turned to face the tapper.

He was about my height, bald, with black-framed glasses that looked old-fashioned five years ago, but were very hip these days. His soft corduroys were dark olive, and his zipper sweater was a shade lighter. I could swear his eyes were green too, but he jumped back so fast I couldn't be sure.

"Oh my, you scared me," he said.

"I scared you? Are you kidding me?" I asked.

"I saw you sitting in your car and wondered if you were lost. That's all," he said. "The Cog & Sprocket is closed. If you are picking up a clock, I can make sure the owners get the note."

"I'm the owner," I said. The words felt odd in my mouth, but they were true enough.

"You? You're Ruth?"

"I am. And you are?"

"Sorry, sorry. Where are my manners? First I scare you, then I accuse you . . . Sorry. I'm Beckett Green. I own the store across the street. Caroline had let me know that you were taking over for Thom."

"I'm not sure I'm taking over. I just found out about . . . everything . . . this morning."

"Oh, I'm so sorry. And I'm so sorry for your loss. Thom was a good man, a pillar in this town."

"Thank you. Have you lived here long?"

"Not long. I was driving through this past spring on my way out to Tanglewood, and I saw that the building was for sale. Well, it's a long story, but to shorten it up, I decided to buy it on the spot. Always dreamed of running a bookstore, and thought now is the time. I'm in the middle of some renovations. Hoping to be open early in the new year."

"Well, that sounds interesting."

"Not really. A very dull midlife crisis, in fact. And here I am prattling on. Are you going to stay here?"

I looked at Beckett Green and considered his question. For him, a polite inquiry. For me, a multilayered potentially life-altering decision. Was I going to stay at the Cog & Sprocket tonight? The exhaustion of the day was catching up to me, so I supposed that staying overnight made sense. Should I be concerned about staying there, given what had happened? I looked back at the building. No, there was nothing to be afraid of at the Cog & Sprocket. I had to believe that. But was I staying at the Cog & Sprocket more permanently? That was too complicated a question to ponder right now.

"I am going to go in and look around."

"Well, that's good. You should know, we are all keeping vigil on the building, and nothing has happened. Pat Reed's been adding more locks to all the windows and doors just to be sure, but it is perfectly safe. Besides, poor Bezel needs the company."

"Bezel?"

"The shop cat. You can't miss her. Ben's been over feeding her, but she and Blue don't get on well."

"Blue?"

"Ben's dog."

"Oh." I felt like Alice in Wonderland, and someone had given me the magic tea. Who were all these people? And where were the people I knew? "Do you know if Pat Reed is here?"

"Last I knew he was out making deliveries. He's been trying to keep up with the shop since, you know. It's difficult to believe it hasn't even been a week yet. We're all reeling, I tell you, reeling."

"G.T. had lived here his whole life. He knew everyone in Orchard."

"G.T.?"

"Grandpa Thom. My nickname for him." I cleared my throat.

"Thom did, indeed, know everyone. Which is why the theft was such a shock. Who would steal from Thom and Caroline? And then that they came back?"

"Is that what they think happened?" I asked.

"Well, it's the current theory. The shop had never been robbed, then twice within a month?"

"Was anything taken the second time?"

"No. Not that anyone can tell. Thom hit the car alarm. It was making a real racket. I was getting dressed to go over and see what the commotion was about. Woke me out of a sound sleep, let me tell you. And it woke Ben up too—he lives next door. You don't hear car alarms that often in Orchard, and never at two o'clock in the morning."

"Why was G.T. here so late?"

"Caroline was out of town, so I guess he was catching up with work at the shop. There are a lot of clocks that need fixing if he was going to meet his goals for the shop and be ready for Thursday."

"Goals? Deadlines?" I asked. Things really had changed around here.

"Look at me, keeping you standing here. You must be exhausted. As I said, you are perfectly safe. Here's my card, call me if you need anything. What say I stop by in a couple of days, and we can get to know each other properly? I look forward to that, I really do." With that he turned and walked back across the street, half turning to wave at me over his shoulder. I watched him go, wondering what was going to happen in six days, on Thursday.

chapter 5

The door was double keyed, so it took me a few minutes to figure it out. I finally opened it and stepped inside. I knew exactly where the lights were. And I knew exactly how it would look once I turned them on. But I paused for a minute, trying to brace myself. The last time I'd been in this shop was three weeks after my grandmother's funeral. I was heading back to London to finish my internship at the World Horological Institute. The two-year program had been a huge expense for my grandparents, but I know G.T. had been as excited as I was about the opportunity. I'd hugged my grandfather tight and promised to write soon. I had no idea that was the last time I would see the shop. Or one of the last times I would see him.

I reached to the left and flipped the switch. Since there was little ambient light from outside seeping in, it was dark. But even in shadow, it was familiar. Shelves of clocks on both sides, starting from five feet up. Glass cases with watches and smaller clocks lining either wall. The wooden counter still cut the front part of the room off from the workshop itself. There were a few batteries out, and a couple of cases of watches on the counter. Halfhearted attempts to get last-minute sales.

I locked the door behind me and put down the bags. I walked over and lifted the counter up. Then I heard it—a noise behind me. I whipped around to see a gray cat nudging my bag with her head.

"Hey, you." I leaned down and reached my hand out. "Bezel, I presume?"

When I'd left, Chime, a huge tabby, was the shop cat. My great-grandfather had started naming cats after clock parts, and my grandfather had continued the tradition. Bezel was a large gray beauty. She looked like she was part Russian Blue. She was eyeing me warily as she inspected my bag, though I could hear her purring from four feet away. She crept forward, stopped about a foot from my hand, and looked at me. I just waited.

"My name is Ruth. I am Thom's granddaughter. Sorry we haven't met before." Bezel walked around my hand and gave my knees a head-butt. She made a hissing sound, but looked up at me with her big, round eyes. She walked in between the curtains that led to the back of the shop, looking over her shoulder as if to say, *"Are you coming or not?"*

"I'm coming." I pulled open the heavy velvet curtains and walked into the back of the shop—the heart of the operation.

Under the best of circumstances, there was never enough room at the Cog & Sprocket. Clock repair required wall space for testing, shelf space for storage, and somewhere to put clock parts and packing cases. G.T. and Pat had always been good about using every possible space for storage, including shelves that ran a foot from the ceiling around the entire perimeter of the shop. Because we backed up to the river, the basement was always deemed too dank for storage. Too dank for much else either.

I'd seen a lot of inventory before, but never anything like this. Clocks were packed on every single shelf. The smaller clocks were double shelved. All three worktables were covered with clocks in varying states of repair. Boxes sat all over the room, some piled on top of one another, some opened, most closed. I peered into one of them, but restrained myself from taking anything out. Was there a method to this madness? Probably. I looked over at the old library card files where G.T. kept his clock filing cards, but wooden crates blocked them.

Bezel stopped about halfway into the workshop and blocked my path back. I walked up to her and looked to my right. More boxes. "You're right—I can look through that later. Should I look upstairs?"

Bezel hissed and then smiled again. Was hissing her way of letting me know who was boss? She certainly owned the place. She walked to the back of the shop, where the curtain to the upstairs was pulled open. Before I went back, she stopped and flicked her head to the left.

So far, I'd avoided looking at the back door, for fear of seeing outside to where it had happened. But Bezel wasn't pointing me there, but rather to the left of the door, behind a wall of boxes. I walked back and gasped. Eight grandfather clocks, beautiful examples of longcases. All different sizes and styles, but all impressive. I took out my cell phone and used the light from the screen for a closer look. There was a card table set up in the corner, and I saw three pendulums laid out. There were weights laid out in front of each clock. Most of the doors were partially open. Were these what G.T. had been working on?

Bezel nudged the back of my knees, waking me from my reverie. She walked over to the staircase and took one step up. She meowed at me, a deep husky meow that wasn't friendly—more "Obey me now." She took one step up, and then looked back at me.

I did as Bezel told me, following her upstairs, ducking as I walked up the first step. Funny, I hadn't walked up or down those stairs in years, but I still remembered that the staircase was only easy to clear if you were five foot six or shorter. I'd outgrown the door when I was fourteen, topping out at five foot ten finally. I reached the top of the stairs, felt around to the right to find the light switch, finding it and flipping it on by rote.

If the shop hadn't changed that much, the same could not be said of the rooms upstairs. Rather than the rabbit warren of four small rooms where my grandparents had started their marriage that I remembered from my childhood, the space was open. I could see the fading light through the window on the back, though the details loomed in darkness. On the right was the galley kitchen, such as it was. A refrigerator, microwave, and deep slop sink. Old metal cabinets that had been there for as long as I remembered, and looked much the worse for the wear. Behind the kitchen was the only room with doors left in the space. I turned on the light and peeked my head in the bathroom. Clean, but still as cramped, with a toilet, tiny sink, and the claw-foot tub. Walking down the hall I reached around the back of the bathroom and found the light switch. And I stood there, gobsmacked.

My grandmother's bedroom set was all there. The sleigh bed, the highboy dresser, the bureau, the wardrobe. More than the bedroom set was in the back of the space. A couple of chairs, both of which I remembered from my grandparents' living room. A dry sink. Books, so many, many books, piled on the furniture. And more clocks. Everywhere I turned there were clocks. Were I not Thom Clagan's granddaughter, I would be overwhelmed. Cuckoo clocks stuck open. Gears exposed on a beautiful but tattered grandfather. Clock guts everywhere. A smell that combined lemon oil, dust, mothballs and motor grease. As I was, indeed, Thom Clagan's granddaughter, I felt comforted and inspired.

I turned and looked on the bed, noticing the box set on it. A piece of yellow legal paper was folded in half and taped to the side. *Ruth* was written in big red letters. I pulled it off and read the note.

Dearest Ruth,

I'm sorry to not be there in person to welcome you back to the Cog & Sprocket, in case you decided to stay here. I've added new locks, and the place is locked up as tight as a drum. I cleared some space for you and hope that you can find some rest. Here are a few things for the night. I look forward to seeing you tomorrow.

All my best,
Pat

I looked in the box and found sheets, towels, a bar of soap, a tin of cookies, and a bottle of wine. I looked over at Bezel, who perched on top of the headboard.

"I'm just going downstairs to get my bags. Do you want to come?" I asked Bezel, hoping the answer would be yes. Instead she climbed up onto the bed and curled herself into a ball.

"Thanks for the support," I said. I took my phone out as I went back down the stairs, ready to dial for help if I needed it. The enormity of today hit me, and I moved around the shop triple-checking the locks. The back door had a crate in front of it. I walked to the front of the shop, and moved a box in front of the door, grabbing an alarm clock from one of the shelves and resting it on top. I realized it was a silly security system, but it made me feel better. I turned off all the lights, my Yankee frugality kicking in. Then I went back and turned one of them back on, common sense taking over. I grabbed my bags and headed upstairs.

chapter 6

I went into the bathroom and splashed some cold water on my face. I stared at my reflection for a while. Any relaxation I'd felt after leaving the retreat, which I will allow was limited, was gone. I pulled out the ponytail holder and ran my wet fingers through my auburn Medusa-like curls. The swollen red marks that rimmed my blue eyes looked permanent. The bags under my eyes had been features these last few months, but at one point last week I thought maybe they'd go away. Not anytime soon, that's for sure. Turning thirty had been quite a journey so far.

I knew a shower would make me feel better, so I turned on the taps. From cold to tepid. Verging on warm. I got undressed and stepped in, fighting the circle of shower curtains that stuck to my wet skin. The clawfoot tub had a shower attachment, but it was too short. I decided to opt out of washing my hair until I had more energy. I pulled on my sleeping T-shirt and a sweatshirt and walked back to the box Pat had left.

I pulled out the bottle of wine. A screw top. Pat always thought of everything. Wine and cookies. Not the healthiest of dinners, but I would have to make do. Bezel peered up at me from the center of the bed, blinking a few times.

"Bezel, I need to make the bed. How about if I give you some dinner? You can come back when I'm done."

I went into the kitchen and poured some fresh dry food from the cabinet into a dish. I rinsed out a clean coffee mug and took it and a small plate back to the bed. I went back to the box and unscrewed the wine.

"I'll let it breathe," I said aloud. I pulled out the sheets that Pat had left, and started to make up the bed. I stopped every few seconds to run my hand along the footboard. I'd heard the story of this bedroom set so many times I knew it by heart, and heard my grandmother's voice telling it to me.

Her grandmother had come from money. But then she fell in love with the farmhand her father had hired. Their love was forbidden, but they wanted to marry anyway. She defied her father and ran away with the love of her life. Her father never spoke to her again, but a year later, after the birth of her first child, this bedroom set was delivered. It was a gift from her mother, who began to visit once a week in order to know her grandchildren. No matter how hard things got, my grandmother held on to this bedroom set. And it had been passed on from generation to generation, through the women in the family. *"And someday,"* I could hear her say, *"it will be yours."*

I guess someday was now. I blinked a few times, and

grabbed a cookie. Yum. I remembered them from my child-hood. Nancy Reed's Kitchen Sink Specials. My grand-mother always named recipes after the person who gave them to her. They were basic oatmeal cookies with anything and everything tossed in. I tasted coconut, chocolate chips, walnuts, and either cherries or cranberries. I took another bite. Cherries. Delicious.

I remembered the armoire that was next to the bed. It used to be in the hall at the cottage, a coat closet of sorts. I tried to pull open the door, but it was locked. I reached around and ran my hand along the back, feeling a small hook. I followed the path of the hook and felt a ribbon hang-ing down. I picked it up and, sure enough, there was a key hanging on it. Clagan family security at its best. Lock your cabinets, but hide the keys where the tall people in our fam-ily could find it easily.

The armoire was packed with stuff. I pulled out a box with notebooks spilling over the top. I put it down next to the bed and then sat on the edge of the bed. Bezel har-rumphed her unhappiness at my intrusion, gathering her paws beneath her, but didn't move. I picked up one of G.T.'s notebooks, running my hand along the cover. I checked the inside, and noted the dates. July 1995–June 1996. I started flipping through the pages. Like my own notebooks, this was as much a journal of his life as the notes of a horologist. The visual musings of a brilliant clockmaker. Notes on materials and orders. Some numbers in the margins that I vaguely remembered as part of his archiving system. I looked through the book, recognizing a couple of pieces that he'd made, but there were dozens of others that had stayed drawings. These were his daydreams. I walked back to the kitchen to get my own notebook. I dragged my entire bag back with me and put it on the side of the bed next to the wall. Bezel hissed and moved away. She gave me quite the look before turning her back and going back to sleep.

I stopped and looked very closely at one of his more elaborate designs. The physical measurements of the clock indicated it was supposed to be a mantel clock, medium sized. But the detail he wanted to create and the movement he envisioned needed a much bigger case. I looked at a couple more sketches and saw the same theme throughout many years. My grandfather was meant to work on a much larger scale. He needed to design a huge clock, the size of a building. He knew it, and I knew it. And we dreamed about it together for years. But looking at these sketches, I realized how much the world had lost because he hadn't done it. His genius was something I aspired to.

I got up and opened the armoire again. I noticed the paper model on the top shelf and pulled it out carefully. I smiled, remembering the summer I helped G.T. build this paper model of the clock tower. I took it out and put it on top of the armoire, stepping back to take it in.

He'd tried to get permission to fix the clock tower at the old Town Hall for years, but something had always stopped it. The designs weren't approved. The funding was cut. Or G.T. and a selectman or a member of the zoning committee or a member of the chamber of commerce had a falling-out and a wrench was thrown in the plans. G.T. had a knack for upsetting folks who could get in the way of getting the clock tower project from paper to reality. But that didn't stop him from planning, dreaming, and designing. I closed the note-book and shuffled through the rest of them, looking on the back-inside covers for the green sticker. Where was the clock tower notebook?

I'd put a shamrock sticker on it one summer day when I was ten or so. I asked G.T. about the figures he'd drawn, and how did the clock tower mechanism work? And what were the drawings of the moving figures? How did they work? And why did this lady look like Grandma? And so he gave me my first lesson in horology, and let me in on his vision. My world changed forever. I started my love affair with the family business. And I also found a way to get to know my busy grandfather. My grandmother had always defined love for me, but he had always scared me a bit. But not after that day.

Here it was. I looked through the notebook, pleased to realize that when I made a comment or did my own drawing, he dutifully included them in the notebook. This particular notebook was a chronology of my long summer visits with my grandparents, the beginning of my life, actually. I flipped through to the end, but I couldn't read a word. The tears came back, flooding my eyes and dripping on the notebook pages. I wept like I hadn't for years. At first I tried to stop. But why? I'd stopped myself from crying so many times in my life, and where had that gotten me?

Funny thing about that. Permission to cry dried my tears. And stiffened my resolve. I pulled my notebook out of my bag and opened it up. When I'd sent that postcard, I'd begun to imagine talking to him about my work and asking him for advice on some of my own designs. I'd wanted to impress him. Too late for that now, but maybe I could honor him in another way. I opened up a new page in my notebook and named it "Clagan Clock Tower." I stood up and took some pictures of the model with my phone. I'd import them into my computer later.

"Game on, G.T.," I said aloud. Bezel woke with a start and hissed irritably. "Sorry, Bezel. Just making a promise. We're going to make this happen."

chapter 7

I woke up to a feeling of pressure on my chest. I opened my eyes and saw a gray ball of fur coming toward me. I stopped the head-butt with a kiss, which Bezel seemed to like. She stepped off my chest and let me sit up. I looked down at the closed notebook on the floor, barely remembering putting it down there. I heard a crash coming from downstairs. I threw on my yoga pants and grabbed my fleece. I picked up my phone again, dialing a nine and a one, with my finger hovering over the other one.

I crept down the stairs, crouching down as I reached the bottom. I pulled back the curtain at the foot just enough to peek through. A woman was bent over the alarm clock toward the front of the shop and the toppled box I'd left in front of the door. Bezel bounded down the stairs beside me, gathering speed as she hurled herself across the shop. She used a box as a springboard and jumped up on the counter-top. She made a terrible sound that was the cross of a yowl, a meow, and a hiss. She jumped down from the counter and slunk over to the woman.

"Good heavens, Bezel! You'd have liked to have given me a heart attack, wouldn't you? No, don't come closer. You know that I can't . . ."

The slim, petite woman looked up and saw me standing at the foot of the stairs. She reached up and patted her perfectly coiffed hair.

"Oh my," she said. "Are you Ruth? I'm Caroline Adler. I didn't realize you were here already. Pat did say he'd gotten a call from Kristen, but I hadn't heard from you."

"I didn't know about any of this until yesterday morning." I walked forward, wishing I'd had time to get dressed and brush my teeth. The light wasn't great, but from what I could see, Caroline Adler was very put together. Black trousers and a black turtleneck with a houndstooth jacket on top. I leaned forward to see her shoes, which were actually black clogs.

"Did you get my messages?" she asked. Her voice was getting raspy, and I could hear her labored breathing.

"I haven't really listened to my voice mail," I admitted. I'd actually skipped her messages, but I wasn't going to tell her that.

"Well, you're here now. That's what matters. Don't come any closer. No, not you, Ruth. Bezel. I'm terribly allergic to her, and didn't take my medications." She took an inhaler out of her purse and had a deep, long pull on it. "I'm so sorry. I just can't. I'll call you later—would that be all right? There's a HEPA filter that we can turn on. Oh my, I really need to leave. We'll talk soon."

I moved toward her, but she was out the door in a flash. I peered behind the window shade, but she was already crossing the street and she didn't look back. Then I saw Pat Reed round the corner with a tray of coffees. I looked down and raced back upstairs to get changed into something more presentable.

chapter 8

"Hello, Pat. I'll be right down," I called out as I heard him open the front door. I pulled on my leggings and added a pair of hand-knit socks, jamming my feet into my boots. I threw on a tunic, added a belt, and pulled my hair back with a large barrette. That was as good as it could get in five minutes. I stopped by the bathroom and quickly brushed my teeth.

I walked down the stairs, instinctively ducking so my head would clear the doorway.

"Ah well, there she is now," he said softly. I walked down the stairs slowly, feeling shy all of a sudden. He brushed his tears aside and opened his arms wide. "There she is indeed. And a beauty she is too."

I ran the final three steps, throwing myself into his arms. His red buffalo plaid shirt felt scratchy and wonderful against my cheek, and I inhaled his aftershave. I held on for a while, but let go first.

"Pat, it is so great to see you."

And it was. I had known Pat my whole life. He and his wife, Nancy, were the parents I always wished I had. Loving, doting parents to Moira and Ryan. And present. Very present. I couldn't even imagine what that was like, though Grandma Mae tried her best. Even when I was a little girl, I had developed a tough shell—a loner with no expectations of anyone else but myself.

"It is good to see you, Ruthie. It has been too long."

"Too long. And too late," I said. I looked over my shoulder toward the back of the shop.

"Don't do that. He wouldn't want you to do that. There's no point. What's done is done."

"It's what you do now that counts," we said at the same time, reciting one of my grandmother's favorite expressions. Easy to say, difficult to live. Funny, I'd thought a lot about that expression last week on the retreat. Even thought about making a sampler of it.

"What do you think of the place?" Pat asked.

"It feels smaller than I remember. And I don't ever remember seeing so much inventory," I said.

"It's a lot and we still haven't started organizing it. We were almost done with inventory when it happened. When Thom passed. We got slowed down when Caroline's son had an emergency appendectomy and she had to go up and take care of him. She was up there when it happened; came right down as soon as she heard."

"Does she have other children?"

"No, just the one son. Levi. Good kid."

I had nothing to say, nothing to add. I barely knew her name. I knew only that she was a few years younger than my grandfather and had married him less than a year after my grandmother died. For the past five years, that had been enough.

"I think she was coming by this morning to drop off some files," Pat said.

"We met. Sort of. She had to run out. She says she's allergic to Bezel."

"I should have turned on the air last night to help clear the space. Let me do it now. See this box? Just flip this switch right here. Usually that helps, plus we keep Bezel upstairs when she's here."

"Why do you have a shop cat if she is so allergic?"

"She hates mice."

I shuddered. We had that in common.

"Well, at least she wasn't allergic to me."

"It's really none of my business, so I am only going to say this once: she's good people. After Mae passed, I never thought I'd see Thom get right. He was in a bad place when you went back to school. But meeting Caroline, it was like a light went on. Not the same light as he had with your grandma, but a light all the same. And she was good for the business. Got Thom to join the chamber. You know how hard your grandma tried to do that."

"Okay," I said. Pat tried staring me down, forcing me to say more, but he had no idea who he was dealing with. I could stare down the best of them. "So tell me more about the clocks."

Pat shrugged and looked around the shop. "They bought out two estates last spring. The Stockbridge lot had three grandfathers and a few more pieces. The plan was to spend the fall working on those and get them sold. Very doable. But then the Winter estate came up. Do you remember the Winters? Their kids were a little older than you, but you knew the Chairman."

Everyone in Orchard knew Grover Winter. He'd been chairman of the Board of Selectmen for years, as close to a mayor as Orchard ever had. Like most towns in the Berkshires, Orchard citizens ran the town, with a Board of Selectmen voted in to administer it. Grover Winter had family money and was a successful lawyer. But his service to the town of Orchard always came first. He'd served in the State House for a few years, first as a representative, then as a senator. He'd come back to Orchard after he'd served two terms, even though he easily could have been elected for a third. Orchard was home, he always said.

"You know what good friends Thom and the Chairman were, don't you? They'd gotten really close these past few years. Anyway, he'd come into the shop a few times to buy a clock or bring one in, so I knew him. And, of course, we'd all gone out to the estate for the Fourth of July picnic."

"I remember those picnics. Out in their orchards, right?"

"Right. But I'd never been through the entire house before I went with Caroline and Thom last month. The Winters were clock collectors. I've never seen so many anniversary clocks in my life. A half-dozen grandfathers. Two dozen Viennas. I lost count of the mantel clocks. And some stunning shelf clocks. Collections of miniatures, intact. At least a dozen cuckoo clocks."

"Wow. I do remember that they had clocks, but I had no idea they were serious collectors."

"They were passionate collectors. Some clocks were very

valuable, but some were collected for the joy of them. It took us a week to do the inventory and for Thom to come up with an offer."

"It must have been a huge offer," I said.

"It took all the cash Thom and Caroline had," Pat said. He paused for a second and regrouped. "They'd talked about going for a second mortgage on the house or the store if they needed to. Jonah Winter, the son, just wanted to get it done. Maybe he could have gotten more, but he trusted your grandfather to give him a good deal."

"Are all the clocks here?" I asked.

"Yes. At least I think so." Pat looked away from me and around the Cog & Sprocket. "We were planning on moving some out to the shop at the cottage for storage after we were done with inventory."

"Shop at the cottage? You mean the one in the barn? Is that good for storage?"

"It is now. They redid it last winter. Airtight, climate controlled. Plan was that Thom could work from there more often."

"Why? For more space?"

"More space. And he'd been making noises about retiring. We're none of us getting any younger. But we both know he'd never stop working. Anyway, we've been doing an inventory to assess what exactly we have. I'm happy to say that the Chairman and his wife kept great records, and several of the clocks were sold or repaired here, so they were already in the system."

"In the system?"

"Caroline's son, Levi, spent one summer working with the clock cards. You remember them, don't you?" Pat gestured toward the old library card catalogs along the wall.

Remember them? I had dreams about them, and not all of them pleasant. The clock cards were G.T.'s filing system on the clocks he'd worked on. He'd inherited the system from his father. Each clock was coded with a series of numbers and letters that made its identity unique. Usually the clockmaker, type of clock, and year we worked on it, with some more specificity added. The numbers were put on index cards, and everything about the clock was recorded on the card. They were then filed, by number. Heaven help the person who misfiled a clock card. She'd have to spend hours finding the mistake. Once it took an entire day.

"I remember them," I said, grimacing.

"Thought you might." Pat winked at me. "Anyway, Levi was always a bit of a brain. He created a database for the inventory, based on the Clagan system. See these labels? We put the number on them and then we'd affix it to the clock in a place where it wouldn't get noticed."

"Wouldn't that take away from the value of the clock? Adding a sticker?"

"No, we were careful. If the clock was of huge value, we wouldn't add the label. But then again, those really valuable clocks are few and far between."

"I heard there was a robbery last month? Five clocks were taken, all around a thousand dollars? That's pretty valuable."

"Who have you been talking to?"

"I think it was Kristen Gauger who told me about the clocks. Or maybe it was Beckett what's his name? From across the street?"

"Beckett Green. He's a troublemaker, that one. I think

those clocks were overvalued, to tell you the truth. But yes, five clocks were taken."

"And do you think the robber came back and attacked G.T.?" I asked quietly.

"No, I don't think it's the same person," Pat said, putting his arm around my shoulder and giving me a quick squeeze. "But the chief will be able to answer your questions better than I can."

"I'll make sure and give him a call today. Do you think he's working on a Saturday?"

"Jeff Paisley works every day even at the best of times, and this isn't the best of times. He'll be more than happy to talk to you whenever, I'm sure.

"Now, what were we talking about?" Pat said, letting go of my shoulder and walking over to the counter. He picked up a coffee and held it out. I took it and removed the lid, savoring the smell. I took a sip and smiled. A nice dark roast, but not at all bitter. Wonderful.

"I think we were talking about all the clocks? Inventory systems?" I was just guessing here, since we'd gone on so many tangents. My hands itched for my notebook so I could start writing some of this down. Stolen clocks. A trouble-maker for a neighbor. A workaholic police chief. I felt com-pelled to start making lists. It was how I dealt with stress.

"And besides," Pat said, as I realized he was still talking. "Thom got a work plan in place, so we will have some of them ready for sale by Christmas."

"Some of what, the clocks? By Christmas? That's less than three months from now."

"Maybe he didn't mean this Christmas." Pat laughed and

then stopped. He stared into the shop, with a far-off look in his eyes. I reached over and rubbed his arm. He looked at me and smiled.

"This must be hard for you. Are you all right here by yourself, Ruthie? Is there someone I can call for you?" Pat asked.

"No one," I said.

"Your husband?"

I shook my head and rubbed the place where my wedding band had been up until last month.

"No husband. Not anymore."

Pat paused, but good New Englander that he was, he didn't press.

"Moira would love to see you," he said, changing the subject.

"I'd love to see her." And I would. I had, so far, resisted using the social media networks that would have helped us reconnect. I lurked on Facebook, but hid my profile. And my Twitter handle had nothing to do with my personal life. @ClaganClocks barely tweeted. My entire life had been hovering on the edges, but now I longed for a connection, any connection.

"She's two doors down."

"At the diner? Were you meeting her there?"

"No, she owns it. The Sleeping Latte. A terrible name, but don't tell her I said that."

"Wow, that's terrific." Terrific, but surprising. Moira had always talked about leaving Orchard in her rearview mirror. I wondered what brought her back.

"I can call Moira and have her bring some food over."

"No, that's all right. I'll walk down and say hello in person."

"Good for you. I'll keep on working on the inventory. And, Ruthie?"

"Yes?"

"When you see Moira don't ask her about Ryan. It's a long story; I'll tell you later. In the meantime, you settle in and call me on this number anytime, day or night." He pulled a card out of his wallet and handed it to me. "Day or night."

chapter 9

I pulled the door of the shop closed, turned, and stood on the porch, surveying the town. I looked over at the new bookstore and had to smile. What a great old building—one of the few in the valley that had survived the floods that ravaged the area until a few strategic dams were put in place. The building was also one of the originals in Orchard. Brick construction, which was not the norm in the day. Legend was the original owner had taken a load of bricks as payment for a debt and he used them here. High ceilings, sturdy post and beam construction. The building took a long time to build and had very special additions. Trapdoors, removable walls, hidden passages, custom-built cabinetry. It started life as a merchant's home, but was turned into a bank in the late 1800s and had stayed one ever since. Until now.

The Cog & Sprocket wasn't quite as grand, but it still had

a rich history. My great-grandfather either bought the building or took over the payments. Or won it in a poker game. That part of the family history was always a little hazy. It was a general store for years until the Clagan family moved in and made it a clock shop, the first in the Berkshires.

My grandfather may have inherited the building and the family business that went with it, but my grandmother made it an Orchard institution. She worked closely with her long-widowed father-in-law to make it more hospitable. She wrestled my grandfather away from the shop long enough to get him to add the two-story porch that ran all along the front. Then she added the rocking chairs and the flowers. I'd spent hours sitting in those chairs, reading, drawing, dreaming. I'd forgotten how wonderful that porch was. I was tempted to just sit, but I was in search of more coffee. And nothing got me moving like a caffeine quest.

Fall in New England was generally glorious, and today was no exception. The cloudless sky was sapphire blue, with the lazy autumn sun just making an appearance, giving just enough light to twinkle on the dew beading on multicolored leaves. A low-lying fog would burn off soon, but for now it gave Orchard an appearance of a ghost town rising from the past, with twinkling dew waking it up.

The fog suited the old Town Hall down the street. The gray siding, white trim, and black front door all melded together. The building was a story higher than any other building in town, but still, it didn't impose. Instead it just held back, serving and keeping watch over the citizens of Orchard. The building was a community center, after-school care venue, and occasional community theater. When I was growing up, the Saturday after Thanksgiving there was always a town pancake breakfast, a benefit for the Winter Citizen Fund. Christmas trees were sold in the parking lot, and the Christmas craft fair was held inside.

"She is the town center, but not well respected," my grandfather would always say. "She needs her works put back."

By that he meant the clock tower, the gift that my great-great-grandfather made to the town almost a hundred years ago. During World War II the clock's workings were stripped and melted down for the war effort. After the war they were reinstalling some of the ironworks and there was a fire in the old clock tower. The tower burned but the rest of the building was saved.

The structure of the tower was rebuilt but the clock was not reinstalled since it had never been a priority for the Board of Selectmen. But rebuilding the clock tower in its entirety was a Clagan family obsession, passed down from my great-grandfather Harry to my grandfather. And from my grandfather to me, skipping a generation past my academic father.

The old clock tower hadn't been just a timepiece. It had been an art piece. Once a month, on the first Saturday at four o'clock, the clock would begin to chime and the show began both outside and in the main chamber of the Town Hall. Doors opened, figures spun, and music played. It lasted for five minutes.

There were still pictures, the initial drawings, and one shaky silent film, but the glorious history was just that, history. My grandfather had been one of the few people in town who still remembered. He'd always dreamed of rebuilding it. I'd stayed up late reading G.T.'s notes. According to them he was sketching out his ideas just weeks ago. In fact, from what I could see, he'd started to work on the project anew, at least on paper, a few months ago. I wasn't sure what had fired up his imagination again, and somehow it felt very important to try and figure that out.

I shook myself out of my daydreams and memories. I needed more caffeine first, and breakfast. But I also needed some questions answered, and I hoped that Moira could take care of all three.

chapter 10

I stepped off the porch and headed to my left. When I was growing up in Orchard, half the town thought the building next door was an eyesore while the other half rooted for the owners, the Parkers. They'd bought the lot and opened a small drugstore with a family apartment upstairs. When the children were a little older, Mr. Parker built an addition and Mrs. Parker opened a beauty shop. A couple of years later Mrs. Parker's brother—I think it was her brother, or maybe a cousin—someone opened a barbershop in a second addition in the back. The Parkers hadn't even tried to make all three spaces look alike. In fact, Mrs. Parker's family had been in construction, so everything was built with leftovers from renovations and new construction. Lots of sinks, but nothing matched. Different countertops. Cabinets that were a little nicked or dinged. "A carpenter's castle" is what my grandfather called it.

I wondered what he'd thought of the renovation. It looked like everything matched, or at least as far as I could tell by looking at the two chairs in front of the shop. I took a step toward the front window, trying to look in. I was about to cup my hands against the window to see better when a dog barked. I turned just as a large gray, black, and white ball of fur came hurtling toward me. I expected him to jump up, but he stopped short and plunked himself down next to me, wagging his tail. And smiling. The dog was smiling at me.

I lowered my hand slowly and kept my voice steady. "Hello, sweetheart, it's nice to meet you more formally. My name is Ruth. We haven't been properly introduced." I held out my hand and he answered by nuzzling it and flipping it over so I would pat his head. I gave in, setting my bag down as I scratched him with both hands. He stood up and leaned into my hands, trying hard to give me a kiss. I kept him at bay for a bit, but soon realized he was just a big sweetheart. I kissed the top of his head and he barked his thanks. I love dogs.

My ex-husband did not like dogs. Or cats. Or, as it turns out, me. He obviously had bad taste.

"Blue, leave her alone!" A tall blond man ran across the street. The guy I'd almost hit when I drove into town. He was hard to forget.

"You know, they have crosswalks here for a reason," I said, continuing to pet the dog.

"What?" He smiled at me while he leaned over and put a leash on Blue.

"We almost met yesterday when I wasn't paying attention

and almost hit you." He took off his glasses and squinted at me. I was right, his eyes were blue.

"Actually, you told me I almost hit this guy. Which would have been terrible. Wouldn't it, sweetheart?"

"Blue has a lot of energy. And gets into a lot of trouble. We're still trying to figure out this whole 'living in town' thing." Mr. Scruffy looked at me, or rather looked at my hair. A mop of auburn curls that I'd piled on top of my head. "You here for a cut? Or a shampoo?"

I raised my hand to my head and tried to pat down my flyaway curls. "No, just looking." Mr. Scruffy looked very disappointed. "Is this your shop?"

"Yes. Just opened it last summer."

"I grew up here. My grandmother used to take me to see Mrs. Parker. It was a little different back then."

"Hopefully a lot different. I moved in last December. It took me a long time to renovate."

"You bought it?"

"Sort of. My uncle Phil owned the drugstore and offered me the barbershop. My aunt Flo was Mrs. Parker. She ran the beauty shop for years, but decided to retire and travel the world, so I combined the two. Want to take a tour? We don't open for another hour, but I'd be happy to show you around."

"I make it a habit not to tour barbershops with strangers."

"It isn't a barbershop. It's a hair salon. A friend found the barber pole in Brimfield and gave it to me as a housewarming. Or salon-warming? Anyway, let us not be strangers. I'm Ben Clover. And you're?" He held out his hand and I took it.

"Ruth Clagan."

"Clagan? Thom's granddaughter?" He put his other hand

on top of mine and held it for a second longer. "I'm so, so sorry. Thom was a great guy."

"How did you know who I was?"

"I didn't until Caroline told me you'd be taking over the shop. Folks around here play it pretty close to the vest. Especially when you aren't from here."

"Yes, they do," I said. Cranky Yankees, as my grandmother called us. Even if you were related to folks, you weren't from here. And being from here mattered.

"If Aunt Flo had been here to introduce me to the town, give me her stamp of approval, that may have helped things. But she and Uncle Phil had a huge blowout and she took off in her RV. That left Uncle Phil to make the introductions, which didn't help things much. He wasn't too popular, but maybe you knew that? Thought maybe the town frost would melt after he died last March, and business would pick up after I renovated, but no such luck."

"I'm sorry, I didn't know he'd passed on."

"Thank you. He was quite a character, and I miss him. But he didn't take to the role of town elder, not like your grandfather. Not sure Phil put much back into Orchard. But Thom Clagan sure did."

The silence that followed should have been awkward, but it wasn't. I was thinking about G.T. and how much he loved Orchard. Of course it helped that I was staring into the stunning blue eyes of Mr. Ben Clover. I finally broke the silence.

"Ben, I'd love to see the shop, but I'm in desperate need of some caffeine. Maybe on my way back?"

"Going to the Latte? How about if I walk you?"

I hesitated, but only for a moment. "Sure, that would be great."

Blue actually walked us, pulling on his leash, chasing some unseen foe. Ben bent over to tie Blue to a post outside the Sleeping Latte, but Blue wasn't having it, despite the dog-friendly parking space, complete with a bowl of water and tin of dog biscuits left by the front door.

"He needs to walk a bit more," Ben said.

"Seems so. He has a lot of energy, doesn't he? He's an Australian shepherd, right?" I bent over and rubbed Blue's ears, returning his smile of contentment.

"Not certain, since I adopted him from the pound, but I think so. Wonderful breed, but they need lots of attention and exercise, otherwise they get into trouble."

"Is it true that owners take on the characteristics of their pets?"

"It is indeed, Ruth. We can discuss the specifics another time, after you and Bezel have gotten to know each other a little better. Don't look so surprised. Bezel loves me. And she's pretty fond of Blue, though she likes to play hard to get." Ben started to smile, then stopped. "Listen, I'm really, really sorry about Thom. He was a good friend to me these past few months. He promised me he'd show me how to repair an old cuckoo clock I found in the shop. Wish I'd taken him up on that." Blue tugged on the leash and Ben gently pulled him back a bit. "I know that Thom didn't want a service, but Caroline said she wanted to talk to you before she made a decision. I'd love to have a chance to honor Thom in some way, so keep me posted on any plans."

"Thank you, I will."

"Let me know if I can be of any help with anything.

Anything at all. I'm right next door, except when I'm walk-ing the beast. Okay, Blue, I'm coming. Are you staying at the shop?"

"For a few days at least. Until I figure out what I'm doing."

"I'll see you around, then." We stared at each other for a second too long, then he turned and walked away. My heart did a little leap, and I couldn't help but smile. I watched Ben and Blue walk away for another minute before going into the Sleeping Latte.

chapter 11

The Sleeping Latte should have been called Ruth's Heaven. The warm air that swept out the door as I walked in carried a mixture of scents that practically made me swoon: fresh-baked goods, strong coffee, and a faint hint of cedar. The bones of the old diner were still what I remembered from childhood—the countertop and stools along the back, the open kitchen with shelves for pickup, tables and chairs in the rest of the room. But the details were completely different. The countertop was made of wood, the pivot stools were replaced by wooden barstools with backs. These, as well as the deep red walls and the expansive and impressive coffee machinery that lined the very back wall, must have been vestiges of the upscale redo.

None of the tables and chairs matched completely, yet they were all perfect in the space. Upholstery in red, green, black, and yellow had different patterns, but they all coordinated. A few small couches and wing-back chairs anchored the area to the left. A half-dozen people sat sprawled with laptops and coffee cups, working away. The area to the right had more tables and chairs, and about half of them were full.

A woman bent over one of the tables, spraying it down and wiping it off. A tub of dirty dishes rested on a table behind her. She didn't look up. "Seat yourself anywhere. Be right with you," she said.

I did as I was told, sitting at one of the cleared tables with no one around me. I watched my old friend Moira Reed make quick work of clearing and cleaning tables, carrying the tub through the swinging doors in the back of the diner. She was back in a moment and attended to the customers at the counter, smiling and chatting with everyone as she refilled coffee cups and water glasses.

I tried to think what Moira had said she wanted to be when she grew up. I'd always wanted to be a horologist, so it was never up for discussion. But Moira had so many interests it was always hard for her to pick just one career. She loved food, so maybe she'd be a chef or a caterer? But she also loved to paint: an artist or illustrator, then? And then there was her curiosity. About everything. Journalist or maybe detective were the options we'd come up with there. But diner owner? We'd never thought of that.

Where I was always on the taller side of average, Moira was a little taller. "Five foot twelve," she used to say, as if that sounded shorter than six foot. Her brown hair was cut in a bob, with highlights. Her jeans were tucked into short boots and she wore a henley T-shirt under a black-and-white plaid flannel shirt. A red SLEEPING LATTE apron offered a splash of color. She looked Berkshire comfortable, but with an urban edge. Whereas I'd kept the boardlike shape I'd had through middle and high school, Moira was curvier, a taller version of her mother. Even in jeans, she was a knockout. She finished up at the counter and walked over to me.

"Good morning! What can I get for . . . Ruthie, is that you?"

"Hi, Moira," I said, feeling shy all of a sudden.

"Don't you 'Hi, Moira' me, missy. Get up and give me a hug." She took both my hands and pulled me into her arms. I returned the hug and was embarrassed by my tears until I pulled away and saw her face covered as well.

"Ah, Ruthie, it has been way too long. Way too long. And I hate that it has to be now, after everything . . ."

"Ruth! Hello, darling! Aren't you a sight!" Nancy Reed came through the swinging doors and made a beeline to the table. Her hair was pulled back into a ponytail and her clothing was just Berkshire comfortable. Still, she looked more like Moira's older sister than her mother, and she hugged as tightly.

"It's wonderful to see you both," I said, meaning every word. Nancy reached up and wiped my tears and then cupped my face in her hands. I leaned forward and she gave me another hug.

A gust of cold air followed a small group of what looked like college-aged students coming in. They laughed and pushed each other until they sat at one of the tables on the other side of the room.

"Moira, I'll take care of them. You visit with Ruth. And make sure to invite her to dinner tonight, you hear me?"

"Thanks, Mum."

We both watched as Nancy walked over and chatted with

the newcomers. Moira moved us to a pair of wing-back chairs in the corner, close to the kitchen and with a full view of the restaurant. Nancy stopped at our table on the way back to the kitchen.

"How do you take your coffee?" she asked, all business.

"Black," Moira and I said at the same time.

"And could you bring us something to eat, Mum?"

"Could I bring you something to eat? Please, Moira. Like I wouldn't feed her?"

"Thanks, Nancy, but don't go to any trouble."

"Please," Nancy said as she turned away, sputtering.

"She's still the same. And you look great, Moira. And this place? Wow, look at you."

"I know, right? Crazy. One of those universe-aligning things. I needed a change, was visiting my folks, saw the 'for sale' sign, and boom. A year later here I am, a business owner."

"Visiting?"

"Yeah, I went to grad school in New York. Went into graphic design, met a guy, living the life, then it all went to hell in a handbasket. Long story for another time. And a bottle of wine. And you? I will admit, I Facebook-stalked you a while back. Saw a picture of that handsome husband of yours in a cute garden. Is he here with you?"

"Another long story. And a second bottle of wine. The divorce papers are still fresh. He and his girlfriend got the garden."

"Yikes, I'm so sorry. Didn't mean to bring it up, especially now. What with G.T. . . . ." Moira's voice broke and she took my hand. "Shoot, I'm so sorry. It keeps creeping up on me. I forget most of the time, and then I remember and I feel like throwing up. He was like another grandfather to me too, you remember. It's so awful."

"I can't believe it either. *Awful* is a good word. Inadequate, but good."

Nancy interrupted us, bringing over mugs of coffee and a large plate of wondrous baked goods. A brioche roll. Blueberry muffins. A turnover that I hoped was apple. I inhaled the aroma of the coffee, and sipped. It tasted even better than it smelled. I picked the turnover from the plate and took a bite. It was apple. The apples were still crisp, with a wonderful spice mixture that included the traditional cinnamon and nutmeg, and something more. Was that ginger? Yum.

"This is amazing," I said, gesturing to the turnover.

"Mum makes most of the food for the Latte, but we do outsource some of it. The turnovers are from a bakery in town. We always use other small businesses if we can, and keep it seasonal and local. Orchard is on a big 'keep it local' trend right now."

"Hasn't it always been like that?"

"Yeah, but the idea has built up some momentum. There's a new town administrator—did you hear about that?"

"Someone mentioned it, but no real details. What is a town administrator? Is that different than what Grover Winter did?"

"A town administrator is a paid position. The first one in Orchard's history. Grover Winter had taken on the role for years, but he was never paid for it. When his wife got sick, he had to cut back on the time he spent on the Board of Selectmen. It made everyone in town realize just how much he'd been doing over the years to keep the town running. He suggested that the town hire an administrator and pay him or, as it turned out, her. Kim Gray. Grover Winter still served on the Board of Selectmen, which was a good thing. One of the first things she did was to come up with the idea to bring in a couple of chain stores, including a coffee franchise."

"How did that go over?"

"Not well. But the brouhaha started a 'buy local' movement. It's one of the reasons I got this location at such a great price. Strong local ties, and I wasn't a franchise. Now the new idea is to make Washington Street a historic district. Some people are taking the whole 'buying local' thing to the extreme though. See the couple by the window?"

"I don't recognize them."

"Ada and Mac Clark. New age hippies. They've taken over the grocery store."

"Taken over? You make it sound like it's been invaded by alien life-forms."

"They're into all things local and organic. Mum bakes for them and we send leftovers over at the end of the day for them to sell as day olds that night since we won't use them. They have an emphasis on seasonal foods and a crazy selection of teas. They are really very nice people and a big improvement over his uncle Matt Clark. Of course, that isn't difficult. The problem with Mac and Ada is that they're the food police."

I laughed a little and moved the brioche over to my plate. Moira hadn't changed a bit. I'd forgotten how she could make me laugh.

"They judge your basket, I swear. All the junk and processed food is in one badly lit aisle. I feel guilty even going there, since half the time I only want corn chips and ready-made onion dip. And they keep trying to host wine tastings and cheese events in the store, to support local. People attend, but the events aren't fun."

"What could possibly make an event in a grocery store fun?" I laughed.

"You know, they need to make it the kind of event you look forward to attending. That makes you smile while you're there. That you don't check your watch during. You know. Fun." Moira sighed and shook her head. "There isn't much fun in Orchard."

"Was there ever fun in Orchard?" I asked.

"You know what I mean."

"Yes, I guess I do. The town seems to have changed a lot while staying exactly the same. Does that even make sense?" Moira nodded her head. "This town administrator, what's her name again?"

"Kim Gray," Moira said quietly, looking around.

"Is Kim Gray doing a good job? Seems like a big step for Orchard, hiring someone."

"Depends on who you ask, I guess. There's a lot of strife these days. She keeps trying to get new businesses in town, which is good, but the businesses she is going after don't sit well with old Orchard. Take the new bookstore going in across from you."

"Beckett Green's shop?"

"Oh, so you've met him already? Yeesh, that was fast, even for him. Yes, Been There, Read That. That building was this close to the wrecking ball, but then Beckett stepped in and bought it. Now Kim Gray has set her sights on the old Town Hall. G.T. was leading the charge to get it declared a historical landmark."

"So where does it stand now?"

"There's a problem with the deed. It was actually in the Winter family for years, but a few years ago they leased it to the town. Now she's making noises about eminent domain, just taking it over. Grover left the deed to G.T. in his will, but no one can find it. If they find the deed, it's a simple decision: the Town Hall would be safe. But if they don't, there's going to be a meeting on Thursday to discuss the next steps."

"Wow, that sounds a little complicated. Why does the town want it?"

"Kim wants to level it and use the front half of the land for an indoor mall of sorts. And then make the back half of the lot a parking structure."

"A parking structure?" I laughed. "For the dozen or so cars that are downtown at any given time?"

"Not downtown, Ruth. Historic district. G.T. used to call it a tourist trap. G.T. and a few other people were fighting the idea of a new building. They were doing a good job keeping her hopping."

"What do you mean?"

"G.T. had made it a habit to go to every town meeting. Called it his new sport, throwing nails in front of the wheels of progress. Jeez, I'm going to really miss him."

"Me too," I said. It hurt my heart that I would never know the grandfather who was taking on town government. The grandfather I remembered voted in every election, but that was about as involved as he got.

"There have been some changes for the good in Orchard over the past couple of years. Like that one." Moira gestured toward the door with a nod. I turned to see a man in uniform walk up to the counter. He had powerfully broad shoulders that stretched the back of his dark blue jacket. I watched as Nancy flirted with him, flicking his arm with her dish towel. When he turned and saw Moira, he nodded at her, a faint smile cracking his brown face, but not for long. He went to the counter, sliding into a stool.

"Who's that?" I asked, though I thought I knew.

"The chief of police. Jeff Paisley."

"He's good at his job?"

"He's by the book. The old chief, you remember Harmon Gibbs, right? He just kept the peace. Did his hours, let the state police take over nights and weekends. Chief Paisley is on twenty-four/seven and doesn't let calls go through to the barracks until he's fielded them first."

"That's good, right?"

"Right. A little obsessive, but good. He's trying to get at least one full-time officer in addition to the three part-timers he's got now. It makes sense. With Harris University buying up parts of Orchard, there's more going on here than ever before."

"Where did he come from?"

"He used to be in the military, and was a SWAT commander. Grover Winter pulled some strings, got him the job and a five-year contract, so he's staying put. Don't get me wrong, he's good at his job, but really hard-core."

"What do you mean, hard-core?"

"Sometimes I feel like he's a robot, not a man. But he's been working day and night since G.T. died." I'd forgotten that she called him by the same nickname I did, but it felt good to hear her say it.

"You don't know of anyone who would want to hurt G.T., do you?" I asked quietly.

"Jeez, Ruth, no. Sure, he was a tough old bird. But he was also one of the most respected men in town. I can't even imagine who would have done this."

"Do you think it had anything to do with the robbery?"

"I guess so, don't you think? It's all too much of a coincidence otherwise."

Before I had a chance to ask what Moira meant, I felt a shadow fall across our breakfast table.

"Sorry to interrupt, ladies. And sorry to listen in on your conversation." I hadn't heard Chief Paisley come up to the table. "Ms. Clagan? I'm Jeff Paisley. First of all, let me say how very sorry I am for your loss. Thom Clagan was a good man and a better friend. He will be missed."

"Thank you. Chief, can you tell me about the investigation and where it stands?"

"I'd be happy to tell you everything I can. When you are done here, perhaps I can walk you back to the shop? Unless you were planning on staying to use Moira's Internet connection?"

"Moira's Internet? Why, is there no Internet at the Cog & Sprocket?" I tried not to sound too horrified at the thought, but honestly, the Internet-less week at the retreat almost did me in. I could use my phone, but my plan didn't allow for a lot of roaming Internet use. E-mail took forever to load. Besides, cell connections in the Berkshires could be spotty.

"Oh, Ruthie, you have no idea," Moira said. "It's like a 1970s time warp in there. They just got a computer, but only because Caroline insisted. Old-fashioned phones."

"You're kidding, right?"

"Wish I were. But you're always welcome to come and

use our Wi-Fi. You go ahead with the chief. I need to get to work anyway. Let me get you both a cup of coffee to go."

"I'm going to go back to say good-bye to your mother."

"Just poke your head in though—otherwise you'll be trapped."

I did as I was told, but Nancy Reed grabbed me and gave me a hug. "We're expecting you for dinner."

"Yes, ma'am."

"See you at six. You remember the way."

"Like I could ever forget it. See you at six."

I knew better than to ask if I could bring anything. I'd need to be creative with a hostess gift. Heading back out to the front of the café from the back, I stopped when I saw Moira and Chief Paisley deep in conversation. I couldn't hear what they were saying, but Moira's body language said a lot, and the finger poking Chief Paisley's chest confirmed it. She was angry and it was personal.

I approached them both, just in time to hear Moira say, "Why did you even bother to ask me if you are always working?"

They both noticed me and stopped talking.

"Sorry, that took a little longer than I thought it would," I said, shrugging awkwardly.

"Of course it did. You know Mum. Here's your coffee," she said, reaching behind the counter to grab a large paper bag. "And I packed up a couple of our to-go sandwiches and threw in some premade salads to keep you fed while you figure things out. Don't give me that look. And put your money away. It's no good here. Chief, be useful and carry this stuff."

He hesitated, but carefully took the handled bag, brimming with food, from Moira's hand. I gave Moira a quick hug and picked up the cardboard tray with the coffees. Together we walked out of the Sleeping Latte and took a right. I slowed down a bit in front of Ben's Barbershop, but I couldn't see through the window.

chapter 12

"Tinted glass. And most of his chairs are set back. He didn't want folks peering in and making customers uncomfortable. Not understanding that in a town like Orchard, peering in is a pastime. For some folks, it's a job," the chief said as we passed Ben's shop.

I glanced over, but no smile from the chief. He didn't strike me as a small talk kind of guy, but I thought I'd keep trying.

"I remember when it was Parker's Emporium. People would reschedule depending on who was in the room. And half the people were just there to gossip. My grandmother included. She went over every day, midmorning, to bring Mrs. Parker a cup of tea."

"That was neighborly of her," he said.

"It was. She'd end up staying for an hour. She also got

her hair done once a week, washed and set. Mrs. Parker did quite the business."

"Well, the karma didn't get passed on to her nephew."

"Business bad? Surprising. Ben seems pretty charming."

"Every time I go in, it's pretty quiet, but you'd have to ask Ben."

"You go there?"

"I need to get my hair cut. Ben does a fine job. Figured I should support the new guy, being new myself. This town isn't easy on new guys."

"This town isn't really easy on anyone."

"Sounds like you speak from experience."

We'd arrived back at the Cog & Sprocket. I searched my pocket for the keys and fumbled to find the right one.

"My grandfather and I had a falling-out. I'm sure you've heard." I looked over at the chief, and he nodded. "And I just knew that Orchard would take his side, so I stayed away. I realize now, that was a mistake. Why don't you come in and we can have a cup of coffee and chat?"

I walked in and found a note from Pat on the counter: *Gone to wind the clock tower over in Marytown. Will be back.*

"Wind the clock tower?" the chief said.

I turned just as he stepped back from looking over my shoulder. He didn't even look abashed. I was surprised to realize we were the same height. He'd seemed much bigger. His short brown hair was very closely cropped, and flecked with gray. Liquid brown eyes held my gaze, but I noticed a lack of laugh lines around them. That said, when I smiled, he returned it.

"Part of the business has always been maintaining the

clock towers in the area. Pat must be keeping up with the jobs, bless him. Tell you what, why don't we go upstairs to chat?"

The chief preferred milk in his coffee, but there was none to be found. In fact, there wasn't much in the refrigerator, just beer and condiments. He shrugged when I told him, and took out his phone.

"Low battery," I heard him mutter.

"What kind of phone is it? Maybe my charger would work?" I walked over and picked up my bag from where it still rested on the other side of the bed. I brought it over to the kitchen table and riffled through it till I found my phone charger. I handed it to the chief and pointed him toward the extension cord on the floor.

"What else do you carry in there? It looks like a bag Mary Poppins would carry if she was a hipster."

"Hey, watch it." I looked down at my messenger bag. I found it online on a steampunk site. Steampunk enthusiasts love clock parts almost as much as horologists do. I loved the different shades of gray gears that created the pattern on the red bag. "My life is in this bag."

"Obviously." The chief pulled out some reading glasses and looked down at his phone. "Ms. Clagan, I thought I'd let you know where the investigation into Thom's death stands. How much do you know?"

"Not much. Just that he died of a heart attack, but had been attacked first?"

"Yes, Thom did suffer a head wound. We didn't know what caused it, but two days ago Ben Clover and his dog . . ."

"Blue."

"Blue." The chief smiled. "They were taking a walk by the river and Blue started barking frenetically. Ben went over to see what was wrong, and Blue had found a pendulum."

"A pendulum?" I asked.

"Yes. Good dog—he wouldn't let Ben touch it, but we couldn't find any prints. I'll spare you the details, but the pendulum was used in the attack against your grandfather."

"Was it from the shop?"

"I'm hoping you can tell me that."

"Maybe," I said, remembering the gutted grandfather clocks. "Do you have a picture of it? Or any details?"

"I can get you the details—weight, size, all of that. Give me your e-mail address before I leave. I do want to reiterate that I am treating this like a murder, since it is a death during a robbery. But according to the coroner, Thom had a fatal heart attack during the attack. He didn't suffer."

I was grateful that Chief Paisley took such care to make me feel better. I wasn't sure if he could really know that, but I didn't push. I had to believe that G.T. didn't suffer.

"There is some evidence that someone was in the shop with Thom that night. Pat confirms that he took out all the garbage before he left work that evening. We found two coffee cups in the trash the next morning. That alone means nothing."

"And DNA?" I asked. Too many crime show reruns had made me an expert.

"DNA testing takes a long time and we'd need DNA to compare it to. And the person in the shop may not be the perpetrator. Pat says he doesn't think any clocks are missing, but he can't be one hundred percent sure. I haven't shared the evidence about the pendulum with him yet. I'd appreciate your checking to see if one is missing."

"I will, as best I can."

"Thank you. If the pendulum came from the shop . . ."

"Then the killer was with G.T. in the shop before the murder," I said, finishing his sentence. He nodded his head, and I felt a shudder.

"Do you have any suspects?" I asked.

"Yes and no. There are a number of people who could have been in the shop. But someone who is also a murderer? I need to figure out the motive before I can find a suspect. And right now, that is challenging."

The shop phone rang.

"Go ahead and take it," the chief said. "I'll just look around up here a bit. Do you mind?"

"No, of course not," I said. I picked up the wall phone that hung to the right of the staircase.

"Hello?" I answered.

"Ruth, it's Caroline Alder."

"Hello, Caroline. Are you feeling better?" I asked. Her voice sounded raspy, but I couldn't hear her breathing.

"Yes, thank you. Listen, I forgot to mention this. Your grandfather had an appointment with Stephanie Lincoln over at the Berkshire Real Estate Group. She's been working on getting the shop appraised."

"Were you planning on selling?" I asked.

"Orchard's been changing. I'm sure you see that. Someone offered Thom a sum for the shop. Thom mentioned it to Ben, who said the shop was worth twice the amount."

"Ben? Barber Ben?" I asked.

"Yes, that Ben. I'm glad you've met him. He and Thom

had become good friends. Of course, it's hard not to like Ben. Anyway, Thom decided he'd see how much it was worth. And then he became a bit obsessed. He started to look into what Orchard property values were and to compare them to other towns."

"Why?" I asked.

"Why." Caroline sighed. "That's a big question. Thom's been restless this past year. Percolating ideas, most of which I didn't know about. Stephanie Lincoln may know more. She specializes in historical properties."

"Historical properties? Like the Cog & Sprocket?"

"Yes. And on the pros and cons of getting a home declared a historical landmark." She paused, waiting for my reply. "Anyway, you may want to keep the appointment. Your choice of course. It's at four o'clock, I think. The appointment card is in the corner of the desk calendar."

"Great, I'll check it."

"Ruth, why don't you plan on coming by for dinner this evening?"

"Oh, I'm sorry, I already promised I'd go to the Reeds for dinner."

She paused for a moment. Did she think I'd cancel the Reeds for her? Not a chance. "Well, how about lunch tomorrow then?" she asked.

"Yes, of course. I'll be there. What time?"

"Would eleven thirty be too early? We could have a meal and then I could come back to the shop to talk you through a few things. How does that sound?"

It sounded like it would be much easier for her to come into town, but I wasn't about to turn down a trip to the cottage.

"Eleven thirty it is, then," I said. I hung up and grabbed

my cell phone. Just a few days before, I couldn't have even imagined willingly having lunch with my grandfather's new wife, but there I was, entering the appointment into my calendar for eleven o'clock sharp. I added three reminder alarms. That way I might be on time.

I turned back to the chief, who was over by one of the tables of clocks. I walked over and looked at them with him.

"Chief, I understand there was a robbery a while back?"

"Three weeks ago. Yes," he said, reaching out to shift a clock so that it lined up neatly with its neighbor.

"What was taken?" I pressed.

"Five clocks. I'll e-mail you the descriptions I got at the time."

"Thank you. Do you think the robber came back?"

"That's the assumption right now. Everyone knew that the shop was chock-full of clocks."

"And so they came by to get more clocks, but hit G.T. over the head instead? Does that make sense?" I asked.

"Yes and no. It's just a theory."

"Do you have a line on the stolen clocks?"

"We aren't looking for them. Or weren't until Thom died. Caroline and Thom dropped the complaint," he said, looking up at me.

"Dropped it? Why?" I said, meeting his steady gaze.

"You'll have to ask Caroline. All I know is, I'll be surprised if one has nothing to do with the other."

We heard a noise at the door, and I got up and looked down the staircase. There was a carefully placed mirror on the wall that let you see the front door from upstairs, as long as the curtains at the bottom of the stairs were open. Pat Reed was coming in the front door.

"Be right down, Pat!" I called. I turned back to the chief. "Is there anything else I should know?" I asked him.

"Not at the moment," he answered, taking one last glance around the room, setting his jaw, and offering me a stiff nod. "But I'll keep you apprised."

chapter 13

I walked down the stairs, with the chief following close behind. Pat's face fell when he saw him.

"I just hung up from a call with Caroline," I said, pretending not to notice the staring contest between Chief Paisley and Pat. Neither man acknowledged the other, nor did they seem inclined to.

"What's all of this?" I asked, pointing to a mop and bucket and a roll of paper towels.

"Thought I would clean up a bit," Pat said.

I looked around and saw the jumbled boxes, the fine film of dust, and smudges of what I assumed was fingerprint powder. I hadn't noticed all of that last night in the lower light. I noticed a new box of paperwork on the counter.

"What's that?" I asked.

"Ask him," Pat said.

"I brought this over earlier this morning." Chief Paisley picked up one of the sheets. "This is all of the paperwork collected the morning of the incident. We've made copies of it all, and I wanted to give it to you since you're here now. And it's your shop now, from what I understand."

"You don't need this?" I said. "I thought you were still investigating."

"Thom's death continues to be an open investigation. As does the theft of the clocks last month. By law, we could keep everything and lock down this building. But a year in Orchard has taught me a few things, and one of them is shutting down a business, even for a few days, doesn't serve the community."

"Wonder how you figured that out?" Pat said under his breath, loud enough for us both to hear.

The silence that followed was icy, so I jumped in.

"Thanks for bringing the cleaning supplies, Pat. It's probably a good idea. Let me just change my jacket."

"No, Ruthie, I can clean up down here. How about if you take the box of papers upstairs and try to make some sense of them. Take the calendar. Make sure we're not missing anything important."

"I don't know if I could be much help with sorting the files," I said as I looked through the box. There were scraps of paper, invoices, and dozens of four-by-six index cards.

"You at least speak the language on them," Chief Paisley said. "Warning wheels, J levers, strike release pins? Some of these look like orders, others seem to be invoices, or repairs that need to be done. There might be something there that could help reconstruct what Thom was working on that night."

I looked around the shop. "Do you have jobs in the shop in addition to the estate sale work?"

Pat nodded. "We had a few jobs that were ready to be picked up, so I've been delivering them. And there were a few outstanding jobs. I could do a few of them, but most need you to look at them, Ruthie. I don't feel confident in doing the work myself."

"Have you become a clockmaker?" I said, smiling.

"An apprentice of sorts." Pat laughed. "Sounds crazy at my age, but Thom was giving me more and more jobs to do on my own, and then he'd look them over. With this much inventory, it was all hands on deck."

"I will look them over. But first, Pat, would you walk me through the inventory system one more time?"

"Fascinating as that sounds, I am going to leave you both to it. Nice to meet you, Ms. Clagan," Chief Paisley said. "Pat, you take care."

"See you soon, Chief," Pat said, not sounding thrilled at the prospect.

"Oh, you can count on that," the chief said. He stared at Pat for a few more seconds. Pat, to his credit, did not blink or look away. I totally would have folded.

"What's that all about?" I asked after the door closed behind the chief.

"I had some outstanding parking tickets and the chief threatened to throw me in jail. He's very by the book, mildly put. Anyway, let's not talk about him. Let me show you the new system we've set up. I think you may be impressed. At least I hope so."

Pat turned to the laptop on the counter. "This isn't completely paper free, but we're trying. See that number in the corner of this index card? That's the coding system Caroline used, the one I showed you this morning. On the clocks that are in for repair, you'll see a blue piece of painter's tape on clocks with that number. Once the repair is done, we put a Cog & Sprocket tag on the clock and include that number on it. Anyway, the number goes here in the database. And then we fill out the rest of the information as we find it. The type of clock, the maker, the history of it—"

"The repairs needed. The repairs made. The owner of the clock. That's terrific. Lots of information," I finished.

Pat nodded and said, "Levi Adler, Caroline's son, says he will work on it some more over the holidays. But for right now, it's been a great way to start to work on all of the new inventory, since the Chairman kept a lot of these records on a spreadsheet already."

"Are you taking pictures of the clocks?"

"Another Levi project."

"Is the database on a network?" I asked.

"Another Levi project," we both said at the same time. I smiled. Baby steps. At least there was a computer system. Sort of.

"How about tracking payments on repairs?" I tried.

"Well, Ruthie, I'm going to let you down on that. See this button here? That's what you click to print an invoice. Course, the computer and the printer need to be connected. Which is a whole other project. Caroline usually takes care of that. Anyway, once the invoice is printed, we're back to paper. We use the ledger, this one here, for the rest of the journey."

Pat handed me a ledger that looked like it was from the early 1900s. "You put the number in this column, a bit of a description, customer name, and amount due. Then you highlight the amount due in yellow and put it with the clock. Once it's paid, you—"

"Mark it paid with a red check."

I opened up the ledger and ran my finger along the familiar handwriting. I looked at the beginning of the ledger. Nineteen ninety-five. Two decades of the Clagan family business all in one book. I shivered a bit.

"Cold?" Pat asked.

"A little, I guess," I said.

"I've got the air on, trying to get it cleared up a bit for Caroline. Makes it chilly. You want to borrow a jacket?" There were wooden pegs on the wall by the back door, and several work shirts and jackets hung there. Pat walked over and picked up a blue and black wool shirt, handing it to me. I held it up to my face. It smelled of machine oil, Brut, pipe smoke, and pancakes. It smelled like my grandfather. I breathed it in, hoping my tears wouldn't dilute the scent.

"So, where are you with the inventory back here? Can we move some of this stuff around?" I asked, pulling the shirt over my shoulders.

"Absolutely. Caroline thought we should wait until you got here to organize it all. It would give you a chance to look things over at the same time."

"Does she want to be here too?"

"Your store now, from what I understand."

I nodded. "I know that's awkward, since I haven't been here for a while."

"No, it's right. It does my heart good to think of you running the old place. You are going to run it, aren't you?"

"Me? Oh wow. I don't know what I'm going to do. I have a life, sort of, back in Boston." Boston felt so far away. I'd been staying in Steve and Rick's guest room for months, ever since the separation. Half of my belongings were in storage. Was it really a life? Or a holding pattern?

"Pat, I promise, you'll be the first to know. So, talk to me about these boxes."

"That's another spreadsheet. Also on the computer. Hold up, it's right here."

I took a breath as he fumbled with the software. I knew I could find and open what he was looking for in a matter of seconds. But I could only understand the business with Pat's help, and the business was more than a spreadsheet. Much more. I looked closely at the nearest crate and noticed a number written in marker on the upper right-hand corner.

"Here it is." I walked around to look at the spreadsheet with him. Sure enough, the crate number was there, along with the clocks that were listed inside. The clock numbers from the database were also included. I realized that the data was all in the same place. I ached to scroll through at a quicker pace, but I patiently let Pat show me how it worked.

"So, if we look in this crate, for example, we should find three banjo clocks, two mantel clocks, and a Vienna wall clock. All from the Winter estate. Should we test the theory?"

"Sure." I was thrilled to see that the crate did, indeed, include those very clocks. I wanted desperately to examine each timepiece more closely, to turn them over in my hands, but there would be time for that later.

I looked around and thought about how best to rearrange things to create enough space to do some work while maintaining some of the order out of the chaos.

"Pat, what do you think about us moving the grandfathers over to that wall?" I pointed to the blank wall on the far side of the shop. "And then moving the crates over there? The clocks are taking up a lot of space, but it's not easy to work on them from back there. I think we need to figure out a game plan for them first, don't you?"

"Sounds like a plan. Let me get the dolly. Are you going to get changed?"

I looked down at my black leggings and black tunic. I took off my belt and then the borrowed plaid shirt, folding both of them over the chair. My Doc Martens boots were my go-to shoes for everything, and excellent work boots. "No, good to go."

I walked over to the grandfather clocks to get a better look at them. Most of them were missing their pendulums and weights, though there were several of each lined up nearby. We cleared wall space first and then moved each one over. We placed them in a pattern that took up the least amount of floor space while giving us enough room to walk around so we could work on them. My hands itched to reassemble each one, to see if they worked. Were they stopped because they ran down or were they stopped because they needed repair? Grandfather clocks were a delicate balance of movement and required many pieces. I promised myself this would be the last time I moved them if I could help it.

"Ruthie, see here? The blue tape on each weight and pendulum? The clocks are labeled A, B, C, and so on. Pendulums are labeled. And the weights are AR, AC, AL, for right, center, and left."

There was a stack of towels on one of the side tables. I took one, put it in front of clock C, and found its missing parts.

"We're missing the guts for clock E," I said, turning to scan every surface in the room for the parts one more time.

"Grover's Folly," Pat said.

"Grover's Folly?"

"Sorry. That's what Thom called it. Grover Winter left it to your grandfather specifically; we didn't buy it with the others. At first, we thought it was a joke, since the old girl had been gutted and it was all electric. There was a pendulum, though. Wonder where that got to?" he said as he straightened a pile of crates against the wall.

A little alarm went off in my brain and it must have showed on my face.

"Ruth? What is it?"

"Nothing," I said slowly, considering. "So tell me, was it a joke gift?"

"No, far from it. This was the Chairman's safe. Hidden pockets with notes. Puzzle drawers that only opened at a certain time of day. Two false bottoms."

"Any hidden treasures?"

"Well, we did find a sea clock, a beauty, a perfect replica of the original Harrison design. We found it in one of the false bottoms."

"The clock wasn't the real thing?"

"Alas, no. Boy, that would be something. From what we could tell, most of the Winter estate was replicas. Good replicas, but replicas. The clock had a note in the case from Grover that said, 'This is the key to it all' or something like that."

"John Harrison was a great clockmaker. Maybe G.T. was working on his own copy of a Harrison?"

"Nope, not that he mentioned. And he would have mentioned it."

"What does it mean?"

"No idea. We have no idea. Thom kept it, brought it home

to look at it more closely, but he didn't find anything. We looked all over the case—didn't find anything else."

"I really look forward to looking at it more closely later. But let's keep organizing. How about if we check each crate and then stack them over along that side of the shop? We can mark where they all are."

"Sounds good. Want me to call over to Caroline's to see if she can help us out?"

"I think we can do it. I'm pretty tall and we can use the stepladder if we need to," I said, not relishing the thought of spending more time with Caroline Adler than I already had to.

We moved the smaller crates from the top of the large ones first. Pat handed them to me and I stacked them to the side of the shop, looking at the markings and checking them against the inventory sheet. Pat was right, they weren't heavy. But there were a lot of them. We got into a routine very quickly.

"So tell me about Moira and the old diner," I said, having confirmed that there were three more banjo clocks in the crate. That made twelve total, and we weren't close to done yet.

"She bought it a little over a year ago. It had a couple of owners since you left. Last folks tried to make it a fancy coffee shop. You can only imagine how well that went over."

I laughed out loud. I could indeed. Orchard didn't take well to two things: chain stores and high-end boutiques. Though the town had its share of tourists, most of the residents were firmly middle class and lived that way. Even the Cog & Sprocket stayed "Old Orchard," as my grandmother used to call it. Well tended, clean, but very New England and utilitarian. New Englanders didn't go in for high style.

"The good news is the owners just walked away, left the machinery in place. The bad news is no one wanted five-dollar coffee. So Moira bought it, brought back the diner menu of burgers and breakfast, but kept the high-end coffee as a choice. It's working real well for her. The locals go there for breakfast, the college kids spend the afternoon drinking coffee. Nancy's working there part-time, helping with the lunch rush during the week. And keeping up with the baking."

"It was great to see them both," I said, smiling at the mention of the Reed family matriarch. I checked off a box of three mantel clocks. It was all I could do to not open the crate and look at the contents, but I stayed focused on the task at hand.

"Pat," I said, stopping for a moment, "are we ever going to know what happened to him?"

"I don't know, Ruthie. I just don't know," he said, shaking his head.

"Nancy invited me over for dinner tonight," I said to fill the heavy silence.

"Good. I'm glad you're back, Ruthie."

Funny, when I was studying in London or making my life in Boston, I barely thought about the Reeds. Now I felt their absence in my life like a toothache. I sighed and pulled my hair out of the ponytail, shook it out, and then gathered it all back up and refastened it. That should last five, maybe ten minutes. I cocked my head to the side. Then I stood back up. The light was definitely catching a sparkle.

"You need to rest a bit, Ruthie?" Pat asked.

"No, just thought I saw something. Yes, I did." I bent down and crawled under the worktable. I backed up and stood up carefully, avoiding the corner of the worktable.

"Look at this, Pat." I held out my palm and showed Pat the pearl and diamond earring I'd found. The three diamond drops must've been what had caught my eye in the light.

"How did you see that way under there?"

"When you moved that last box, the light hit the corner. I thought I saw something and apparently I did. Wow. Is it Caroline's?"

"I've never seen her with them on, but I can't say I'd notice one way or the other."

"I'll ask her about it. It's lovely. I really hope someone has the mate." I put it in the pocket of my tunic. "I really appreciate your help, Pat. You must have a million other things to do."

"Nothing more important than this. Well, that's the last one. Not sure it made more space though."

"Well, at least I got a sense of what was in the crates."

"Do you want to look over the shelves next?" Pat asked.

I glanced over at Pat, who looked as tired as I felt. "Maybe tomorrow? I am having lunch with Caroline, then she's coming by the shop."

"Sounds good. Listen, I'm going to clean up a bit and then head home. I hear we've got company coming tonight. Why don't you head upstairs and get some rest?"

"Mind if I take the computer with me?"

"She's all yours. See you tonight."

chapter 14

I ate one of the sandwiches Moira sent over and put the second one in the refrigerator. My sandwich had slabs of turkey, shaved Swiss cheese, and some amazing cranberry chutney that added a little heat. Delicious. I sat at the kitchen table in my traditional spot at the end of the table looking over to the kitchen, in full view of the door from the shop. When I was in high school I had rigged several systems in addition to the mirror to help me know when someone was coming up. I'd need to reinstall a few of them.

I ate every bite of the sandwich despite Bezel's intermittent mewing requests for a taste as she wove her body around my legs and the chair. I resisted the temptation to eat the second one. Tempting as eating three meals a day at the Sleeping Latte was, there were two problems with that plan. First, I'd gain ten pounds in a week. And second? I craved being alone.

I liked people, but the thought of eating three meals a day publicly held no appeal. I'd try and get to the store in between the real estate appointment and going to the Reeds' house for dinner. What time was the real estate meeting? Four? I should have put the appointment in my phone.

My phone calendar was set to e-mail me a reminder of appointments an hour in advance and then to ring ten minutes before a meeting. I sighed. It didn't help. My inability to keep time for myself was just plain embarrassing. I studied time. I built timepieces. Accuracy was an obsession. But I was perpetually late for everything. Or hopelessly early. It wasn't that I couldn't keep time, I just couldn't remember it in time.

I took the calendar off the top of the box the chief had brought up. True to Caroline's word, I found the real estate agent's card clipped to the corner. I took it and slid it into the card slot on the other side of my phone case. Google told me it was a twenty-minute drive to the Marytown office. I factored in a longer drive because of leaf peepers, and another twenty minutes just in case. It was almost two. I had over an hour; might as well start looking things over.

The Cog & Sprocket system must have been in my DNA. It took me about five minutes to remember my grandfather's shorthand. I flipped through the pages of the general ledger, trying to get a sense of how the business was doing. There were jobs off-site, tending to clock towers or tuning up a grandfather that couldn't be moved. Some regular winding appointments. But most of the work still came into the shop. That had stayed steady. What had been slowing down were the clock sales. G.T. hadn't embraced the Internet yet, and I'd bet that was impacting the business.

I looked at the calendar again. Never one for pretty pictures, my grandfather's plain calendar had big blocks for writing appointments. They also included G.T.'s plans for the future and notes on the past. A lunch with Ben last Tuesday, with the notation *in* next to it. A call made to Stephanie last Thursday, with a *time* notation. Stephanie? Stephanie Lincoln? Yeesh. I looked down at my own watch. Ten minutes of four. Could I make the twenty-minute drive in ten? I could sure try.

I ran out the door, shouting to Bezel I'd be back. I went down to the shop, shouting to Pat that I'd see him later, at his house. I doubted he'd hear me over the drone of the shop vac. What was he doing back there? No time to check. Late!

chapter 15

I barreled out the front door and clambered into the car, tossing my bag on the other seat. I took a deep breath and pulled out my cell phone case. Living in the land of two bars drained my battery. I plugged it into the lighter and put the address of the real estate agent into my GPS. Predicted arrival: 4:23. Hah! You'd think the GPS would know better by now. I'd be five minutes late, tops.

I put on my seat belt, put the car in reverse, and started to move in one, fluid, well-practiced move. A person in grayish blue clothes jumped out of the way at the last possible moment, grazing the corner of my car with a hip. Or a leg. Maybe a head. I couldn't tell. The figure disappeared as quickly as it appeared.

I swallowed hard, throwing the car into park and jumping out to see what happened.

"Please no, please no, please no," I whispered. I ran to the back of the car.

"Are you okay? I'm so sorry," I said.

I bent over the figure that was knocked on the ground on her side. Definitely a she. Maybe ten years older than I was, but I couldn't be sure. Her hair was a mess of brown, blond streaks, and gray. Her mascara was smudged and her lipstick was slightly crooked. I realized the gray was a Safety Service delivery uniform. Twenty-four-hour delivery anytime, anywhere. I hoped she wasn't on a deadline.

"I didn't see you," she said as she shifted, testing her body's limits.

"I didn't see you. Should I call an ambulance? Where'd you come from?" I looked around.

Where did she come from? I was parked in front of the shop in our small lot. No other cars or trucks were there. I looked around, but didn't see the familiar gray and yellow truck anywhere. Since this side of the shop was on a corner with no parking, where had she been? Was she parked out back?

"Look, I'm really very sorry. I didn't see you. Are you all right? Can I help you up?" I asked.

"I'm fine. I'm fine. I was just startled," she said, slowly gathering herself in a crouch. "You're Ruth Clagan, aren't you?" She looked up at me and then looked away quickly as she stood. She steadied herself with one hand on my car.

"Do I know you?" I asked. She looked familiar, but most people in Orchard sort of looked alike, at least to my Boston-focused eyes. She just stared at me.

"I don't think so. My name's Aggie Kurt. I grew up here in Orchard. I heard Thom's granddaughter was in town, taking over the shop. Put two and two together."

"Did you know my grandfather?"

"Of course. I made regular deliveries here. He always had time for me. Always. He was a good man." She started to weep. I reached out to touch her shoulder, but she turned away.

"Aggie, are you parked out back? Where's your truck? Are you on duty? Can I call someone?" I asked frantically, anxious to be sure she was physically all right and also desperate to get on my way.

"I'm fine," she repeated firmly, brushing the dust from her uniform.

I took a deep breath. "Listen, why don't I call the police. Just in case you're hurt. Maybe they can bring an ambulance with them." I bent down and reached for my phone, which was charging on the dash.

"No!" She reached out and clasped my arm. "No cops. I'm fine. Just fine. No cops. You've got to promise me. No cops."

"All right. No cops." I pulled my arm back and watched helplessly as she tried to pull herself together.

"Sorry, sorry," she said as she stepped back, looking like she was trying to smile. "No cops, okay? I've got a dozen parking tickets; they're just waiting to arrest me. I know they are. Listen, it was nice to meet you. I'm sure I'll see you around."

I watched Aggie walk toward Ben's shop and then hook a left to the rear access road. I was tempted to follow her partly to be sure she was safe and partly to see where she was headed in such a hurry, but a quick glance at my watch propelled me back to the car.

chapter 16

I pulled up in front of the real estate agency. Four twenty-five. Time was not on my side, but hopefully the real estate agent was. There were a few different companies in the Berkshires, but these gray and burgundy signs were omnipresent. I swiped on some lip gloss and walked up to the office.

"Hello. How can we help you today?" the very cheery blonde said, looking up from her laptop as I walked in.

"I have an appointment with Stephanie Lincoln?"

"With Steph? Really? And you are?"

"Ruth Clagan."

"Ms. Clagan? Your appointment was for two o'clock."

"Two? I thought it was for four."

"No." The blonde tapped on a few keys. "It says right here the appointment was for two o'clock on Saturday—that's today—for Thom Clagan. Steph called to change it on Monday. It says so, right here. I keep records of everything."

"I'm sure you do. He didn't note the change on his calendar. I'm Thom Clagan's granddaughter. I'm not even sure what the appointment was for, but his wife asked me to keep it. Would it be possible to reschedule it?"

"The appointment was with Thom Clagan. As he is the client, I'm not sure if I should be talking to you. Is Mr. Clagan under the weather?" she asked, not looking up from the screen.

"Mr. Clagan passed away on Wednesday."

"Oh, I'm so sorry." She didn't sound that sorry, but she did sound surprised.

"Thank you," I said. "Perhaps I can reschedule the appointment?"

"I'm sorry to say that Steph is out of the office for a couple of weeks. This appointment was her last before she left for the airport," she chirped. "Going on a cruise and off the grid. She did put a package in the mail for Mr. Clagan."

"Perhaps I can take it? Are you mailing it to the Cog & Sprocket or to his house?"

"The Cog & Sprocket? Oh, I know that shop. I took my mother's mantel clock over to be fixed. They did a wonderful job. I think I just saw the shop in the news. Oh, wait. Was that your grandfather? Oh, I'm sorry." This time she sounded sorry.

I pulled out my wallet and slid my license out of its sleeve, pushing it across the desk. "Here is my license. See, same last name." Not for the first time I was grateful that I hadn't changed my name when I got married. "I'm staying at the shop and will get the package anyway. Surely you could just give it to me."

"I'm so sorry, Ms. Clagan, but Steph already sent it out with a delivery service. Did it herself, right before she left."

"Do you know what's in it?"

"I think Steph sent him some comparables, for other businesses in the area. And there must have been other information—it was pretty thick. I know they'd spoken several times over the past few weeks. A terrible time for Stephanie to be out of the office, but who am I to say anything? I just run the office, that's all. Anyway, you'll get the envelope soon enough. Tuesday, Wednesday at the latest. Sorry I couldn't be more help."

So was I. I wondered what G.T. and Stephanie had been up to.

chapter 17

Imeandered back toward Orchard with my GPS on, even though I knew where I was going. I always drove with my GPS these days, just so if I took a wrong turn, I could get back on track. I never really minded getting lost, but there is something comforting in knowing your latitude and longitude no matter what. It was all so odd, coming back all these years later to a town that was both familiar and foreign to me. G.T. had always been a bit of an outsider, even though he'd lived in Orchard his entire life. You had to earn his respect and once it was gone, it was gone for good. Things that lost his respect included the obvious: lying and cheating. But I remembered his disdain for old Mr. Clark, who ran the Corner Market. Whenever I visited we were one of the only families in Orchard who went the next town over for groceries. It was a pain in the neck and I told my grandmother so one particularly sullen summer Saturday when I was about sixteen.

"Why do we have to go all the way to Marytown for milk?" I whined. "The Corner Market has milk. All we have to do is walk down the block. I'll do it."

"Ruth Ann," my grandmother said. She always called me Ruth Ann when she wanted to end a conversation with no argument. "You know that we don't give the Corner Market Clagan business. Now get in the car."

"But why not?" I asked with my hand on the car door. "Everyone else does."

"Not everyone," she said, lowering her voice. "No, not everyone. Listen, Mr. Clark and his brother owned the store together for years. Your grandfather was friends with them both. When his brother died in that horrible accident, Mr. Clark bought out his sister-in-law for a fraction of the business's worth and never offered a penny to his brother's kids. They struggled and had to move in with her family down in Rhode Island. That didn't sit right with your grandfather. So we don't give him our money."

"How long ago was that?"

"Five years."

"That's a long time to hold a grudge," I said, my hand still gripping the door handle.

"Ruth, this should tell you something about your grandfather," she said, reaching across and opening the door for me. "He's an honorable man and has a strict code. He expects a lot from himself and as much from others. I for one am proud to be married to such a man."

My grandparents were a unit. My parents were also devoted to each other, in their own absentminded professor sort of way. I thought about my ex-husband. Even in our honeymoon phase, which was pretty short, I'm not sure I was devoted to him. I thought I was, but in retrospect, not so much. I think that G.T. knew that the first time he met my ex, but I wasn't willing to listen to him. Not getting G.T.'s blessing bothered me more than I'd been willing to admit.

"We're family now, baby," my ex said one day. "We don't need anyone else. We're all we'll ever need."

Ha! Until you met the younger, cuter version of me, jerk. I still couldn't believe it. He'd left me for the grad assistant for his British literature course—what a cliché. I felt a mixture of anger, and relief. Which probably wasn't a good sign. The divorce itself was finally done and the paperwork was finished. That was the whole reason I went on that silly retreat and part of the conversation I'd wanted to have with G.T. And now I couldn't ever tell him about the marriage or my divorce.

I was almost back in Orchard by the time I realized I still needed to grocery shop while I was out and about. Though I told myself that my reasons were to fill my cupboards and growling belly, in truth I did want to see if past resentments still existed between my grandfather and the little shop. So I broke with tradition and headed toward Clarks' Corner Market.

chapter 18

I tried to pull into the parking lot, but it was full—all six spots. Looked like things were hopping at the Corner Market. I parked my car at the Cog & Sprocket and walked back. I was careful to use the crosswalk and looked back at Ben's Barbershop to see if he'd notice, but I couldn't see if he was there. Shaded glass. I shook my head. Maybe I'd explain how small towns worked, the next time I saw him. Which I hoped was soon, much to my own surprise.

I slowed down and took a long look at the Corner Market as I walked toward the front door. This Corner Market was different than the Corner Market of my youth. Not that there was anything wrong with that Corner Market, aside from the family feud my grandfather had with the previous owner. From the outside, the changes were subtle, but significant. The siding was gone, replaced by cedar shingles. The front porch was a porch, not just a cement slab that provided an entrance. The new porch was also cement, but it went across the entire front of the building, with a ramp that turned on one side, allowing for greater access to the doors. The doors themselves were still double-sided wooden doors that swung in when you pushed. I grabbed a basket, pushed through the doors onto the mat, and immediately saw that the changes were not only cosmetic.

I defied my grandfather and went to the Corner Market with Moira a few times when I was in high school. I remembered the creamy penuche fudge with fondness, but that was my only good memory. It was mostly aisles of canned goods, some halfway-decent dairy without much variety, and a depressing produce section in case you needed a potato or two. The aisles were tight, the lighting was bad, and you had to know where you were going in order to get there.

But even if the food was subpar, the Corner Market was the place to go to meet folks and catch up on "news" or, if you were honest, the gossip. My grandmother didn't mind missing out on the food once we'd started boycotting, but I know she missed out on the gossip, which is one of the reasons she started bringing tea over to Parker's Emporium.

The new Corner Market felt old-fashioned and fresh all at once. Gone were the linoleum floors, replaced by wide pine floors that I suspected had been there all the time, since the building was one of the oldest in Orchard. The aisles had been replaced with large sections of shelving that suited the old-time feel of the store: more wood, less metal. To the right of the entrance were large wooden bins of fresh produce, all locally grown, according to the signage. When I looked closer, I saw the name of the local farm on the tag.

I grabbed a few potatoes and walked around to the other side. NOT LOCAL, BUT ORGANIC, the sign said. I browsed the lemons and limes. And were those mangoes? I picked one up, smelled it, and dropped it in the basket.

Behind the produce the refrigerator section spanned the side wall, filled with locally produced and organic food choices. I hovered my hand above the nice cheese selection, yogurts, and local eggs. I added a few more items, and was sorry I hadn't taken a cart. I noticed the rotisserie chickens in the meat section and made a mental note to come back tomorrow when I wasn't going out to dinner. Cooking for one had made me a boring eater of late. A roasted chicken frequently got me through several days' worth of meals.

I noticed a half dozen people crowded around a table in the middle of the store, dodging shoppers on their way to check out. Beckett Green was busy sampling the wine. I thought about going over and saying hello, but decided against it. I didn't have the energy. I recognized the couple Moira had pointed out at the Sleeping Latte: the owners and apparently the Orchard food police. He stood behind a small table with paper cups and open bottles of wine, talking to Beckett. What was his name? I looked over at his full beard and longish hair. Less a hippie, more of a hipster. His clothes were casual but expensive. He smiled while he topped off Beckett's cup. She handed out napkins to people who nibbled on heaps of cheese, olives, and crackers on the table to her left. There were a couple of other employees talking to the crowd, gesturing toward the items and handing out coupons. I tried to figure out how to navigate around the crowd to get to the wine racks, dry goods, and ready-made sections behind them, when the woman approached me. I put my heavy basket down.

"Hello, I don't think we've met yet. I'm Ada Clark. Are you new in town?" She reached out her hand and I took it.

Ada Clark looked like she was in her mid to late twenties, a couple of years younger than I was. I felt freakishly tall next to her. Long, dark curls framed her face, and her layered outfit of a flowing top and leggings could have been fashionable were it not for the heavy wool socks and Birkenstocks she sported on her feet. She had a beautiful smile, sparkling brown eyes, and a reassuring handshake. I glanced at her pregnant belly, and the world seemed to stop for just a second. A year ago, the plan had been for my ex-husband and me to start a family soon. Now I was glad that hadn't happened, especially given the way everything had turned out. Still, I felt a pang as I shook Ada's hand, and tried to smile.

"No, we haven't met. I'm Ruth Clagan."

"Oh, you're Ruth. Oh." Ada brought up her other hand and covered mine, holding it. "Oh, Ruth, I'm so sorry. I didn't know you were here, otherwise I would have come by the shop."

I drew my hand from her grasp, gently.

"Thank you," I said. "I just thought I'd come by and pick up some groceries. There isn't much food at the apartment above the shop."

"At the shop?" Ada asked. "You're staying there?"

"Yes, of course. Where else would I stay?" I asked. Where indeed? There were alternatives, of course. I could stay with the Reeds, try and find a hotel, or even go back to Boston. But there was so much work to be done, and what better way was there to honor my grandfather but to finish the jobs that were in the shop? Besides, the Cog & Sprocket and I needed to make peace before I could decide what to do with her.

And besides, Bezel needed a roommate. I couldn't bring her back to Boston, since my landlords had dogs, and I couldn't just leave her in the shop. We'd figure out what to do.

"I'm sorry. The whole thing has me in a bit of a state. And I can't imagine what you're going through. I really can't."

I wasn't about to try to tell her. First of all, I don't know that I could describe it adequately. And secondly, something in her tone made me feel that she was less concerned than curious.

"I haven't been to the store in years," I said. "It looks wonderful."

"Oh, thank you. We've done a lot of work on it. It seems to be coming together, though it's hard to get folks to come in because of Uncle Matthew, Mac's uncle, did you know him?"

I nodded. "Not well, but I did know him. Or I knew of him."

"Well, of course, your grandfather and Uncle Matthew had a falling-out of some sort, didn't they? And when Thom stopped coming to the store, it seemed like most of the town stopped for a few years. It's really quite remarkable that poor Uncle Matthew was able to stay in business, it really is."

I must have made a face even though I was trying not to react.

"Not that I blame your grandfather for ruining the store—of course not," she added. "I'm sure he had his reasons."

Yeesh. Ruining the store? Please. "I think it is wonderful that your husband was able to forgive his uncle for the way he treated his mother after Mac's father passed," I said. "And it's great that Matt Clark did the right thing and left you both the store." I faked a smile and then faltered. Maybe she didn't know the family history?

"Thom was always cordial to Mac and me. And those days are finally past us now, aren't they? We can't let one old man's petty grudge—oh dear, you know what I mean. It's just that, oh dear."

I just stared at Ada for a second. Was she seriously calling my grandfather an old man with a petty grudge? And "past us"? Did she mean that now that my grandfather was dead, all of this history was going to be forgotten? I looked at her guileless face and saw a flicker of something more. She knew the history; I could tell. She was just determined to rewrite it. And with Thom Clagan gone, her version might finally stick. Poor Uncle Matt indeed.

My hackles started to rise but I took a deep breath. I could harrumph off and leave my basket, starting a second generation of feuds in the process, or I could be the better woman, ignore her, get my food, and go back to my own store. It really wasn't my business, but if she was going to be dragging my grandfather's name through the mud, it soon would be. I'd make sure I was prepared for her, though.

I bent down to pick up my basket. "It was nice to meet you."

I moved around Ada, looking to my right and grabbing a few cans of cat food and a box of dry food. I couldn't remember the specific brands of cat food at the shop, but Bezel needed to eat. I hoped she wasn't picky. As Ada walked back to her husband I kept breathing slowly, trying to focus on my shopping rather than the subtext of our conversation. Surely there weren't any real hard feelings? Or were there? Did my grandfather's boycott of the Corner Market really impact the store that much? Enough to cause someone to seek revenge? I wondered if Caroline shopped there.

When I turned again to look in another case, a couple of other people had joined Ada and Mac, and all four stared at me. Again, I smiled my fake smile. Five years as a faculty wife meant I'd mastered a really great fake smile that I could pull out at a moment's notice. Unless you knew me, you'd think it was real. And none of these people knew me. At all.

I glanced at the "ready to go" case, expecting to turn on my heel and make my grand exit, but the contents of the case stopped me. Containers of salads and spreads. Wrapped sandwiches. Ready-made microwavable meals. My stomach growled. I loaded up my basket with a container of chicken salad with walnuts and cranberry and a curried tuna salad with currants. I hoped they didn't taste as good as they looked, because boycotting a store with good food was going to be tough. On my way to the checkout counter with my overloaded basket I picked up some bread and a half a pumpkin pie. I deserved it.

The checkout counter was the same as it had always been, without a moving belt. I put my items on the counter.

"Do you have a bag?" the cashier asked.

"Just one, I'm afraid. Here it is." I grabbed the balled-up nylon bag and shook it open, handing it to the young man bagging the groceries.

"This won't be big enough. Do you want to buy another?" the clerk asked, pointing to the pile of canvas bags with THE CORNER MARKET emblazoned on them.

"No thanks," I said. I wasn't going to be a walking billboard for the Clark family until I knew what the status of the feud was. "I'll take paper."

chapter 19

The bags were full and heavy and I began to regret not buying a canvas bag. I felt the paper handles strain with each step. I put both bags down and tried to redistribute the weight a bit better. Wine in nylon bag, bread in paper. Potatoes in nylon, mango in paper.

As I refocused on walking home, I looked up the next block at Ben's Barbershop. The lights were on. I bet I could see inside now. Not that I wanted to stare, but in the dark, who could tell? The best part of twilight walking was looking in windows, since people inside couldn't necessarily see out. I loved getting glimpses of people and trying to figure out what was really going on. The waitress washing down tables at the Sleeping Latte, dancing with her earbuds on? From what I could see, she didn't have a care in the world.

Who was she? Was Moira there? I could stop by and find out, but I'd see her soon enough at her parents' house.

I crossed the street in the crosswalk, having looked both ways. I felt a bit ridiculous at first, but then a delivery truck barreled down the street, making me glad I'd stopped. Aggie Kurt was at the wheel, oblivious. Or so I thought until she waved. I needed to ask someone about Aggie Kurt. I'd bet Moira would know all.

I slowed a bit as I approached Ben's. I resisted the desire to check on my hair, which probably looked as if I had just stuck a fork into an electrical socket anyway. I licked my lips, wishing my lip gloss was in my jean jacket pocket. The rest of my uniform—black leggings tucked into Doc Martens, my tunic loosely belted, long earrings made out of clock parts—were what they were.

The shirt colors changed, I'd made five pairs of the earrings, and sometimes I added some variation of a skirt, but I'd worn the same style for a few months now, and loved it. The freedom of not having to be the staid faculty wife, wearing suits, sweater sets, and nice pants, defined only by my career-conscious husband, was a joy that I swore I'd never forget. I shook my head, still wondering how it all went so wrong. But I'd stopped blaming myself, which was a good sign.

I slowed down before I got to the barbershop and stood up a little straighter. I tried for a casual glance, in case Ben was looking out. I needn't have worried. He was in the throes of a passionate embrace. Or at least a big hug. The lucky recipient? Moira.

I sighed and kept walking. Maybe Moira would be lucky in love with the handsome barber. At least I had Bezel.

chapter 20

I carried the grocery bags up the front stairs of the shop. I wrestled with the keys again. Why were there so many keys on this ring? What did they all go to? I needed to ask Pat Reed if he knew, which he probably did. I found the one, relieved that I didn't have to go in through the back door. I couldn't bear to go in the shop that way. Not yet. Too many ghosts.

Thankfully, Pat had left some lights on, which helped. I hated it when the days got shorter. There were a couple of streetlights, but not close enough to the Cog & Sprocket to cut through the night. Back in Boston, it was never that dark out, but darkness redefined itself out in the Berkshires. As I walked in, I noticed a piece of paper in the middle of the foyer. I put down my bags and turned on more lights.

Ruth, so sorry, but we need to postpone dinner till

tomorrow. I don't have your cell phone number. Mine is 413-555-3511. Come to the Latte for coffee in the morning. xoxo Moira

I texted her back, *Ruth here, see you tomorrow.* Was she ditching me for Ben? Did I care?

Frankly, I was more relieved than anything. It had been a long day and I needed to settle in. Not to mention I had lunch with Caroline looming tomorrow. I brought in the bags and then closed and locked the front door of the shop. Bezel came down the stairs, blinking her eyes and meowing loudly. No hissing this time. And no yowling. Just a conversational husky meow.

"Of course I bought you something," I said, smiling at the cat.

She really was a beauty. A good-sized cat with beautiful blue-gray fur, but surprisingly delicate on her feet. She meowed again, walked over, and head-butted my knees. She was pretty strong—they buckled a bit when she hit them just right. She looked at me, squished her eyes, and walked toward the back of the shop. I hesitated for a second but followed her, taking my grocery bags, turning lights off and on as I went through the shop.

We were almost at the staircase when Bezel turned and stood in the middle of the shop. She looked at me and then she jumped up on the back workbench and looked out the window. I looked at her, my heart pounding in my chest. I walked over and looked out the back window for the first time. There was nothing there. Not even G.T.'s ghost.

"What are you trying to show me, sweetheart?" She wouldn't let me get too close. Instead she walked me around the shop, to every corner. "You're telling me I'm home, aren't you?"

Bezel squished her eyes, came over to me. I knelt down and petted her head. I felt a tear stream down my face, and I wiped it with the back of my hand. When I looked around the shop, I saw G.T. bent over the workbench, lovingly bringing a clock back to life. One way I could honor his life was by continuing his work. Maybe it was a little bit for me too, since that was also my dream, and the idea of doing it in the Cog & Sprocket was perfect. But I also wanted G.T. to rest in peace. What could I do to help that along and get my own life back on track?

"Bezel, I think everything is going to be okay, don't you? See, the back door is locked." I double-checked that and pulled at the door. "I'll put these crates in front of it." I took the dolly and moved one of the stacks of crates over against the door. I checked on the windows and was relieved to see that they had extra locks on them. They looked new, with bits of sawdust still on the panes. No note, but an obvious Pat Reed effort.

"Tell you what, Bezel. Let's leave this light on, so people know we're home. How does that sound?"

Bezel meowed again and turned to walk back to the front of the shop. Talking to Bezel made me feel a lot less lonely. It helped that she talked back. I left the desk light on and rechecked every door and window on my way upstairs, to make sure they were locked. Then I did the same to the front of the shop.

Tight as a drum, as my grandfather used to say. I picked up the bags of groceries and carried them upstairs. I put the bags on the floor near the kitchen table and then turned to shut the door that went down to the shop. It was a beautiful eight-pane window door, with side lights on either side. I remembered helping my grandfather put the door in after I'd complained about being shut up in the dreary upstairs room. The door kept the noise out, so I could do homework or read. But the windows let me watch the comings and goings, especially after I put a mirror on the staircase. I was always interested in observing the comings and goings of Orchard. I was a little winded after hauling the groceries up the stairs. Pitiful. I needed to get back to the gym. Or, to be honest, start going to the gym. Or take a walk. Something.

I'd left in such a hurry that there was still the chaos of paperwork on the kitchen table. All part of my new world. I was tempted to leave it, but I could hear my grandmother's admonition: *"No work at the dinner table."* I compromised, piling the papers on one side, clearing off the other for eating. I unpacked the groceries and looked around. This afternoon the apartment looked like a disaster, but in the gentler evening light, the charm came back.

What a beautiful place the Cog & Sprocket was. I'd never really noticed it until I moved to Boston and saw the same architectural details being highlighted in the high-end rehabs of friends'. Crown molding, end caps, wainscoting. High-end architectural elements that I'd grown up with at the Cog & Sprocket, but never really appreciated. The tall ceilings were mostly tin up here and gave the space some charm. A little bit too shabby on the shabby chic scale, but still lovely. I had a couple of friends who would swoon over the chance to redo this space. It was small, but with a better layout? Perfect.

After I put my groceries away, I poured myself a glass of wine. I picked up my bag again. Oof. It was heavy. What was in there anyway? I looked in it—computer, cords, notebooks, a box of pencils, protein bars, a water bottle. I closed it back up. I'd tried to carry a purse, but it just didn't work for me. My life required a bigger bag. Hipster Mary Poppins. I smiled thinking of the chief's remark, and shouldered the bag, carefully picking up the glass of wine.

I put my wine on the dresser and took stock. I opened the drawers in the dresser. They were all empty and clean. I put my clothes away and laid out my jewelry and toiletries on the top. Then I moved over to the armoire, hoping to make some room to hang up a few of my skirts.

I took out boxes of notebooks and bent down to look at what was filling up the bottom of the wardrobe. On the bottom there were boxes that were marked with my grandfather's handwriting. *Knitting Patterns* and *Cookbooks* and *Tea Cups* were three of the boxes. Some of my grandmother's things. I recognized her knitting bag and also saw one of her afghans resting on top. If I wanted to make room for clothing, I needed to move all of that. Right now, I couldn't take that trip down memory lane. Besides, there weren't any hangers.

While I looked around for another place to hang my clothes, I rested them on top of a couple of boxes that were stacked up. I decided to add a third box so that my longer skirt wouldn't hit the floor. As I moved a box from one stack to another, a large envelope dislodged from somewhere, hitting the floor right in front of me. I picked it up, noting it was addressed to my grandfather, from someone named J. Harrison with no return address. I peeked in and saw a picture of the Cog & Sprocket that must have dated back from the turn of the last century. Another rabbit hole that I didn't want to fall into. I added the envelope to the pile in the wardrobe. I spied a coatrack in the corner and dragged it over.

"This place is a mess," I said to Bezel, who appeared in the doorway. She meowed in response, resting comfortably on my pile of skirts. "Get off those, please. Good thing you've got gray fur; it goes with most of my clothes. I can already tell I'm going to be wearing you all day."

I really didn't mind. I'd missed having a pet and already felt less alone than I had in a while. I looked through boxes and started to move them into some semblance of order. Since I'd looked over the papers from downstairs, it all made a little more sense. I had assumed that this was more inventory that needed to be repaired, but then I found a few clocks that I recognized. They'd been in older crates than the other clocks, more showpieces than anything. From the look of things, they'd been put away with some care, wrapped in old tea towels I remembered from my childhood. These had always been "Grandma's clocks," stronger on beauty than the art of horology. Some of them, many of them, had been electrified at one point in their history. Others were attached to neon signs, part of the vintage collections that my grandmother had loved so. My grandfather had been less of a fan, but indulged her.

I separated the clocks out as best I could. It might be nice to use some of them up here once the space got in better shape. I liked the potential of the wide openness of the room, but it needed some work to make it someone's home. Like getting rid of the clock guts spewed all over tables. Creating a better storage system for the clocks. Taking down the rest of the walls or putting them back up. Lots to think about.

I poured another glass of wine, fed Bezel, and then made

a sandwich. Thick slices of homemade bread. Chicken salad with a little bit of mayonnaise, some toasted walnuts, and dried cranberries. There was a hint of sage in the salad as well. It was delicious.

"Looks like I can't boycott the Corner Market after all, Bezel. Food's too good."

She looked up at me and squished her eyes, then went back to her own dinner. She obviously was enjoying her food as well.

I walked back to the bedroom area, finally exhausted. I went in to take a shower and to wash my hair. I fought back the curtains as I raked my fingers through the knots in my mess of curls. Being cleaner felt good, though. I braided my wet hair, hoping that would help keep it tangle free. I brushed my teeth and climbed into bed, bringing my notebook with me. I started to write without editing myself. I made lists of what I had done today. I made a task list for Monday. I opened to a blank page, and drew a line down the middle, listing with the pros of keeping the Cog & Sprocket on one side and cons on the other. I stopped after a few minutes. My heart wasn't in it. Instead I opened to another page, and titled it "What Happened to G.T."

The first thing I wrote was *G.T. was murdered*. Just spelling out the words caused me pain like I'd never known. Bezel jumped up on the bed and picked her way over to me, getting in as close as she could before rubbing against my upper arm. I looked down at her and put my head down. She gave me a head-butt and then flopped down next to me, purring like a lawn mower.

"Thanks, Bezel. I needed that." I went back to the notebook. I made notes on the people I'd met. Beckett Green.

The chief. The Clarks. Aggie Kurt. Ben Clover. The Reeds. I made notes on all of them, and the stories I'd heard. There were some questions, but I hoped the notes from the real estate agent would answer some of them. What was G.T. up to? And how could any of this lead to him being killed?

I worked until I couldn't keep my eyes open anymore. I closed the notebook, and laid it under the pillow on the other side of the bed. I finally fell asleep with Bezel curled up on the other side of the bed.

chapter 21

I woke up early, too early, and couldn't get back to sleep, so I got up and made some terrible coffee. I decided the coffeemaker was beyond hope. My coffee was never stellar, but this was ridiculous. I was afraid it was going to eat through the mug. Nonetheless, I finished my first cup and went back for a second.

I went to the bedroom to get my notebook and looked at the model of the Clagan clock tower sitting on top of the wardrobe. I felt my grandfather's presence, urging me to get everything in order before I began to dream his dreams. I opened the lists I'd started last night and read them all over. Especially the last one. I needed to let G.T. rest in peace, find him some semblance of justice. Or maybe I was the one who needed the peace and the closure. That meant finding out what had happened, as difficult as that was. I opened a blank page and made one more list, of the things Caroline and I had to talk about. *Funeral? Cog & Sprocket. Clocks.* The categories were a little broad, but there was time to get more details in place before Caroline and I met for lunch.

G.T. was always a big believer in planning and preparation. I'd partially inherited that trait, though I tended to move forward before every *t* was crossed and every *i* was dotted, too worried about waiting too long and missing my moment. I'd seen that happen to my grandfather too often, especially around the clock tower project.

As I thought about the vast inventory he'd accrued, I wondered if he'd rethought his strategy of caution as well. Eight grandfather clocks in the shop? At once? I needed to spend more time looking at them, but the longcases themselves were worth a few thousand dollars apiece. And if the workings were original, or close? They could be worth ten times that. At least. When Caroline came by, I'd need to ask her about what the plan was for these clocks: to fully restore or to turn them around for sale. If my grandfather was the only horologist in the shop, I couldn't imagine him taking on all of these projects himself. Even if Pat could help out with minor repairs, getting all of these clocks ready for sale would take some serious effort. Did he have other staff that no one mentioned?

I went downstairs and walked around the shop with my cell phone, snapping pictures. Later, I'd add some descriptive tags and add them to the database Pat had showed me. But to make all that work easily, I needed the Internet.

I looked for Wi-Fi, but saw only BBSHOP listed nearby. Sigh. If I moved back to Orchard, I needed to get this place wired. If I moved back. Three days ago, that wasn't even on my wildest dreams list. Back in Boston, there was a chance that a job at the museum was going to get grant funding. A chance. I'd been relying on that for weeks now, but this time it might really happen. It wasn't my dream job, but it was a job that could lead to a career. Granted, that career wasn't what I'd expected when I'd studied horology, but being a clockmaker was a difficult career path and not a particularly glamorous one. I'd worked on expanding my skills by creating larger clocks that were installation pieces in offices and worked for rich clients on my own, but since my divorce, I needed to figure out how to make a living.

But now I also had the Cog & Sprocket. The question was, did I want to come back to Orchard? My grandfather was gone. I didn't even know his wife. Moira and I'd been friends back in the day, but even though yesterday had been great, was there anything left after the reminiscing? She had her life and I had mine. And judging from what I'd seen through the window last night, she and Ben had a relationship. I'd be a third wheel.

I could also sell the Cog & Sprocket and use the proceeds to start my career in Boston. Maybe buy my own shop or buy into a business? Too many choices. Not a bad problem to have after the past year.

Did Orchard want me back? The town's welcome was hardly robust. Unless you counted nutty Aggie Kurt or the stares of Ada and Mac Clark. Or Beckett Green's welcome, though he hadn't been back since I arrived. Even last night at the market he didn't come over to say hello. The only people who hadn't treated me like I was radioactive were Chief Paisley, the Reeds, and Ben. And Chief Paisley was only nice to me because I was off his suspect list.

I heard footsteps on the porch. We weren't open for

business, but I pulled the shade aside and looked out. A man was turned away from me, lifting plants off pots to peer underneath. I opened the door and put my hands on my hips.

"May I help you?" I asked.

I startled him and he dropped the potted mum. He half smiled and tried to pick it back up, scooping the dirt back in the pot. I just stared.

"Whoa, sorry. I didn't know anyone was here."

I looked at the tall, reed-thin man in front of me. Very pale skin, pale eyes, dishwater blond hair. His glasses were slightly askew. A few years ago I might have found his look somewhat attractive, but dollars to donuts he was an academic, and I was never going down that road again. I made a bet with myself. History, or maybe English?

"What are you looking for?" I asked. My tone was flat, but I felt my face flush. Was he trying to break in?

"A key." He shrugged, at least pretending to be abashed. "I have some things to drop off and I didn't want to have to make a trip back."

"Do you always let yourself into people's stores?"

"No, of course not. Who do you think I am?" he said, squinting at me as he brushed the dirt off his hands.

"I think you're someone who is breaking in."

"My father and Thom were good friends. I've been to this store a million times over the years. We were doing business together, Thom and I. Just wanted to make sure Caroline got the rest of the inventory is all."

Now I saw it. He looked like a pale, thin imitation of his father.

"Was your father the Chairman, I mean Grover, Winter?" I asked.

"He was. Did you know him?" he asked.

"Yes, I did. I'm Ruth Clagan. I was sorry to hear that he had passed."

"You're Ruthie?" he said, taking a step back with a glimmer of recognition in his eye. "Wow, you've changed. It's been a long time. I'm Jonah. Maybe you remember me?"

Remember you? My first crush ever? Jonah of the swim team? Jonah, homecoming hero? Jonah, the church usher who always winked and smiled at me when he handed me my program? This was Jonah? Even though he wasn't that much older than I was, maybe seven or eight years, he looked older. Still handsome, but very weary. Of course, I wasn't looking my best either. Stress was not kind to either of us.

"Of course I remember you, Jonah," I said, plastering a smile.

"I have a couple of boxes I wanted to drop off. May I?" he asked, looking behind me.

"Sure," I said. I stepped to the side and held the door open.

Jonah brought in a large box and set it on the counter. It was from a liquor store and didn't have a top. He went back outside to the porch, got another liquor box, and put it up next to the first. Both boxes were packed to the brim. I shifted the boxes and tried to take stock of the contents: several loose papers, small timepieces wrapped in Bubble Wrap, a mantel clock or two wrapped in dishcloths. It was all a bit jumbled, so hard to assess what the value was of each piece. My hands itched to open them up, but I held off.

"You know about the deal I made with your grandfather?" he asked, huffing and puffing a bit, leaning heavily on the counter.

"A little, but why don't you tell me about it?"

"I wonder if I could trouble you for a glass of water? I've had this flu I haven't been able to shake."

I looked at Jonah Winter and assessed the threat of inviting him upstairs. It seemed limited. And besides, I could take him, that much was clear.

"Why don't we go upstairs and I'll make you some tea," I said, closing and locking the front door. I grabbed one of the boxes, the heavy one, and headed toward the staircase.

"I don't want to trouble you," he said, picking up the other box and following me up the stairs.

"No trouble. I was about to take a break myself. Put the box over here." I sat my box down on one of the card tables I'd set up. He put his beside mine and then looked around the space.

"I've never been up here."

"It is, was, the family apartment way back in the day."

I put some water in the electric kettle and turned back to offer Jonah his choices. He looked through some of the boxes I'd put aside last night, moving things around a bit.

"Jonah, English Breakfast or Earl Grey? That's all I've got."

"English Breakfast is fine, thanks. Sorry I'm wandering. Just that some of these clocks, they bring back memories."

"Seller's remorse?" I asked.

"Oh no, none," he said, settling in a chair. "I can't tell you how grateful I am that Thom helped me out. He bought the entire collection and promised to do right by us."

"Do right by you?" I asked.

"Caroline hasn't filled you in?"

"No, not yet. We're having lunch later today, but we haven't had a chance to discuss the business yet."

"Well, I guess since the shop is yours, you might as well know."

"How did you know the shop is mine?"

"I was the witness to the will, the most recent will. Well, at least I assume it was the most recent will. Anyway, let me go back. My parents were clock collectors. But you may have known that?"

"I did know that. Your father and my grandfather spent a lot of time together, talking about clocks."

"And clock towers. And town governments. And everything else. They'd always been friends, but Thom really stepped in after my mother died and kept Dad company," he said, his eyes unfocused.

"He knew what your dad was going through," I said. Boy, did he know.

"When my dad passed away last summer, he made Thom one of the executors of the estate, which was a godsend. My sisters and I couldn't agree about anything, especially what to do with the clocks. So I talked to Thom, asking his advice. I was surprised, but he came up with a deal I couldn't refuse." Jonah tried to make the last line sound like something out of a Mafia movie, but it didn't really work. I laughed anyway.

"Thom paid us seventy-five thousand dollars cash for the entire collection. If it made over two hundred thousand, he'd split the proceeds with us, keeping eighty percent for himself and giving us ten percent. Sort of our legacy. We had a couple of other dealers come through and no one came close to his offer. Everyone wanted to break up the collection and it was all just too much. So we took him up on it."

Wow. Was my grandfather being kind to his friend's

family, or had he spotted a couple of gems in the collection? I hoped Caroline would have some answers for me. This wasn't the G.T. I knew growing up. That G.T. was much more cautious and far less sentimental.

"What about the other ten percent?"

"That would go to the Clock Tower Fund."

"He was still talking about that?" I asked.

"More than talking. He and my father had gotten some steam behind the project, then last summer Dad died and the wind went out of Thom's sails. He was just starting to talk about it again, actually. There's some interest now that Orchard is turning itself around a bit. The clock tower could become a destination."

"Wouldn't that be great? What a wonderful legacy." My lower lip began to quiver and, with a pained expression, Jonah looked away.

Jonah cleared his throat. "That's why I brought over these boxes. There are documents going back years about the clock tower and its history. Your grandfather may have the same documents, but I wanted to make sure."

"You don't want to keep them?"

"No, if the clock tower is going to happen, the Cog & Sprocket is going to be the home base. I don't have the energy for it. Thom was looking for a title to the old Town Hall that my father supposedly had, but I haven't found that yet. I'll keep looking. There are some other documents that may be helpful for his work on getting this block marked as a historical landmark, but I'm not sure. It's tricky, since the Board of Selectmen need to vote on landmarking, and there are a lot of loose ends we need to take care of before the vote Thursday."

"Thursday?" So that was the mysterious event. Historical landmarking? Was that what he was meeting with real estate agents about? I wonder how other folks in town felt about that. I'd have to remember to ask Moira. Or maybe Ben knew?

"Yes. Don't you know? There's a special Town Hall meeting called to talk about rezoning this area of town, and making it a historical district."

"What kind of historical district?"

"That depends on the meeting. Thom and some other folks were able to get the meeting called to help save the old Town Hall. But Kim Gray has proposed more language saying that if the Town Hall gets landmarked, then any other building in the district couldn't be changed without permission of the zoning commission."

"Which adds a layer to any project."

"A layer to any decision controlled by the zoning board. That means that Beckett Green would have to stop construction. It could mean that if you wanted to upgrade this shop, inside or out, you'd need permission. It all became a big political game in town. Thom was doing his best to fight it, but life would be a lot easier if he could find the deed to the old Town Hall."

"I can't imagine this made people like Beckett Green happy."

"No, it didn't. Or the Clarks either. They were planning on putting an addition on the back of the Corner Market."

"Do you think it made anyone so angry he, or she, would have wanted to harm my grandfather?" I said, before I could stop myself. There were so many questions and with all of these grudges and political machinations, I just couldn't help but think of the chief's investigation and my promise to myself to see G.T. at peace.

"Jeez, Ruth, I can't say. I can't imagine anyone in Orchard wanting to hurt Thom."

"Yet someone did," I said quietly.

"I don't know who. If I did, I'd tell you, trust me. I lost a good friend last week."

We both sipped our tea a bit for a moment, gathering ourselves.

"So any hidden treasures in these boxes?" I asked after I'd regrouped a bit.

Jonah laughed. "Not in these boxes. These are just the last of the clocks that I found lying around the house while I was packing. I didn't want them to get lost in all the chaos. We're already having trouble finding my mother's jewelry and a couple of paintings. I think they got misplaced somehow, but I sure couldn't tell you where these things disappear to. I figure we'll find them when we unpack."

"Are you moving?" I asked.

"We sold the house. There are three of us, I have two older sisters, and no one was in a position to buy the other two out. So we sold it to Harris University. We included most of the furniture but we divided up the family heirlooms, as the will indicated."

"Isn't your house a ways away from the Harris University campus at Marytown?"

"Yes and no. They are going to use it to house the development and alumni offices. I'm on the faculty there and I knew they'd been looking for a space for a while."

"What do you teach?"

"Political science."

"Really?" I said. Political science was a little better than history or English.

"Yeah. I realized early on I wasn't the politician that my father was, or wanted me to be. And I had no interest in being a lawyer. Figured I'd sort of stay in the family business in my own way."

"It sounds so funny, 'the family business.' But it really was, wasn't it? How long was he on the Board of Selectmen?"

"Twenty years total. There was a chunk of time in the middle when he was in the State House, then he came back and became chairman of the Board of Selectmen. Never lost a race in his life."

"I hear that they have a town administrator now?"

"Yes, Kim Gray. Handpicked by my father, though I think he regretted it toward the end. She has a very different opinion on the direction Orchard should be taking that wasn't apparent when she was being hired. Sort of a mess, especially with Dad passing on before he could make any real changes."

"Do you think he was going to try and get rid of her?"

"I'm certain he was. Thom was working on it too, but didn't have the same clout as Dad did."

"I'd like to meet Kim Gray," I said. Someone needed to help me understand what my grandfather was up to, and she seemed as likely as the next person.

Jonah looked surprised, but recovered quickly. "She's been traveling these past couple of weeks at some conference or another. She spends a lot of time outside of Orchard."

"Really? That seems odd."

"That is part of the problem my father had with her. I know she'll be back at the end of the week and will come to any service you have planned for Thom. Are there any plans yet?"

"Not yet. Caroline and I are having lunch today to talk it out. I know he didn't want one, but I think we should plan a memorial service."

"I agree. There are a lot of folks who'd like to pay their respects. Please make sure and let me know. We'll all want to be there. He was a good man, was Thom Clagan. I really liked Thom." He shook his head and played with his tea-spoon. "It's just so awful."

"The chief tells me that he had a heart attack, so he didn't suffer."

He looked very relieved. "Well, I'm glad to hear that. Dad really had a tough time there at the end."

"I remember your father coming by the shop once in a while. He was one of the few people who could really make my grandfather laugh out loud."

"Your grandfather was with my dad at the end. He did his best to try and help us all get through the last few months, which wasn't easy. Families, you know? He was determined to do right by his friend, no matter what. Anyway, I'm ashamed of myself for not coming by earlier and offering my condolences, but I didn't know you were staying here. Thom Clagan was a good man. And I know he'd be thrilled that you're settling in."

"Not sure if I'm settling in or not," I said, trying to avoid Bezel's gaze from the top of the stairs. "You're very kind to say that about my grandfather. I'm sorry to say that we've been out of touch for the past few years."

Jonah nodded. "I know. But he was very proud of you."

"Thank you," I said, grabbing a napkin and blotting my leaky eyes. "This is hard."

"Of course it is. Especially given everything. I'm sure the chief is on the case. And he's as good as they come. My father hired him right before he retired. Got him a five-year contract too." Jonah took a swig of tea and then pushed himself up from his chair. He winced a bit as he straightened up.

"Listen, I've kept you too long. Here's my contact information and here's my cell phone number." He pulled out a pen and scratched the number onto the back of a small white business card.

"Please let me know if there's anything I can do to help with the arrangements," he added as he started toward the stairs. "Don't hesitate for a minute."

chapter 22

I walked Jonah downstairs, locked the door, and went back upstairs to look at the boxes he left. I carefully lifted out the timepieces. Three alarm clocks, dating back to the 1930s. Two carriage clocks. Three pocket watches in their original cases. I opened up one of the Bubble Wrapped packages to find a Seth Thomas mantel clock. I always loved these clocks. They were mass-produced down in Connecticut starting in the mid-1800s. There were many different types of clocks, but this one was fairly common. Just ten inches tall, with a steeple top, made of oak. There was lovely detail on the door. The face looked original. This looked like it was an eight-day clock, but I couldn't be sure. I turned it over gently and winced when I heard a slight clank. I tried to open it up, but didn't have my tools handy. I stopped myself just in time.

These clocks could suck me in for the rest of the day. Instead I rewrapped it in the Bubble Wrap and put it back in the box.

I couldn't help but unwrap another one of the clocks though, just to take a quick peek. This one was also a Seth Thomas, but a miniature. The rest of the packets looked similar. Were they all Seth Thomases? I smiled at the thought. Lovely clocks. Using my new zoning system, I put the box under the "estate to get ready to sell" table. The Seth Thomas line of clocks had been mass-produced since the 1800s, and varied in worth. The one I looked at didn't have tremendous value at first glimpse, but if there was a lot that could be sold together, that might be a different story. That sort of evaluation took time, and I was still working on making sense of what I was dealing with. My exploration of the miniatures would be a treat I would savor another day.

Instead, I pulled out the files that Jonah had brought. Four brown accordion folders' worth, stuffed to the gills. I took them all back to the kitchen table. I looked inside one of the files, flipping through the pages in each section without taking them out of the folder. It wasn't as if each section had a specific topic that tied it all together. Instead each seemed like a mishmash of different articles, printouts, and forms. I suspected they were put in the file pockets in no particular order, but since I couldn't be sure, I left them in place and just flipped through. I didn't want to risk not being able to crack the code, if there was indeed a method to this madness.

Code. That was a little melodramatic. But then again, this last week had redefined *dramatic* for me. I looked at the files some more, but my mind wandered. What was going on in Orchard? I didn't expect to be welcomed back with a parade, but folks weren't rushing over to give their condolences.

And what about the clock tower? Clearly it had become a bit of an obsession for my grandfather. I walked over to the clock tower model and leaned over it, running my fingers gently along the side of the tiny building. Then I looked back at the files, the reams of paper that all seemed to be about the old Town Hall. From the looks of these files, the clock tower was an obsession for Grover Winter as well.

I felt it all beginning to suck me in. The lure of the Cog & Sprocket. All these wonderful clocks to examine, restore, and sell. No supervisor to report to. Complete control over what I worked on and when. In fact, it was what I dreamed of re-creating back in Boston. The question was, could I come home again? And would it ever be home, without my grandparents?

I took all four accordion files and put them in the wardrobe. I locked it all up and put the key in my dress pocket. Something told me to proceed with caution.

I looked at the clock on the wall. It wasn't running. Ironic, but that's what happened when clocks weren't tended to and wound. I checked my cell phone and saw that it was only ten o'clock. Still some time to look around a bit before I needed to go to the cottage for lunch with Caroline.

I grabbed the account books and took them down to the first floor workroom. According to them, there were several clocks in for repair, but only four had specific customer names. Two mantel clocks that needed new electrics, one wall clock that wasn't keeping time, and an anniversary clock that needed a repair estimate. I'd hold off on the estimate until Caroline came in, since I hoped that she would be able to give me some guidance on how G.T. priced his work, especially on anniversary clocks. They were always tricky to fix, since the repairs often cost more than the clock was worth.

One more glance at my cell phone told me that I needed to get changed and head out to the cottage to meet Caroline Adler. This was one time I really didn't want to be late.

chapter 23

I was due to meet Caroline at eleven thirty at her house. Her house. Not my grandparents' house or even G.T.'s house. Caroline's house.

Caroline Adler. I knew nothing about her. I'd tried to Google her a couple of times in the past but couldn't even find a picture. I knew of her through my grandfather and our brief conversations. She had a son, but I'd just found that out. She was ten years younger than G.T. They'd met through a mutual friend. All I really knew was that she married my grandfather very quickly, and I hadn't taken that well.

I wondered about that sometimes. Should I have been more sympathetic? Did I overreact? Now, at the ripe old age of thirty, I'd answer those questions yes and yes, but I still didn't blame my younger self for freaking out. My grandmother's death was unexpected—a heart attack—and my entire world collapsed, as did my grandfather's. I guess I had hoped we would be there for each other and that would be enough to get us through the grief. Instead he took Caroline Adler in and it felt as if he didn't have a place for me anymore. I never really could get past the feeling that he was trying to replace us with a shiny new family.

I was a little late meeting Caroline. It wasn't like I didn't know the route. I'd spent every summer in that house for as long as I could remember and I'd lived there for most of high school. But maybe it was because I did know the route that it took so long to get there. I slowed down to look at every house, every stone fence, every tree. They all contained memories of bike rides and long walks. These were the places a very unhappy little girl started to find some peace and happiness.

When I drove up, I let go of a breath I didn't even know I'd been holding. The long driveway looked the same. I slowed down to look at the twists and turns. Even the beautiful gardens my grandmother had kept were still in wonderful shape. That had to be at the hand of Caroline. My grandfather could never be bothered. I turned the corner and the house came into view. A simple Cape with dormers on the second floor, weathered shingles, Federal blue trim, and a black front door. As I pulled up, I saw Chief Paisley and Caroline Adler embracing on the front steps, but stepped apart when they heard my car.

Now, this wasn't some sort of torrid embrace you'd see on the cover of a romance novel. It looked like a hug between friends, one giving comfort to the other. At least I hoped that's what it was. While I parked the car, Caroline wiped her eyes and stepped into the house. Chief Paisley waited for me at the front door.

"Chief," I called out as I shut the car door and ambled toward the house. I was always good at small talk. My faculty wife days taught me how to fill quiet spaces easily.

"Ms. Clagan. Thought I'd stop by and fill you both in on where the investigation is right now when Caroline told me you were coming over. Hope you don't mind the intrusion."

"No, of course not."

"Caroline went in ahead of us. Needed to pull herself together a bit. She's in the kitchen. She's one of my favorite people in Orchard," he said, holding my eye contact for a moment.

His implicit recommendation was strengthened by the protective note in his tone. I took a deep breath. This past week had upended my life. I was still navigating the results. Maybe the best thing to do right now was to act less like myself and more like the person I wanted to be? Yeesh, turning thirty was changing my game.

I stepped into the foyer and took in the dining room on my right, the living room on my left. They both looked different from what I remembered: new paint on the walls and beautiful antique furniture that was more suited to a Victorian than a Cape. I resisted the urge to peer into more rooms as I followed the chief down the center hall.

"You seem to know your way around here," I observed.

It took me a beat, but I realized that the chief had stopped. I took a step back toward him, my eyebrow cocked.

"I know my way to the kitchen. Been coming here once a week since I moved to Orchard. Thom and Caroline are my friends. I don't use that word lightly, Ms. Clagan."

I didn't imagine he did. I walked back down the familiar path to my favorite room in the house, dreading what I might find. The heart of any home is the kitchen and that was certainly true of my grandmother's home. I wasn't sure if I could handle that sacred space being changed. My grandparents had built this house themselves, replacing a summer camp on the lake once electricity was brought out that far from town. The Cape was traditional, but spacious. Living room with a three-season porch taking up half the downstairs, a dining room, kitchen, and half bath taking up the other half. On the second floor, I knew there were three bedrooms and a full bath. A breezeway off the kitchen went out to a barn where my grandfather had a small workroom and did cabinet restoration on the clocks. The home shop wasn't as well equipped as the Cog & Sprocket, but it was lovely, with huge windows that looked out at the lake.

The back of the kitchen also looked out toward the lake. I stopped for a moment to take it in. Caroline finished pouring water into the coffeemaker, and then turned toward me, offering her hand.

"Caroline, have you met Ruth?" Chief Paisley stepped back, as if a referee in a boxing ring, ready to jump in if needed.

Caroline Adler's brown hair had lighter roots, which were evident given her hairstyle that was pulled back into a twist with a bit of a bump in the front. She was fit, trim, and polished. She had pearl earrings that matched a pearl choker, a tan sweater set, and black dress pants. Even though she wore black leather clogs, she was still a few inches shorter than I was. I took all of that in, in the three seconds it took for her to walk across the room and take my outstretched hand. When she came closer, I looked into her brown eyes, rimmed from either lack of sleep, crying, or likely both. The dark marks underneath them matched my own.

Her eyes caught me, filled with emotion and a world of pain. No matter how unsure I was about her, making someone cry was not on my to-do list for the day, so I forced a smile and put my other hand on top of hers.

"Caroline, it is very nice to see you," I said awkwardly, not sure what to do next.

"Ruth, it is wonderful to officially meet you," she replied.

"The house looks wonderful," I said, trying to fill in the awkward pause with the first thought that popped into my head. This was even harder than I'd imagined.

"Thank you," she said, smiling.

"I noticed a few changes."

"Just a few. I hope you don't find them too disconcerting," she said, casting her eyes around the room.

"No, the house looks well lived in. This room looks the same," I said. And it did. She let go of my hand and I looked around. The same range, restaurant quality, was a huge investment back in the day, but well used by my grandmother, who employed all six burners and both ovens for family dinners, even when it was just the three of us. The large farmhouse sink sat below the recessed window, where she'd kept herbs growing year round.

The round kitchen table, where we'd eaten most of our meals, was still there. Eating meals together was a family rule. The wide pine floors, which ran through the entire house, glowed. The braided rugs by the sink and under the table were beautiful additions, with colors that complemented the rest of the house: greens, rose pinks, purples, and yellows. The cushions on the chairs and tablecloth gave the room a more decorated air than it had when I was growing up. But I had to admit, it was lovely and familiar.

The tears threatened to flow again. Honestly, I hadn't cried this much in years. Years. Even when I found out my husband cheated on me, I didn't shed a tear. Not sure if that said more about me or about the state of my marriage. I'd come to realize, with despair, that I'd married a man who offered me stability. Not love, but strong opinions and ideas which suited me, especially at twenty-three. They suited me less as I got older, so I got traded in for a new model. And bless his new girlfriend, who was the same age I was when they met. I rolled my shoulders back, shed thoughts of Eric, and kept the tears in check.

"Please, both of you, have a seat," Caroline said. "Do you mind the kitchen? I'm getting lunch ready. Chief, you are welcome to join us."

"Can I help?" I asked.

"You can pour us all some sweet tea. The pitcher's in the refrigerator."

"I'll take the tea, but I need to pass on the lunch," the chief said. "I have a couple more appointments this afternoon. Rain check?"

"You know you're always welcome here, Jeff."

"Let me get the tea," I said, anxious to make myself useful. The pitcher was full, with slices of lemon floating in it. I poured out the tea and handed the chief a glass. He took a long swig. When he put his glass down, I refilled it. I took a sip and understood his enthusiasm.

Caroline was taking plastic off the quiche. "Ruth, I'd try and pretend that my quiche was homemade, but I'd be lying. I bought it at the Corner Market this morning."

"I went there last night. The new owners seem to have a nice selection of food."

"Yes, they do," she said distractedly. "An interesting couple, the Clarks."

One look told me that she knew that this talk about groceries was just to avoid the subject of G.T.

"Jeff, what brought you by this morning?" Caroline said.

Caroline had a bit of a Southern accent, but I could tell she worked hard at sounding like she had no accent. But since no Northerner made sweet tea that tasted like this, her Southern roots were showing. I loved sweet tea. Recipes I'd seen said it was just tea, water, and sugar, but there was more to it than that. The tea had to be strong, but not acrid. The sweetness couldn't tip over too far on the sugary side, but it did need to be sweet. This concoction was perfect.

"Caroline, I wanted to ask you about the five clocks that were stolen last month," the chief said.

"Again? Jeff, I thought you were here to tell us about what happened to Thom. Have there been any new leads, any clue as to who has done this?" Caroline said. She looked strained. She was trying to keep it together, but anyone could see that she was having a hard time with this.

"I am. I think they may be related. What kinds of clocks were they again?" he asked.

"They were all from the 1800s. Wall clocks, mantel clocks. A gingerbread clock. All American, made by the Seth Thomas Clock Company."

"Seth Thomases?" I asked, thinking about the clocks I'd looked at this morning.

"Last month Caroline reported a burglary of five clocks from the shop, but Thom withdrew the report soon after," Chief Paisley told me. "Said that he didn't want to deal with the insurance claims, especially since there were so many new clocks in the shop. Even though they were all pretty valuable, close to a thousand dollars each—am I right?

"Someone knew what they were doing," he continued. "But those clocks, collectors specifically would be interested, right? Who would know about the value of those clocks? Aside from you and Thom? And Pat Reed."

"Anyone who knew clocks would know that they were valuable," I said. "Or even people who had access to a computer."

"Well, Ms. Clagan, that's true." The chief leaned forward as he spoke. "But I went back to the original report that Caroline filed. It was carefully detailed, written with hope we could get those valuable pieces back. And I've been doing some research on them. These five clocks were really something special."

"I told you, Chief, I barely remember them. We have a significant number of clocks in the shop, as you know. You can't expect me to remember every single clock," Caroline said, clenching her glass tightly in her fist.

"Caroline, the shop was broken into, twice. I think Pat Reed knows more than he's telling."

"And I think you're wrong, Jeff. Wrong." Caroline looked as if she was about to start crying, and grabbed a napkin from the table.

"Chief Paisley, do you have any more specific questions that we haven't covered yet? Because I think Caroline has told you everything she knows," I said. The last thing I expected to do was feel protective over Caroline, but here I was. And I didn't like the way this conversation was going. Best to stop it now. Surely Pat Reed wasn't a suspect, was he? That was impossible. I needed to process this. "And I certainly have. Now, do you have any more information about when you're going to be releasing my grandfather's body? Caroline and I need to talk about planning a service."

"I'm hoping the coroner will release the body by the end of the week. I'll check again today." Chief Paisley looked at us both and shrugged his shoulders. He picked up his glass and drained it. He stood up and took it over to the sink, then turned around.

"Caroline, I don't want to upset you," he said. "But you have to know, I'm not going to rest until I figure out what happened to Thom. Or rather, who happened to him. I think the missing clocks from last month have something to do with his death. What, I'm not sure. But I'm going to find out. Thank you for the sweet tea. I'll let myself out."

We sat for a moment after he left. I wasn't sure what to say. Caroline got up quietly, got the quiche out of the oven, and brought it over to the table. Her hand shook as she served us each a slice. I served us each a bit of salad and took a bite of the quiche.

"This is really delicious. Do the Clarks make the quiches themselves?"

"No, they outsource locally to a couple of restaurants. I think this is a Nancy Reed quiche. Nancy uses the kitchens at the Sleeping Latte."

"She must work long hours. She always was a bundle of energy."

"She is indeed a bundle of energy, but I suspect that her extra work is more to do with helping pay the bills and less to do with a desire to fill her time," she said, pushing a few leaves of lettuce around her plate.

"Are they having troubles?" I asked, taking a bite of quiche.

The Reeds had always been a hardworking family and I'd never thought of them as struggling, but I hadn't been around for a while and times had been tough for everyone. I couldn't help but think about Chief Paisley's bringing up Pat's name. He wasn't wrong. Pat would know the value. The idea that he had something, anything, to do with the robbery? Crazy.

"I really don't know," Caroline said, setting down her fork and leaning back in her chair. "Pat and I talk, of course, though not about much else besides the business."

"Pat speaks very highly of you and how well you took care of my grandfather," I said.

"I've been thinking a lot about that these past few days, Ruth. I always felt terrible about your break with him. I know it was partly my fault. I wish it hadn't happened, and I would give anything to make it right. It's too late for that now, I know, but please believe me, I cared about your grandfather, deeply. He was the best man I've ever known. And likely ever will know. I'd give anything for him to be sitting here right now, and for me to be in his place."

"Please, please don't go there. I've been doing a lot of thinking these past few days too. I could go back and regret what can never be, or move forward. Trust me when I say, living in the past is my norm."

"That's where we're different. I avoid thinking about the past." She didn't elaborate, so I went on.

"This could derail me, easily. I could blame you for everything. But I'm sitting here, in this wonderful kitchen, where my grandmother, one of the most loving and stable people I've ever known, made my life so much better by living."

"Thom said that the two of you were very close," she said.

"She meant everything to me. My grandfather didn't want me to get stuck in grief after she passed, and he pushed me out into the world. And now I understand that he wanted to be alone with his own grief. We processed her death differently, but I like to think we are so much alike in so many ways."

"I can see that," she said.

"I can't believe I missed all these years with him. Maybe you can help me and tell me about him and what his life has been like lately."

"Maybe a little at a time? I am still getting used to the idea that he isn't here. I hate it." Caroline looked down at the napkin she was shredding. "Let's start with this. You were his pride and joy. He marveled that you had followed in his footsteps, and was thrilled to hear from you." Caroline cleared her throat and dabbed her eyes with what was left of the napkin.

"I never felt as safe and content as I have these past few years with Thom. I owe him a great deal, more than I could ever pay back. So, let me say this up front. I'm happy to support you in any decisions you make about the shop. Can I come in and show you the accounts and explain a few things about the inventory and record keeping?"

"That would be wonderful. I already missed the appointment with the real estate agent. Apparently she'd changed the time earlier in the week. What was the meeting for?"

"I'm not exactly sure."

"Do you think he planned on selling the shop?"

"I honestly don't know anymore," she said, sighing. "There's a lot going on in Orchard. There were some outside folks who were bidding on some of the businesses on Washington Street. I'd heard about a strip mall, also heard that

Harris University was trying to buy up the town to create a second campus. Thom and Grover had a plan to stop the buying and building spree, but it stalled when Grover Winter passed on."

"I thought he'd retired."

"He'd rejoined the Board of Selectmen and was making Kim Gray's life very difficult. Oh my, listen to me. I sound like Thom. Grover's death really upset him. And, in a way, gave him a new purpose."

"Wow. I've got to say that doesn't sound like my grandfather. He was always so private."

"He was still a private man and kept his cards close to his vest. But he was curious about a few things and had started asking questions."

"And taking notes," I said.

"Of course. He took notes on everything." She smiled.

"I know. I do the same thing. You haven't found his most recent notebook, have you?"

"No, I haven't, and I've been looking. No luck at the shop?"

"Not so far. Do you have any idea what some of the recent notes might have been?"

"I have some idea. He wanted to invite Jeff, Chief Paisley, over for dinner to talk, but we needed to postpone when I had to leave town to take care of my son. He said he wanted me there when they met."

"What did he want to talk to the chief about?"

"He thought that Grover Winter had been murdered. But by whom, and how? He took his theories on that with him."

chapter 24

Well, that was some lunch. G.T. thought Grover Winter was murdered? I couldn't help but wonder where his notes were on that as I helped Caroline carry the dishes over to the sink. In the missing notebook? Because, of course there were notes. *"Take notes on everything. Every idea, every thought, every account, every possible business lead; write everything down,"* was what he always said. My grandfather had taught me well. For a while I'd taken to making my notes on my computer and keeping them in the cloud, but lately I'd taken to writing things down again. My grandfather was old school and I needed to find his notebook.

Much to my own surprise, Caroline Adler wasn't a bad egg. She was genuinely mourning my grandfather. It made me feel better somehow, to think my grandfather was cared for these past few years.

I also liked that she was nothing like my grandmother, though I found I wanted to know Caroline Adler better. Where my own grandmother was warm and open, it seemed that each time I brought up something personal or asked about her past, Caroline steered the conversation back to clocks or pies or anything else. Of course, I didn't offer any details on my life either.

Before I left, Caroline and I'd agreed to both look around, she at the house and me in the store, to see if we could find his missing notebook or anything else that might help fill in some of the gaps of knowledge that were developing for me, especially when it came to the business of Orchard.

"I have no idea where to even begin. Jeff, Chief Paisley, is incredibly capable, but I wonder if he has all the facts? He seems stuck on the theft and Thom's death being related, but I'm just not so sure," she said, as she walked me out to my car. "I keep thinking about the business dealings in Orchard."

"There is some sort of hearing on Thursday. Do you know anything about it?"

"This Thursday?" she said, shocked. "I'd assumed they'd postponed it, given everything. I'll make some calls this afternoon."

"I wonder what else G.T. was working on while you were away," I said. "If we can figure out what he was thinking about these past few weeks, we owe it to him to move forward. At the very least, we can pass on anything we find to the chief."

"Maybe that would get Chief Paisley off of Pat Reed's case. Do you think?" she asked, looking hopeful.

I didn't answer because I didn't know how to. Chief

Paisley didn't strike me as someone who would jump to conclusions. He worked with facts. But what happened if he had the wrong facts?

As I drove back to Orchard, I checked my cell phone. Dead. Of course. I pulled over and plugged it into the car jack. It took a moment for it to get enough power to turn back on, so I sat and waited. Orchard was still a lovely little town, but it was a lot more complicated than I remembered. Town politics gone awry. Stolen clocks.

When I was finally able to turn the phone on, there was a message from Jonah Winter.

"Ruth, Jonah here. Listen, there was a little more drama around the clocks than I expected. I wonder if you could bring the two boxes back I dropped by this morning? It would go a great distance to keeping the peace if I could give them back to my sister, soon. Sorry about the confusion. Thanks."

By the time I got back to the shop, I had one bar of power on the phone. First things first: I needed to get Jonah's boxes. I went upstairs and took out the two liquor boxes full of clocks. I unwrapped the one I'd spent some time mooning over earlier, and sighed. Getting to know this little gem wasn't to be. I always fell a little in love with the clocks I worked on, so I decided I needed to move these out of the shop. I carried both boxes down the stairs and put them in the back of my car, covering them with a blanket. I called Jonah's phone. No answer. I tried once more, but still no answer. No sense in making the trip if no one was home. I considered bringing them back into the shop, but leaving them in the car made more sense. I'd drive them out as soon as he called back. In the meantime, I'd turn on the car alarm. Probably the only person in Orchard who even bothered.

Since there was still daylight, I decided to explore the rest of the Cog & Sprocket. I went to the attic first. The attic scared me when I was a kid, full of monsters covered by sheets and the sound of the wind whistling through the attic vents. Courage, Ruth. Time to explore. I picked up the hook, which looked like a fireplace poker, from where it was resting by the door, and used it to pull down the hatch. Bezel, who had been casually observing from the doorway, yowled and shot off into the bedroom as the ladder smoothly came down and unfolded.

"Wimp," I said. Even though I really wanted to join her.

I walked up and pulled the cord dangling from above. The bulb illuminated just a small part of the attic, but the windows on each end also brought in some light. Once I stepped off the ladder I was able to stand easily. The peak of the roof made the sides shorter, but there was still a great deal of space.

I might have even been able to walk around, were it not for the impossibly haphazard piles of stuff that lined the edges. Not junk, but stuff. I walked over to look at a grandfather clock that was probably five feet high. When I looked more closely, I realized that the case was fairly new. I looked for a marking of the manufacturer. There was a metal plate on the bottom. I used my cell phone as a flashlight and read it more closely. T. CLAGAN, COG & SPROCKET was all it said. I sat back and looked around me. I opened one of the crates farther back from the attic stairs. A crate covered with a thin layer of dust. Inside, a lovely shelf clock, complete with the T. CLAGAN plate on the bottom.

I sat down in the middle of the crates and looked around. Dozens of Thom Clagan clocks, none of which had been sold. This didn't make any sense. I knew he sold some of his own work for a very good price. But what about these pieces? Were they rejects? Or were they waiting for someone to ask for them? More questions with no answers.

There was furniture covered in sheets and more boxes of books. I looked at a few of them, but no more notebooks. It was getting dark. I decided to continue my exploration later when there was more light. I went back down the stairs and closed the hatch on the attic. I rested the hook on a pile of boxes and watched the hatch close. I loved the way the stairs disappeared into the ceiling.

The musty smell hit my nose the minute I opened the basement door. The basement was dank, but not damp thanks to the dehumidifier. During the great flood the basement had been flooded, but the river hadn't come up that high since, and thanks to some new dams, it wasn't likely to. G.T. had moved some plastic crates down here. I sat down on a stool and opened up one of them. I looked at old files, some of which dated back a hundred years. A history of the work the Clagan family had done. I needed to move these files upstairs, where they'd be safer. Holding on to the family history felt very important these days. The words started to swim in front of my eyes and I decided to call it a day. One more look around. No notebooks.

I went back upstairs to feed Bezel, who was nowhere to be found since the incident with the ladder. Then I went back downstairs to explore the bins in the workroom. Maybe the notebook was there.

chapter 25

The bin system had been in place forever. When you walked back into the workroom, there was a wall of bins along the left-hand wall. When a clock came in for repair, it was put in a bin along with all its pieces. Each bin had a sheet, detailing all the work. Back in the old days, once a job was done, the notes were all transcribed onto an index card and the card was filed in the shop. The infamous clock cards. Now it looked like they were moving to a computer database, but I wondered if they still filled out the clock cards. The filing system of these cards was always a little convoluted. Clock type, manufacturer, owner. In paper files? I'd spent a lot of time in the basement looking for misfiled clock cards back when I was a kid.

Sure enough, I found two clocks in bins. All of the parts needed to fix them were also included. A pang tore through me when I saw my grandfather's handwriting, estimating the cost of the job. I thought he undervalued his work, but that was his way. Hook them with a battery change or a new electric cord and then let them look at the rest of the inventory while they waited. Two out of every five customers would make a bigger purchase in the future. He believed clocks were contagious, and I agreed. There was something about trying to manage the everyday drudgery of time with an object of beauty. Man's folly, and the family business.

Still no notebooks. I decided to do what I always did when stressed. Look at a clock. The repairs were simple enough. It would take me five minutes, tops. Plenty of time before dinner at the Reeds'. I almost went upstairs for my own tool kit, but instead I put on my grandfather's vision visor and adjusted it to fit my own head. I took out his beautiful screwdriver set, which he'd inherited from his own father, and set to work. The walnut handles felt warm in my hands. I let the tools rest in their worn spots. They fit my hands perfectly. Both clocks had already been polished and cleaned and were just waiting for the new electrics to be installed. I did the jobs, putting the old electrics in the box that the new parts came in. Both would be returned to the customer, as was the Cog & Sprocket way. I made notes on the sheets and entered them in the account book, marking them with a Post-it so Caroline could check my work. Then I put them back in the bins and brought them out front and put them in a cubby for pickup. So satisfying to get a job done, though I ached to work on one of the grandfather clocks.

I looked through all the bins once more and even pulled them all out of the cubbies. No notebook. Maybe there wasn't a notebook, but I knew in my gut there was. The notes from the final days of G.T.'s life would surely give me some answers. As I walked through to the front of the shop the doorbell rang. Then again. Was it always this busy on Sundays? I walked out front and created a gap in the blinds on the front door. Ben greeted me with a smile and a wave. I couldn't help but smile back. It was impossible not to.

"Hi, Ruth. Sorry to intrude," he said, shoving his hands in his coat pockets.

"No worries. I'm just doing a little work. Catching up on outstanding jobs in the shop, and looking for a notebook."

"You sound just like Thom. And you look like him too, with that thing on your head." He grinned.

I reached up and pulled the visor off my head. Half of my hair pulled out of my ponytail, and the visor got stuck.

"Don't move. Let me help. I'm a professional," Ben said, reaching to untangle my hair. "Here you go."

"I've got it. Thanks. Yeesh. I must look like a mess."

"You look great." Ben grinned again and shook his head. "So, I thought we could drive to the Reeds' house together."

"The Reeds' house?" I asked.

"You were invited for dinner? It got postponed till tonight. Moira hasn't heard back from you, so I told her I'd come by and check in on you. She invited me to come along."

"Dinner." Yikes. I needed to start setting more alarms on my cell phone to remind me of things. Like that would help. "But it isn't dinnertime yet, is it?" I looked around and all of the clocks told me a slightly different time. Not a great business advertisement, but I'd deal with that later.

"Ruth, it's close to dinnertime here in the Berkshires. You folks from Boston probably eat later, but out here, six is a respectable dinnertime. I take it you aren't ready to go?"

I laughed out loud. "Not nearly, no. I need a shower and to get dressed. I've forgotten how long it takes to get to the Reeds' house from here."

"About twenty minutes, give or take. You've got time. Unless you don't want to ride with me?"

"No, I mean, yes, that would be great. Thank you."

"I've got a few more calls I need to make to confirm appointments. I'll be back in a half hour, all right?"

"Fine, I'll be ready!"

A half hour to get dressed and get ready to take a trip down memory lane. With Ben at the wheel. Thirty minutes was not enough time. When I went upstairs and looked at myself in the mirror, I was horrified to see streaks of dirt and dust all over my face in addition to the red marks left by my grandfather's vision visor. My hair looked like a red, curly nest. Couple that with the purple bags under my eyes and the slightly swollen lids, and I was hardly looking my best. The shower helped a little, though I almost got a black eye from the showerhead when I was trying to rinse the conditioner out of my hair.

I dressed carefully, wearing my only pair of flats with tights, along with a black-and-white wrap dress and cardigan. I added one of my more subdued pair of earrings, comprised of wheels, gears, and springs, all in silver tones. I'd started to create the earrings to help me perfect my soldering techniques. It worked, and had become a way to unwind. I gave them out as gifts to friends. I did what I could with my hair, resorting, once again, to tying it up in a knot.

I checked Bezel's food bowl. She rubbed against my leg, covering me with a light dusting of gray fur. I just smiled and shook my head. I'm sure Ben would be wearing some of Blue's fur too. I wished I had a hostess gift to bring, but bringing any food items was ridiculous, and I didn't have time to search out flowers. I tucked two pairs of earrings I'd made into my purse for Moira and her mother, but felt a little shy about giving them out.

I left a few lights on both upstairs and downstairs. I locked the door and went out on the porch to wait for Ben to close up his shop. I sat down on one of the porch rockers. While the cold enveloped me, I gently rocked and looked at the Town Hall outlined gently in the darkness. I wondered how often G.T. had sat here, imagining the glory of a new clock tower.

I hadn't been sitting long when Ben drove up in what looked like a bad 1970s flashback. My car wasn't much better, but at least my 2004 Scion xB was from this century. Ben's car looked like it might have started life as a Volkswagen Bug, the old model, and then been pieced together with different parts over the years. The doors didn't match the body, which didn't match the hood, which didn't match the trunk. When I climbed in, I noted the feeling of springs popping through the plaid seat cover, which someone had designed to go over the seats, sort of. I looked in the backseat, but it wasn't there. Instead there was a dog bed on one side and a milk crate on the other. Both were bungeed in place. I happened to glance down at my feet and thought I saw the spill from the streetlight between the floorboards. I kept my bag in my lap and tried not to rest my feet on the ground.

"It is perfectly safe," Ben said, a wicked grin flashing as he walked around the car and opened the creaky door for me. "Perfectly safe. You'll note the seat belts are new."

Indeed they were. Lap belts only, but they were new. I didn't even bother asking about air bags. But the interior seemed in pretty good shape. And besides, how fast could this thing go?

"What year is this?" I asked, buckling up.

"Nineteen seventy-seven. You weren't even born then, were you?" he said as we pulled out onto the road.

"Nope. Not for another eight years."

"Well neither was I, but I got this car when I was in college. Been keeping her in shape ever since. If the business picks up, I may even get her painted."

"Her?"

"Betty. Named after my grandmother. Don't laugh—it's the truth. She gave me the money to buy her."

"Winter must be tough for Betty," I said, patting the dashboard gently.

"I don't drive her much in the winter. Don't really need to. I can get my groceries right in town, the library is right down the street, the shop has Internet, and Aggie Kurt makes deliveries all year. Plus, I cut my own hair."

"No urge to take a trip into Boston or down to New York? Or even over to Marytown?" I asked.

"Nope. And if the need arises, I'll hitch a ride with someone else. Or take Betty out. She actually handles pretty well in the snow. It's the cold that she can't take."

"Betty and I have that in common." I smiled, suddenly wishing I had remembered to swipe on some of that lip gloss.

Ben laughed. "Orchard has everything I need. At least for now, while I try and get the business off the ground."

"Any buyer's remorse?"

"Well, I inherited it, indirectly. Since Aunt Flo, there have been three attempts to make the shop work. The other two failed. I'm trying something new and hoping it catches on."

"What's your new way look like?"

"Unisex," he said brightly.

"As in?"

"As in I can, and do, cut men's and women's hair. Both are welcome."

"How's that working?"

"Not well, honestly. Aunt Flo says I need to have men-only and women-only hours so that the gossip mill can start churning again. I also lowered my prices. I'd been thinking about being an upscale salon, but I think I need to be a bit more mainstream."

"A hair emporium," I said.

"Exactly. See, I'm learning. I can still do high-end treatments, but I also do rollers and rinses if I need to. Whatever makes the customer happy."

"How's it going?" I asked.

"The town folk are all still checking me out, so business is pretty slow. Your grandfather made a point out of coming over every week for a trim and a shave. And Caroline's a regular customer. Trust me, that helped. I have a few regulars, just not enough." He downshifted and slowed down to weave through the curves. "I've been thinking about your grandfather a lot." Ben looked over at me. "Is it okay to talk about him?"

"It is," I said. "I'm thinking about him a lot too."

"Thom Clagan was one of the most important people in Orchard, I think. Kept the town steady, if that makes sense."

"I guess it does. I don't remember him playing that role when I was younger."

"I didn't know him then, of course. But now he even said he was going to run for the Board of Selectmen."

"What? No, I don't believe you," I said, straining against my lap belt to look over at him.

"Thom and I had lunch once a week. We talked about a

lot of things. And this was his latest plan for fighting for old Orchard."

"How big was this fight? I keep thinking about what happened to G.T., and I can't help but think this whole business fight had something to do with his death. I have to figure this out. It's the only way he's going to be at rest and the only way I am going to get some rest." I looked out my window at the dense trees. "Sorry, didn't mean to dump all this on you."

"Thom was my friend. Anything I can do to help, let me know."

"Thanks," I said. I wanted to trust Ben, but needed to have ideas better formed before I talked to him. "Tell me more about Ben's Barbershop. Is that the name?"

"That's the name I am thinking about using. What do you think?"

"It is confusing, if it is unisex. But I sort of like it." I smiled over at him, feeling my face flush. "So who else goes to your shop?"

"Jeff Paisley comes over once a week so that his fade is always perfect. And the Reeds come over a lot. Hopefully I'll get some more customers soon. I may start having a bingo night, see if that drums up business."

I laughed. "Bingo night?"

"Yeah. There were a few folks who tried to get Orchard to go upscale, my uncle included. They all lost their shirts. It was partly because the recession hit at the same time. But it was mostly because Orchard isn't going upscale. Ever. It's a town of hardworking folks, college students, and weekenders who pass through on their way to destinations that aren't Orchard."

"Same as when I was growing up. I would have thought they would have figured out something else by now."

"We are getting a little more artsy, which is cool. And there is talk of a microbrewery opening up in town. But for the most part, Orchard is as it always has been. And that's great."

"Wow, you really love it here."

"Coming to Orchard saved me," he said, suddenly very serious.

I wanted to ask how, but I could tell Ben wasn't going to tell me by the way his jaw was clenched and his grip on his steering wheel. He was fighting something.

"How well do you know the Reeds?" I asked, carefully changing the subject.

"I eat most of my meals at the Sleeping Latte, so I know Moira and Nancy pretty well. Why do you ask?"

"Pat mentioned I shouldn't ask Moira about her brother, Ryan. I hadn't thought about it, but if there is something I should know . . . Just wanted a heads-up before I showed up for dinner."

"Ryan's the reason last night got canceled, but I'm hazy on the details. The Reeds are a private family. I'm just there to lend a shoulder when Moira needs it. Ryan lost his football scholarship last spring after he busted his knee. The whole family has been hustling, trying to figure out how to keep him in school. The only person who isn't hustling is Ryan, or so it seems. I think Moira is getting a little fed up."

I wasn't surprised. Ryan was always a great guy, lots of fun to be around, and the anointed male child in the Reed family. But I remembered when Pat asked my grandfather to give him an after-school job to keep him out of trouble, and my grandfather had to fire him after a couple of weeks of missed shifts and shoddy work. Pat had stopped working with my grandfather for a while after that, but by then I was really interested in learning the trade and I stepped in more to help. By Christmas Pat was back in the shop. I'm pretty sure my grandmother had everything to do with the detente. Thankfully, after a couple of months, everything was back to normal between G.T. and Pat.

Moira and I never talked about it or about Ryan. I didn't talk about my parents either. That wasn't what our friendship was about. It was just about us and being the best friends we could be. Again, I was struck by what I'd left behind in Orchard and how easily I'd let it go.

"Ruth, you still here?" Ben asked.

"I am. Just thinking about how complicated families can be. And how hard regret is."

"This is none of my business, but you should know how proud your grandfather was of you. When he got your post-card last week, he about popped a button."

"He told you about the postcard?"

"It made his week. And that's a quote," Ben said.

I stared hard out the window. "I'll never forgive myself for staying away so long."

"Ruth, I don't know you well. I don't know you at all. But I knew Thom. That's not the way he'd want to be remembered by you. You know what he would want? For you to figure out what happened, take care of Caroline and the shop, and have a great life. In that order."

I hated that the tears were threatening to flow again. Ben reached behind me and took out a tissue box, handing it to me. "Here's a tissue. I'm just rambling. I hate it when people cry. Just know that if you need help, I'm right next door. Okay?"

By now Ben had pulled up to the curb in front of the Reeds' house and stopped the car. He reached over and took my hand, giving it a squeeze.

"Let's go let Nancy feed our feelings," he said.

chapter 26

"Ruth, you come right in here this minute," Nancy Reed said when she opened the door. She gave me a big hug and then turned toward Ben, slapping him on the shoulder.

"What were you thinking, driving her over in that death trap? We could hear you coming a mile away."

"Nance, I keep telling you, it's one of the great rides. I'd be happy to take you out for a spin anytime."

"Oh, you!" Nancy said, giving him another swat, this time more gently.

"Stop flirting with my mother, Ben," Moira said, coming out of the kitchen, wiping her hands on a dish towel, which she tossed at Ben. He caught it and smiled.

"Hi, Ruthie. Sorry about last night. Hope you got the message. I lost your cell phone number and Chief Paisley wasn't giving it up." Moira gave me a quick hug and then guided me into the living room.

"No worries," I said, sitting on the couch. "I went by the Corner Market and got some food."

"The store looks good, doesn't it?" Pat said, coming into the room. I stood up and gave him a hug.

"It does," I agreed. "And I met Ada Clark."

"Ada's a nice young woman," Pat said. He didn't sound overly convinced.

"She seems nice enough. Though she was a little weird with me."

"Weird, how?" Nancy asked, glancing over at her husband.

"I don't know. I'm likely being paranoid. She kept saying how sorry she was about G.T.'s passing, but I got the sense that she wasn't really that sorry. It's probably just me."

"No, probably not just you," Nancy said. "Stop looking at me like that, Pat, you know it's true. They blamed Thom for putting a hold on their building permit, even though he didn't have a thing to do with it. And then Thom had some words with them after that slick developer met with them, and they were none too pleased with that, let me tell you."

"How do you know, Mum?" Moira asked.

"Moira, I do work for them. While I'm making my deliveries, I can't help if I overhear conversations, can I?"

"I wish you wouldn't do business with the Clarks, Nancy," Pat said.

"Their money is just as green as everyone else's, and it helps us all make ends meet. What's wrong with that, may I ask?"

"Nothing. Nothing. Listen, we'll talk about this later. How you holding up, Ruthie?" Pat asked.

"I'm holding up. How about you?"

Pat didn't answer right away. Instead his lips moved in and out and he cleared his throat.

"Enough of that now," Nancy said. "Ruth, I don't want to rush anyone, but dinner's ready. And honestly, I didn't make any appetizers. Would it be rude to suggest that we eat?"

"No, of course not," I said.

"Good. Let's go in then, shall we?"

We walked through the double arch into the dining room. I always loved the Reeds' house. Their post–World War II colonial was just so normal. And it was always so full of love. These were two concepts that my childhood lacked for a bit. I noticed that there were only five place settings on the table, so no Ryan tonight.

I moved toward the single seat on one side of the table, but Moira moved me. "No, sit here, next to Ben," she said. I complied, plopping down between Ben and Pat as Nancy ladled out pumpkin soup. Between the smell and my first sip, I was transported back to when I was about twelve and Nancy taught me how to make this very soup. I'd wanted to make it for my grandmother, since it was always her favorite. Tears pricked the corners of my eyes.

"Is it all right?" Nancy asked, sounding anxious.

"It's perfect, thank you. I was just remembering when you taught me to make it, so I could surprise Grandma."

"Well, don't fill up," Moira said. "Mum's been cooking all day. Turkey, corn bread stuffing, maple brussels sprouts, Boston cream pie."

"Thank you for going to all this trouble, Nancy."

"Please, no trouble. I only wish it was under happier circumstances."

"I wish it was too." I picked up my spoon, but couldn't bear to take another sip. I looked around the table. Everyone appeared transfixed by their own bowls, but no one was eating.

"So, tell us what you've been up to for the past few years, Ruth. We all lost track," Nancy said, breaking the silence the way only she could.

"Mum!" "Nancy!" Pat and Moira both called out at the same time.

"Wow," Ben said under his breath.

"What?" Nancy said, waving her spoon in the air. "I'm making conversation!"

I looked at Nancy and then around the table.

"It's fine, really. Lots to tell, but told pretty simply. I got married, he left me, I got divorced. I've been leading a freelance life, working for different shops on a project-by-project basis."

"Okay, I'll admit it. I did some more Internet stalking," Moira said. "I saw a picture of you with this beautiful clock you designed. Is that something you're doing?"

"Yes, sort of. I have been working on my own pieces, more art pieces than clocks, but clocks are part of them. Hard to explain."

"It's great that you are making a living doing the family business," Pat said.

"None of this pays the bills, but that's all right for now, because I'm living with friends. And I had a job that I loved at a museum, but there are some funding issues, so they had to lay me off for a bit while they try and find more money. Basically, you know the rest."

I grabbed a roll from a basket Pat passed to me. Ben slid

the butter dish over to me and gave me another reassuring smile.

Pat turned to me. "Sounds like you've had a bit of a rough go, Ruthie. I am sorry to hear that. We knew bits and pieces, of course. The Internet is a wonderful thing, even if Moira is the only one of us who uses it. I'm sorry about your marriage. Is that recent?"

"The divorce was final last month." I started to break off small chunks of bread and nibble it slowly.

"Are you in touch with your parents?" Nancy asked. Pat glared at her. "What? They need to be contacted." She got up and cleared the soup dishes. Moira helped.

"We've e-mailed, but I haven't spoken to them about G.T. yet. But Caroline talked to them."

"So they won't make it back for the funeral?"

"No, they won't make it back for the funeral or whatever service we decide to have. Or, put it this way, we won't hold off on having it until they arrive."

"So there's going to be a funeral after all?" Nancy asked. "I thought Thom didn't want one."

"Caroline and I are going to talk about it some more tomorrow when she comes to the shop. But yes, I think we should have some sort of service, don't you?"

"Of course I do. People will want to pay their respects. Thom was a good man," Nancy said with a nod. "So tell me, you've never met Caroline, is that right? What did you think? What are you looking at, Moira? We need to catch up." Nancy went back in the kitchen, which allowed me time to regroup. Nancy Reed had always been forthright. That was the term my grandmother always used. My grandfather said she spoke her mind. Moira was always embarrassed by her while we were growing up. I never minded. And didn't really mind now. I always figured she cared enough to ask. Besides, I had nothing to hide.

"Caroline was not what I expected."

"Well, Ruth," Pat said, passing me a plate with turkey on it. It looked like the rest of the sides were going to be served family style. "I think you'll like her. She's not much like your grandmother, except that she also took good care of your grandfather. She made him happy. And kept him from being lonely these past few years."

"And she helped run the business," I added.

"She did. For a while, we all thought Thom was going to sell, but she got him reinspired to stay with it."

"But he may have been thinking about selling again recently. Did he mention that? He was talking to a real estate agent."

"He got an offer recently, yes. He wanted to know how the offer stacked up. But he wasn't going to sell, not for a while. Wanted to build up the nest egg a bit more."

"I talked to Jonah Winter about that. It didn't seem like the sort of thing my grandfather would do, buying up all that inventory."

"There were lots of reasons for him to want to get some more clocks in the shop," Pat said. "Thom had a master plan. The clocks were part of it. Also, getting some capital, trying to get interest around the clock tower. He was working on that with Grover Winter, right up until Grover passed. Lots of folks thought Thom would let it go, but he kept at it."

"I knew about the clock tower idea back in the day, but why was he so focused on it now?"

"We've got a new boss in town, acts like she's the mayor

and not a hired hand. Anyway, Kim Gray, she has big plans for Orchard. Rebuilding part of Washington Street is part of her plan. She was trying to get a community center built. That meant tearing down the old Town Hall. But Grover and Thom, they had plans to restore the clock tower. They'd filed paperwork to make the Town Hall a historical site a while ago, and Grover had kept it up. The title to the building was lost, so it's all at a standstill right now, though Grover Winter claimed he owned the building. Thom and Grover were working with the Board of Selectmen, trying to get that passed."

"Where does it stand now?"

"Your grandfather was never a great politician. But Caroline was helping, at least before she had to leave town. They were making headway. Now, without Thom, I'm not sure what's going to happen at the vote on Thursday. It could go either way. It would be a lot cleaner if someone found the deed to the Town Hall."

"What about the Winter family? Are they helping?"

"Jonah isn't much of a leader. And that sister of his? She's had her own difficulties. We're not in a position to help right now either. It looks like the clock tower dream is going to die, right along with Thom."

"Maybe not," Ben said. "Some of us newer residents think it's a good idea. Thom was winning us over. Even the Clarks were coming around. The more folks look into Kim's building plans, the less they like them. We just have to keep the pressure up, and someone needs to step in for Thom. And we need to find the deed."

Everyone turned to look at me. I focused on my plate.

chapter 27

I took a long sip of coffee. It was all I could do to swallow it.

"This is terrible, Bezel," I said. She looked up at me and squished her eyes quizzically.

"I think it's the coffeemaker. I wonder if cleaning it would help?"

Bezel meowed and circled my ankles.

"You're right, this one has seen better days. I'll think about getting a new one."

Bezel gave me a short meow and then went back to her own breakfast. Her sympathy only went so far.

"Well, I think I need to go down to the Sleeping Latte and get some real coffee." Instead of taking my entire bag, I grabbed my phone and put some money in my pocket.

"Caroline's coming over this morning, so I'm going to lock

you up here. Oh, don't act so put out. You spend all your time up here anyway," I said as I spent a couple of extra minutes trying to tame my hair and putting on a bit of makeup. Was I going to the Sleeping Latte looking for coffee or looking for Ben? I shook my head. Maybe a bit of both.

The Sleeping Latte was packed. Most of the people in the shop were getting coffee to go, and looked like students. The wait wasn't long, but there was a wait.

"May I help you? Oh, Ruth, it's you," Moira said after she looked up. "Good morning."

"Good morning. Thanks again for a great dinner last night."

"It was a lot of fun," Moira said. "Though I thought you'd be sick of seeing Reeds by now."

"Never. Besides, I need good coffee. How's it going this morning?"

"Busy, but that's nothing new. Between the leaf peepers, the students, and the thirsty citizens of Orchard, this has been a really busy fall."

"That's great," I said, turning to look at the line forming behind me. "Could I have a French roast and a bacon breakfast sandwich?"

"On bread, bagel, or English muffin?" she asked.

"Bagel," I answered without thinking much about it. I wasn't a foodie by any means, but between the Sleeping Latte and the Corner Market I was getting a more discerning palate. I was also going to have trouble fastening my skirts if I kept it up.

"The bagels are a little stale," Moira whispered. "The

Italian bread is really fresh. And the chef prefers making it on bread anyway. It's great."

"Sounds wonderful, thanks. With your mother in the kitchen, I should just say 'chef's choice' every time I come in."

"Good choice. Here's your coffee mug. Go sit down and we'll call you when it's up."

"How much do I owe?"

"Pay on your way out," Moira said, pushing my money back toward me.

I had the sense that paying wouldn't be easy, but I was going to keep trying. The diner was busy, but I could only imagine what the profit margins were like when you ran a restaurant. I'd taken several small business courses over the past few months, trying to figure out how I could open my own shop or studio. I understood how hard it was for a small business to stay open, and comping your friends wouldn't help. Maybe I'd just leave a really big tip.

I did a quick scan and saw a table by the window open up. I made a beeline for it, nearly colliding with Ben.

"Were you going to sit there?" he asked. He looked like he'd just rolled out of bed. If I had a type, and I'm not sure I did, Ben wasn't it, at least on paper. He wore a paisley shirt that I normally wouldn't find attractive, but he managed to make it work. The shirt hadn't seen the hot side of an iron and was half tucked into his jeans. The cowboy boots and brown bomber jacket were well worn, his hair was a little too long, and he had facial hair that was more than scruff but less than a beard. Ben was the least well-groomed barber in existence. Handsome and confusing all at once.

"I was," I said. "Happy to share."

Ben pulled my chair out for me and then went to the other side of the table and got settled.

"Glad this is working out. Real estate around here is tough to come by, especially at this time of the morning. But you still need to come by the shop. I'd love to show you around."

"Maybe on my way back to the Cog. Caroline's coming by this morning and I want to make sure I'm there to meet her." I looked around. "Is it always this busy?"

Ben nodded and swallowed his coffee. "It is, now. It took folks a while to warm up to the new decor, but Moira won them over. And so did Nancy."

"So did Nancy what?" said the woman herself, placing two sandwiches in front of us.

"So did Nancy prove herself to be a goddess of the kitchen, so all of Orchard and the students of Marytown came to worship at her feet. Thanks, Nancy, this looks like just what the doctor ordered," Ben proclaimed, hand over his heart.

"Ben Clover, you look like ten miles of bad road."

"Feel like eleven," he said, dropping the false bravado as he took a sip of coffee.

"Did you go out last night sowing your wild oats?"

"Sowing my wild oats? How old are you, Nancy, eighty? I dropped Ruth home around nine thirty. Where would I sow my wild oats in Orchard at nine thirty on a Sunday night? If you must know, I have terrible insomnia that kicks in every once in a while. It has kicked in this week, ever since Thom was"—he stopped and cleared his throat—"ever since Thom passed."

Nancy put her hand on my shoulder. "We're all having

trouble sleeping these days. I saw the chief a little while ago. He says there's no news, but I don't see how that's possible. How could it take so long?"

"Mum!" Moira bellowed over the crowd.

"Back to it. Enjoy your food."

Ben watched her go, then turned, picked up his sandwich, and took a bite.

"Is there something wrong with your food?" he asked with his mouth full, looking meaningfully at my untouched sandwich.

"No, I'm sure it's great. I just keep thinking of all the things I have to get done before Caroline comes by this morning. Maybe I'll get this to go," I said, starting to lift up my plate.

"Oh no you don't," Ben said, reaching out and gently pressing the plate back to the table. "Not allowed."

"Not allowed?" I asked.

"Three reasons. First, you need to respect the food. And it demands to be eaten right away, while it's hot. Second, you need to eat. I'd imagine you have a full day ahead, and breakfast is the most important meal of the day. And third, I'd like the company. What do you say?"

What could I say? I picked up my sandwich and took a bite. Wow. The bread was fresh Italian bread, pan toasted in butter. The egg was over easy, the cheese a mixture of cheddar and something sharp, maybe Asiago, and the bacon was crispy, but not overcooked. Just perfection.

"See what I'm saying?" Ben asked. "If you'd waited till you got home, the cheese would have started to congeal. Not good. Trust me, you need to eat these when they are fresh. Some of the other food is to-go worthy, but not these."

"Thanks for the food lesson," I said, taking another bite.

"Anytime. These are the things I can give lessons on. Food, baseball, and the best places to buy treats for your dog."

"And barbering? Is that the word?" I said, taking another bite.

"It is. I've still got a lot to learn about barbering, but I'm learning."

"It's hard to run a business," I said. "Sounds like you're trying to adapt, though."

"I think the changes Aunt Flo suggested will help with the folks from Orchard. And I'm running a student special at Harris University that's starting to kick in. I'm figuring it all out. What? You look like you want to say something."

"I don't want you to take this the wrong way," I said.

"Go ahead."

"I remember your aunt and uncle. She always had perfectly coiffed hair. It was a little crazy, but it was done. And your uncle? Perfectly shaved, hair trimmed."

"And I'm, what?" At least he was smiling.

"A little scruffy," I said, hating that I was blushing.

"A little scruffy? I'm alone in the shop, no one there to cut my hair. No matter how good I am, it looks like I cut it myself. And the beard? I hate shaving with the passion of a solar flare."

"Ha. Well, that explains it."

"Not a great advertisement for a barbershop owner," he said.

"Can I tell you a secret?" I asked.

"Anything," he said, looking very serious.

"I'm a very good horologist. I fix a mean clock. But I can't keep time to save my soul. I'm late for everything. And when I get going on work, I completely lose track of time. It used to drive my husband crazy."

"Well, he must have been crazy to let you go."

I laughed out loud. "Boy, that's quite a line, Barber Ben," I said.

"You have a great laugh. You should use it more often."

"Another great line."

"Not a line, the truth." I looked at Ben and sobered up again. It'd been a long time since someone had tried a line on me. A long, long time.

"Darn, it's back," Ben said.

"What?"

"The shadow that comes across your face every once in a while. It's like I can see your memories creeping in and causing you pain. I really hope it all gets easier for you soon, Ruth Clagan."

"I do too, thanks," I said. I fumbled with my coffee mug, but finally took a long sip. Ben Clover was a nice guy. I thought they were extinct.

"Caroline and I are going to talk about the business. It's more complicated than I expected. I've been trying to piece together G.T.'s intentions for the Cog & Sprocket. Was he going to sell it? Or not? Was he trying to rebuild the clock tower? Why'd he buy so many clocks?

"I looked at his calendar, and it looked like he met with you several times. Maybe you could help me understand him better."

"Met with me? Not meetings, really. We ate dinner pretty regularly when Caroline was out of town. And had lunch once a week. I really enjoyed his company. And I loved hearing about Orchard back in the day."

"It seems like it's changed a lot since I left."

"Times have been tough. I think folks are tired of struggling, and when someone offers them an easy way out, it's tough not to take it."

"An easy way out?"

"Like buying up property to rebuild Orchard into the model of a modern Berkshire town. Thom called it an amusement park for city folks who wanted small-town charm. They even wanted to build bus depots so they could park after they'd shipped in tourists."

"Who's they?"

"Kim Gray and some of the so-called business leaders in town. Thom was working on convincing people to see beyond dollar signs into what it would mean long-term for Orchard."

"Did they offer you money?"

"They did, and I turned them down flat. So did Moira. But across the street, they were making headway. Money was pitting neighbor against neighbor, and it wasn't pretty. I was trying to help Thom get the rest of the town on his side, but it was slow going. Kim's a good chess player. Every time Thom would make a move, Kim would have anticipated it and be ready for a zoning commission meeting or a vote by the board. I asked Aunt Flo to come back and help me run the business and to help Thom and me make a case for keeping the old Town Hall."

"Is she going to?"

"She has some things to wrap up, but then she's coming back. Sorry to say, it's too late to work with Thom. They would have been a great team."

I didn't doubt it.

"Listen, I know you have a lot on your plate right now and I don't want to add to it. But you'll let me know if you're going to sell, won't you?"

"Why, are you interested in buying a clock shop?" I asked.

"I'm interested in trying to save Orchard. And I think the Cog & Sprocket is critical to that plan."

We ate in silence for a few minutes and then Ben got up to refill his coffee. He took my mug as well and I watched him walk across the diner, saying hello to many of the people, smiling at everyone. He looked like a modern-day cowboy. Maybe he could save Orchard after all.

Ben almost ran into Aggie Kurt at the coffee urn. Even she ended up talking to him for a moment, and smiling while she watched him walk back toward me.

"It must have been a heck of a line to get Aggie Kurt to laugh," I said.

"She's a tough audience, that's for sure. But she loves dirty jokes."

"Dirty jokes?"

"Yeah, well, don't judge. A happy Aggie is good for everyone, trust me."

"Oh, I do. She seems like she's got a lot on her mind. I've only met her once, but I've seen her around town a couple more times. She always seems sad and a little distracted."

"Aggie has had a really bad run of luck. She lost her husband, her business, and both her parents within a two-year span of time. People were sympathetic at first, but she wore most everyone out. Your grandfather was one of the best friends she had left. Thom always treated everyone with respect. And he also had strong opinions and a unique way of looking at the world."

"I've been learning about his vision this week. It sounds like he was taking on a much more public role. That wasn't typical of the G.T. I grew up with," I said.

"Did you know about the historical landmarking he was proposing?"

"I found some paperwork, but I have no idea where it all stood. There's a meeting this Thursday, so I need to catch up soon. Caroline was going to try and get it moved."

"Good luck with that. Kim Gray sees her opportunity. That sounds cold, but then that's Kim. Here's my understanding of what's going on. Thom got a bee in his bonnet when the old camp back on Route 143 was turned into a dorm for Harris. Thom worried about Harris taking over Orchard and the town losing its soul. His words."

"That doesn't surprise me, that part about wanting to keep Orchard true to itself."

"He thought making it difficult to build would be a step. Plus, his personal goal was to save the old Town Hall. With big money being offered, Thom decided to take another approach and make some of the buildings in town landmarks. But Kim outmaneuvered him and decided that landmarking a building meant that it couldn't be modified. At all."

"Isn't that typical for landmarking?"

"No. Every town, county, state, has its own set of rules. Landmarking in Orchard used to mean a plaque, and the need for a series of town meetings before a building could be torn down."

"Modifications were all right?"

"They required a permit, but yes. Especially if it involved making the building safer or more accessible.

"Problem was that Kim's new rules got in the way of some folks. Ada and Mac Clark had to hold off expanding the Corner Market out the back, and they weren't happy. Beckett Green just stopped working on his building and has said he would sell it to the developer who was interested in the old Town Hall if the rules didn't change. This developer, Henry Smith, was going to pull it down and build a community center. Of course, it was his definition of a community center, complete with a chain coffee shop and pool hall."

"Sounds lovely," I said, rolling my eyes. "Who is this Henry Smith character?"

"No one knows. Kim's the only person who's met him. I've tried doing some research, but haven't found anything. Thom thinks . . . thought . . . the name is just a front, but he couldn't prove it. So he decided to really focus on saving the Town Hall.

"The Winter family had leased the building over to the town for fifty years at a dollar a year. The lease is up at the end of this year. Kim thinks the town can take it over, since no one can find the deed. On paper, Grover Winter left it to your grandfather. But paper doesn't count for much these days and without the deed it's worth even less. Thursday's meeting is the first step in the takeover."

"Did all of this upset anyone so much that they might have harmed G.T.?" I asked.

"He wasn't the most popular guy these days. I just can't imagine who was pushed that far."

chapter 28

I was mulling over what Ben had said. It's a leap from ruffling feathers to murder, but passions run high when money is involved. I thought about Ada and Mac Clark. Were they really the locavore hipsters they seemed or were they less than scrupulous businesspeople like Mac's uncle? What about Beckett Green? Had he sunk his fortune into the bookstore or was this a hobby for him? Who was Henry Smith? Who else in town had money riding on change? Did Caroline know about all of this or had G.T. been waiting until she got home to tell her?

On my way out, I went back to the counter and ordered two cups of coffee.

"Two more cups?" Ben asked. He sounded impressed. I noticed he ordered a decaf.

"Caroline's coming by this morning so we can go over the books. I've tried to make some coffee in the coffeemaker, but it isn't good. That's an understatement. I've been thinking of using it to remove varnish on some of the clocks. It may be the coffeepot or the coffee. I'm doing what I always do. And making coffee is one of my true talents."

Ben laughed and I did too. It was nice to share a laugh with someone. I'd forgotten.

"Bad coffee and terrible showers are the two things I'll never get used to, and that apartment has both in spades," I said.

Moira handed me a tray with three cups of coffee and a bag of baked goods.

"Caroline's a coffee drinker. She'll want a second cup. And if I know the both of you, you won't break for lunch, so there are a couple of sandwiches in there."

"How much do I owe you?"

"Your money's no good here. We can argue about it later. You, Ben Clover, your money's welcome."

"You cut me to the quick, Moira, you really do," Ben said as he reached into his back pocket for his wallet.

"Oh, you know I'm just playing with you," Moira said. "Thanks again for taking care of me the other night. Ruth, if you ever need a shoulder to cry on, Ben's got the best one in town. Very broad and manly. Ben, I'll see you this afternoon, right?"

"Right, see you then."

Ben held the door for me and we walked out into the street. Orchard was starting to wake up, for Orchard. Compared to Boston, it was still in a slumber for a Monday. We saw Aggie Kurt and her truck making deliveries to the Corner Market across the street. Ben waved to a half-dozen people in cars, none of whom I knew. He wasn't in any rush to get back to his shop, and I didn't walk any faster.

"So a new coffeemaker may require a trip to Marytown, but that can be done. What's this about the shower?"

"It isn't a real shower. It is a contraption to make a claw-foot tub into a shower. It's okay, but it's short. And I'm tall. And my hair is thick and curly, as you can see."

"And auburn. And lovely."

I chose to ignore him, but I felt the blush start again.

"Under the best of circumstances it's hard to get it rinsed out," I said. "But these are not the best of circumstances. Far from it. Very far from it." I felt the pressure of tears behind my eyes. I didn't have a free hand to wipe the tear that was brimming and so I wouldn't be able to stop them if they fell. I blinked them back and cleared my throat.

Ben had the good grace to look forward.

"You know, I could help with that. Come by the shop. I'll wash your hair for you."

I drew a sharp breath. Getting my hair washed by a handsome barber was an offer I might not be able to refuse. Or might not want to.

"I'm great at hair washing. Brilliant, in fact. Ask Moira. She comes by once a week for a wash and a flat iron."

"Maybe I'll take you up on that," I said, a little disappointed that I wasn't the only girl whose hair he offered to wash. "But no flat iron. Keep that thing away from me!"

"She'll be by around four thirty, after the shop closes."

"I'd hate to be a third wheel."

Ben laughed. "Me and Moira? Not likely. We'd probably kill each other. Just good friends. Anyway, come by before or after. Anytime. You have a good day, Ruth Clagan. Give Caroline my best. And you take care of yourself."

"Thanks, Ben. Maybe I'll see you later," I said, continuing on next door to the Cog & Sprocket, a stupid smile on my face.

chapter 29

I called Caroline's name out when I came into the shop. I'd seen her car parked out in front. I put the coffee down on the countertop and called her name again.

"In here," she said. I walked through the gap in the counter and into the workroom. No Caroline. Then I noticed that the tower of clocks was a bit higher, and there was a path cleared. I walked to the right, through the path, and was pleased to see a clock-free area.

Caroline had set up a card table and had moved in two chairs. I didn't recognize them from the attic, but they did look familiar. She had a laptop plugged in and was setting up a printer.

"What's all this?" I asked. "Where did the clocks go?"

"Pat took a few of the crates out to the cottage. Here's a list. They're yours, of course. Apparently he's been thinking about ways to create more space and that seemed like the best plan, especially with you staying upstairs. I hope it's all right."

I looked down at the list of clocks, with the dates they were moved. Very thorough and very official-looking.

"Of course, that makes sense."

"You're always welcome to come out to the cottage to work in the barn. I hope you know that."

"Thank you," I said. I actually hadn't known that. Our relationship felt like an arranged marriage. We were both dancing about, trying to get to know each other, even after our chat the day before. "Where did you get the card table?"

"I brought it from home. I thought we could work in here. Upstairs is your space. And I can't work in the workroom—too many memories right now. So I thought we could settle in here for the day. Is that all right with you?"

"It's fine with me," I said, and I meant it. "Were these chairs upstairs?"

Caroline nodded. "Thom was going to re-cover them."

"They look heavy. How did you get them downstairs?"

"Pat," we both said at the same time.

"What would I do without Pat?" Caroline asked. Her voice sounded shaky and she turned away from me. "How about if we open up these front shutters?"

I looked at the front window. Sure enough, the shutters had been pulled across the front. I went over and unfastened them. They opened easily enough, but the dust on the windowsill told me they hadn't been opened for a good long while.

I looked around and sighed. For such a tiny shop, there were a lot of pockets of space. Years ago someone had decided the shop itself should be small, so they'd put up a half wall that made the downstairs more of a U shape. Every few years my grandmother brought up the idea of taking the wall down, but my grandfather had always refused. He called the front area useful space for clock making. He was right. The natural light made the room look shabbier and more wonderful. I heard a noise coming from the back of the shop.

"Is someone else here?" I asked.

"Pat's here. Apparently Thom wanted to surprise me, and they were putting in a bathroom on this level. Of course, it was as much for him as it was for me. He was starting to have trouble going upstairs several times a day."

"Was there something wrong?"

"Nothing more than a lifetime of work catching up to him. His knees were bothering him more and more. Arthritis. Anyway, Pat's going to be working on the bathroom today, and a couple of other odd jobs. I hope that's all right."

"Of course," I said. I walked back around to the shop and I grabbed the tray of coffees from the counter.

"Oh, thank you. This looks wonderful."

"Thank Moira. She's taking good care of us. And she and Ben both send their best."

"I'll take a walk later and say hello to them both. Do you know what's in the bag?"

"Sandwiches, she said. But that's a big bag for two sandwiches."

"But not for two sandwiches, three muffins, cookies, and a couple of Danishes," Caroline said, rummaging through the bag. She put it on the table and ripped it open, creating a makeshift tray. "These sandwiches should go in the fridge."

"I'll take them up. I need to get my computer anyway."

When I went up, Bezel came out to say hello. She leaned against my legs and purred. I petted her, rubbed behind her ears, and gave her a kiss on top of her head. She purred up until the kiss, which earned me flattened ears and a look of utter contempt before she stalked off.

I grabbed my computer, my cell phone, and a tangle of power cords. Upstairs at the Cog & Sprocket was basically a dead zone, but both my phone and laptop kept trying to get signals and that wore them down quickly. When I headed for the door, Bezel made a move to follow me.

"Sorry, Bezz," I said. "We talked about this. Caroline's here. I need to lock you in." I leaned over and locked the cat door that usually allowed her free rein.

Bezel stopped and stared at me for a moment and then she seemed to shrug before she walked back to the bed. One final yowl let me know that I was on her bad side.

"Bezel wanted to come visit, but I told her to stay upstairs," I said as I turned the corner into the front part of the shop. Pat sat in my chair, drinking the third cup of coffee. He made a move to get up, but I waved him off, putting the computer on the table and then plugging in my phone. I looked down at the wireless connections available, frustrated because none were available here in the building.

"I don't suppose either of you know what Ben's wireless password is, do you?" I asked.

"B-e-n-C-l-o-v-e-r. Capitals on the names. Zero for the *o*," Pat said without hesitation.

I typed it in. "Fabulous! That worked. Pat, you've been holding out on me," I said.

"Not really. Ben gave it to Moira. I figured he wouldn't mind giving it to you, even indirectly, so I asked Moira for it last night."

"Why didn't I think of that?" I said. "This will make life easier." I checked my business account and immersed myself in the e-mails I'd missed over the past few days. Lots of friends had written wondering where I was. I deleted an e-mail from my ex without even reading it. Boy, did that feel good. I noticed a couple from the museum, but then I heard my name. Pat must have said it a few times before I looked up at his amused half smile.

"Sorry, Pat, what were you saying?" I said.

"I said I was going to take Caroline's car in for servicing. I'll call in and let you know how it's going, but just in case, can you drive her home this afternoon?"

"Pat, this can wait for a few more days, honestly. I thought it had been fixed, but I guess not. I've been fine for this long," Caroline protested from the table, where she had been updating the paper log books and nibbling on a Danish.

"Caroline, slipping brakes aren't to be trifled with. If I'd known how bad it was, I never would have let you drive up to Vermont, sick son or no. I'll give you a call and an estimate."

"Call me with the estimate before they do the work."

"Fred owes me a favor. You'll be able to afford it, I promise."

"Pat," she warned, standing.

"Caroline. Let folks do for you right now."

"Thank you, Pat. I don't know what I would do without you, honestly I don't." She sat back down.

"Well, you won't have to worry about that, for a bit at least." Pat Reed was more than a fix-it man. He was part of the Cog & Sprocket. I wondered if he worked anywhere else these days, and guessed not. Had G.T. been paying him enough? Another life in turmoil, and more for me to think about.

Pat stood up, drained his cup of coffee, and grabbed a cookie. "And you, Ruthie, are you hanging in there?"

"I am, thank you, Pat."

"I'll leave you both to it then."

"Don't let the door hit you." I sat down in the chair Pat had abandoned and plugged in my computer.

"I never realized how dependent on the Internet I was before I came back here," I said. "It's probably not healthy, but I use it for work and for connecting with folks. Whoa, Caroline, are you all right? What's the matter?"

The older woman looked at me and wiped her eyes. "This is so silly, but that phrase? 'Don't let the door hit you'? Your grandfather used it all the time. You reminded me of him just then. Actually, you remind me of him a lot. I noticed how you've been organizing the shop, taking care of the clocks. You love them as much as he does. Did."

"That's one of the nicest things anyone has ever said to me," I said, concentrating on keeping my own tears in check. "I understand clocks. I treasure the workmanship. And I really love learning about the history of each clock. Not just how it was made or by whom, but how it was used, who repaired it over the years, and who owned it."

"Your grandfather always said that the most ordinary of clocks was extraordinary once you got to know it. I often thought that people disappointed him, but clocks never did."

"I used to think he loved clocks more than anyone else in the world, except for . . ."

"Your grandmother, right?"

"Right," I said, feeling a bit self-conscious.

"And you too. You know that, I hope. He called you his girls. It broke his heart that he lost you both. Getting back in touch with you meant the world to him."

"I just wish I hadn't waited so long, and that we'd had a chance to talk."

"Oh, Ruth, I lived with a long list of wishes and regrets that kept me from being happy for so, so long. Too long. Your grandfather helped me realize that. He rescued me. I know that sounds old-fashioned, but so be it."

"You must have made him very happy," I said. And it wasn't a question. As much as my grandfather's presence was in the shop, Caroline was here too, now that I knew where to look. A shorter stool at the back workbench. The selection of teas upstairs. Post-it notes with reminders, likely from her, on the wall calendar.

"Happy? I don't know. I think I made him less lonely, and that was good. And he enjoyed being part of my son, Levi's, life. He was a wonderful role model for him."

"He was good at stepping in for missing parents."

We both concentrated on our coffee. I was a little uncomfortable with how much I'd shared, and maybe Caroline was too. I was a hard person to get to know. I'd been told that several times, most recently by my boss at the museum. And I was, but it was less of a character flaw and more of a layer of protection, sort of like a turtle's shell. In Caroline I recognized a fellow turtle. The half-answered questions. Vague pronouns. Maybe someday she'd tell me her secrets, but I wouldn't push. I had some of my own.

"So Pat's putting in a bathroom? I didn't know he was a plumber too," I said.

"While I was away, they brought a plumber in, hoping to surprise me. Pat's doing all of the finish work, and is moving right along. He did the same thing out at the house, oversaw a bathroom project. He's good at it, so it is a good solution for both of us."

"What do you mean?"

"Well, the work at the house needed to be done on a budget, but done well. Pat had the time and needed the work. And we could live with some flexibility in the schedule."

"Caroline, I appreciate your going over the business records with me. And your understanding about the will and the shop. But we need to talk about this a little, if you don't mind. You're showing me the books, but tell me about the business. All these clocks? I hate to even ask how you could afford them all."

"We took a mortgage out on the cottage," Caroline said.

"What? You mortgaged your home?"

"We thought if we turned the clocks around, we could pay it back. But, of course, the clocks go with the store. Which is as it should be. You're the only one who can get them ready for sale."

"But you need the money in order to pay back the mortgage," I said, stunned.

"Ruth, we don't need to talk about this now."

"Of course we do. Are you going to lose the house?"

"No. I can get through the next couple of months. And then, who knows, perhaps I'll move up to be closer to Levi."

"I want you to do what you want to do. But G.T. wouldn't want you to be forced to make a decision because of his business deal. We'll figure this out."

Caroline smiled and nodded. It was a taciturn agreement, the "we." But I meant it. Caroline being homeless was not part of my grand plan. Not that I had a grand plan, though doing what G.T. would have wanted had become my focus.

"I called Jeff Paisley on my way over," Caroline said. "Still no idea when they are going to release Thom's body. I know he didn't want one, but I think we should schedule a memorial service soon. I want to make a few more calls first and let people know."

"If they haven't heard already," I said. "It's been in the news."

"I know. But a phone call is still a nice gesture."

It was a nice gesture. And it bought us some time. I know it wasn't rational, but I didn't want to have a memorial service before we knew what happened. It didn't seem right to say farewell to him until we could really let him rest in peace.

"Let's go back to the workroom," I said. "I'll show you some of the work I've been doing." Caroline didn't comment on the changes in the space, but I could tell she was taking them all in. We walked over to the desk area, and Caroline stared at it.

"The accounting logs, did you find them?" she asked.

"The log is upstairs. Pat also showed me the database Levi set up. I'm glad you were starting to computerize."

"We were keeping paper shadow systems until Thom trusted the computers. He wasn't a big fan of technology. Though I do understand his reluctance on one level. Looking through his notebooks, and thinking about the way his mind worked, I don't know if a computer could have kept up with him," she said, smiling a little.

"I was surprised to see digital watches in the store. Yesterday I did a couple of electric repairs. I suppose that was more of the business these days. I'm surprised he was selling electric wall clocks, though. He never would have let them in the front door back in the day."

"I let them in the back door, and he pretended not to see them. Before the investment in the clocks, we had some lean times. Not selling electric clocks just didn't make sense."

"I was looking around the attic yesterday and saw a bunch of clocks that G.T. had made. Why didn't you sell those?"

"They weren't perfect. Your grandfather could admire the craftsmanship of other people's clocks, including the imperfections, but he wasn't as kind to himself. I kept trying to tell him that perfect was the enemy of good, but he wouldn't budge. This hole was off-center. That clock face was crooked. The tone of the chime wasn't satisfactory. A million excuses for them to go upstairs to the Clagan clock graveyard. His term. So, anyway, we needed to start to get creative about the work we brought in."

"What do you mean?"

"We started to try and do a volume business. Pat would create cases, almost as a side business, and Thom taught him how to put electrics into them. Then Thom checked them. The clocks in the attic were more traditional. These new clocks could be built to order. To match cabinetry in a high-end kitchen, for example."

"Did it help business?"

"It did, actually. Pat got a few custom orders, which we filled. People coming into the shop to pick them up saw the rest of the merchandise. And then, of course, there was the new inventory from the estate. I was starting to think about opening up the entire front of the shop, making it a showroom."

"There's a lot of merchandise," I said. "What were the plans for all of it? I met Jonah on Sunday and he mentioned the deal he had with you and G.T."

"He and his sister Delia. Did you know Delia? She was the oldest daughter."

"I think I do remember Delia, but more by reputation. She got sent to boarding school when she was in high school."

"Probably the best thing that happened to her. She lives down in New York now, barely ever came up to visit her folks. But she seems to have made her way in the world, not like Aggie."

"Aggie?"

"Aggie Kurt. She drives a delivery truck."

"We met the other day. She's Jonah's sister? I just didn't make that connection."

"She would have been long out of high school by the time you moved to Orchard. Jonah is the youngest," Caroline said.

"This is going to sound terrible, but she seems a little off."

"Far be it from me to speak ill of anyone, but I agree. She certainly put her poor parents through it. She married badly by all accounts. I never met her husband; he died a couple of years ago. She used her poor mother like a bank. After Harriet passed, Aggie asked her father to fund her latest venture, a high-end clothing store in Marytown. He agreed, but told her that was it, her inheritance."

"I take it by the fact that she's driving a truck that didn't go well?"

"Not at all. By high-end she was talking New York and Boston prices, high fashion."

"In Marytown?"

"In Marytown. Marytown is a college town. And high fashion and the Berkshires don't go hand in hand. Plus, her merchandise was ugly. I couldn't even find a scarf to buy the first time I went in, but Thom told me to patronize the store, talk it up."

"I can't imagine Aggie running a high fashion store."

"She cleaned up well. But her taste was suspect. Once a month I went over and bought a small piece and then tried to use it for a couple of days until I could put it away."

"How long did the store stay open?"

"Longer than it should have. She took the closing hard, but her father was true to his word and finally turned the taps off. She was cut out of his will for the most part. Now, why were we talking about Aggie? I'd hate you to think I was a gossip."

"We were talking about the deal you had with Jonah."

"Ah yes, poor Jonah. His sisters both had legacies, but Jonah is the executor along with Thom. He was stuck in the middle of a family feud. He didn't know how to get rid of the clock collection while honoring his father's wishes, so he and Thom came up with a deal. We bought the collection, will sell it, and once we make a profit, they'll get a cut."

"Sounds fair."

"More than fair. Thom was taking care of his friend's family. Even Aggie saw that, after a fashion. It took her a while. She kept hammering at Thom, wanted to look at the clocks, questioning when they would go on sale, how he was going to price them, all of it."

"Did you have a plan for selling them, aside from opening up the shop and putting more clocks on display?" I asked gently. I didn't want to sound like I was judging, but at the same time, having a crowded showroom would not get rid of dozens of clocks. I hadn't decided what to do with the shop, but no matter what, the merchandise needed to be dealt with—and soon. I had to help Caroline pay that second mortgage back. It felt like a heavy burden that the sooner I figured out the better.

"I was trying to get more information on each piece when I had to leave town. I worked on it while I was up in Vermont. My son taught me how to use the Internet to do the searches. It saved me hours on research."

"Not just the research," I said. "A webpage could help sell some of the clocks online. Do you have a webpage yet?"

"Levi set one up. I was going to show it to Thom. Sounds like you two are going to gang up on me. He said the same thing about going online."

"No ganging up, just helping however I can," I said, laughing, and silently thanking heaven, and Levi, that I didn't have to teach Caroline how to Google.

"Well, I'd also done some sketches for Thom to look at. I thought we should take this wall down," she said. I wondered if Caroline would have more success than my grandmother had?

chapter 30

The Cog & Sprocket was more than just a clock shop, and it always had been. Back in the day, horologists were a commodity, so people started to travel to Orchard to get their timepieces tended to. And Simon Clagan built clocks as well, which brought a higher-scale clientele into town. The shop didn't turn Orchard around on its own, but it played a part.

Simon's son was my great-grandfather Harry. From the stories I knew, the tradition of the horological gene skipping a generation started with Harry and continued with my father. My grandmother called Harry a bon vivant, but she always smiled when she said it. Harry was the reason the Cog & Sprocket still stood.

Harry was not a gifted clockmaker but he was a great salesman. Rumor had it that during Prohibition, the front of the store was a speakeasy, serving a special "tea" that was offered after business hours and was hidden in grandfather clock cases during business hours. After Prohibition, he made it a real tearoom, creating a secondary business during the Great Depression. G.T. once told me that the Cog & Sprocket did pretty well in those days even though Harry didn't charge half of the people who came by for repairs or tea. Clocks were the family business, but keeping the business had required inventive thinking over the years. Harry may have been an average clockmaker but he was a very creative businessman.

I looked around; my grandmother had always kept a few historical pictures of the Cog & Sprocket on the wall. These walls were bare, but I could see the shadows where they'd been. I didn't really need to see them; they were etched in my memory. A picture of the old clock tower, before the fire. Another one of Harry on his wedding day. Another one of Harry and his father outside the Cog & Sprocket, sometime in the late 1800s. Harry had a smile that made him look like he was going to pop out of the picture.

I remembered being in the parlor one afternoon, helping my grandmother clean up after a demonstration on how to wind an eight-day clock. I was looking at the picture of Harry beaming outside the shop and told her that sometimes I felt him in the shop with us, especially when we were having events.

"I do too," she said. "I knew him later in life, but he was still so charming and handsome the room stopped when he walked in. He was a wonderful man. And he did a lot of good in this town. A lot of good."

"What do you mean?" I asked.

"The Berkshires have seen their share of challenges over the years. Floods. A couple of mill fires that shut towns down completely. Orchard could have gotten lost, been taken over by the shadow of Harris University. But Harry, and your grandfather, have dug in over the years, making sure Orchard stands on its own and stays a place for people to have a small business, raise a family, be part of a community, have a good life. Not everyone appreciates what they've done, but they will someday."

When I was going into high school, my parents got the opportunity to go to Dubai to teach. I didn't go with them, preferring to stay in the United States with my grandparents. The day my grandparents officially became my guardians when I was fifteen, my grandmother baked a cake and declared that henceforth every May 15 would be Family Day. My grandfather gave me a mantel clock that was broken, and a tool kit. I often wondered if my parents dumped me or if my grandparents rescued me, but whatever the reason, moving to Orchard saved me. I'd found a place to belong, and where I could just be a kid.

"I love the idea of opening up the shop," I said, pulling myself out of my memories and turning to Caroline. I hope she didn't take that wrong. I still hadn't decided if I should move out here or go back to Boston and face that set of demons. "Yesterday, when I was poking around upstairs in the attic, I saw some old pieces of furniture. When I was a kid, I always thought of it all as so heavy and terribly old-fashioned. But now I seek that kind of furniture out and get it re-covered with more modern fabrics. That mixed style would work really well in here. And get some of the inventory up on the walls."

"Sounds like a good plan," Caroline said.

"I am really surprised that G.T. left me the store," I said. It felt like I was finally greeting the elephant in the room with a big wave.

"Thom changed his will a few times over the years, but you always inherited the Cog & Sprocket. Even though I worked here, it's your family's business. I know that. He seemed to think you loved it as much as he did."

"I did. I do. I'd forgotten how much." I turned on the shop computer and pulled up the database. "We need to get this in the cloud so you can start inputting your research and I can work on getting photos of the clocks taken and attached to the database. That's our best hope of getting the clocks online and sold."

"Our best hope?"

"Caroline, I'm not sure what I am going to do with the shop. But whatever I decide, there are a lot of clocks that need to be accounted for. I can't begin to think of selling it yet, with so much money tied into the clocks themselves. I can't do that alone and am hoping you'll help. You and Pat.

"Why don't we walk through the shop and you can tell me what you were thinking."

We both grabbed our notebooks and walked back around to the front door of the shop. I'd turned the corner when someone banged on the front door and rattled the doorknob.

Caroline walked around me and we met at the front door.

"There's still a sign on the door," she said, sounding perplexed.

"I know—I saw it," I said. The blinds covering the windows weren't the cheap, plastic mini blinds everyone was used to these days. These were old, heavy, metal blinds.

Really old. They predated me, I think. The Clagan family motto had always been "fix, don't replace."

I opened the blinds a bit and peered out. I hated the squeak that came out of me, but the large set of eyeballs staring back at me would have stopped anyone's heart. The banging started again, and Caroline stepped in and looked out the window.

"Aggie Kurt. Just what I need today," she muttered. "May as well open the door. Woman's like a dog with a bone when she has a delivery to make." Caroline turned the locks and pulled the door open.

"Aggie," Caroline said, opening the door.

"Caroline. I didn't know you were here." The two women were the same height, but whereas Caroline looked like she'd stepped out of a catalog, with her perfectly coiffed hair, timeless fashion sense, and perfect accessories, the angular delivery woman looked like she was attempting to mirror Caroline, but had failed miserably. It wasn't just the ill-fitting uniform. Today her hair was barely brushed and her lipstick was even more crooked than it was when I first met her. She looked like she hadn't slept in days, and she stumbled a bit when she came into the shop, heading toward the countertop. She stopped when she saw me.

"You're both here," she said.

"Where else would we be?" I asked.

She stopped and stared at me. Caroline stepped forward.

"Ruth, I see you've already met Aggie."

"We met a couple of days ago," I said.

"Saturday. Around two in the afternoon," Aggie said.

"You have an amazing memory," I said.

"I keep track of time and location. Have to. The bosses

keep track of me, all the time. Where I am, was. They keep these records via a computer and then they make me keep the records and then they compare. I'm always where I say I am."

"Aggie, we are in the middle of some business. Did you stop by for a reason?" Caroline asked gently.

"Yes, sure, of course. I wouldn't come by for no reason, would I?" she asked. "I have a package for Mr. Thom Clagan. Or is it Mrs. Thom Clagan? That's one of you now, isn't it? As far as packages go?"

"Yes, it is." I held my hand out.

"I should really ask for an ID, but I'll take Caroline's word for it. Can she receive packages sent to Thom, Caroline? Or do you want it? Since you're technically Mrs. Clagan, even if you never changed your name."

"Oh for heaven's sake, just give her the package," Caroline said, opening the door again and stepping back with her hand on the knob. "We'll be open for business again next week. Come back then and we'll have a cup of tea."

"Opening again. That's good, Caroline. That's really good. So you think the meeting on Thursday will go well? I'm so glad to hear it. Orchard wouldn't be the same without the old Cog & Sprocket. Or the Town Hall. Just wouldn't be the same." Aggie handed me the package and backed up out the door. "Just wouldn't be the same."

"We aren't going anywhere," Caroline said. She closed the door behind Aggie and then leaned on it as she threw all the locks again.

"What was that?" I asked.

"Aggie?"

"I meant more the conversation. She seemed a little, shall we say, strange, don't you think?"

Caroline sighed and started back up the stairs. "*Strange* is one word for it. Thom had never-ending patience with her. I don't. She has had a difficult time of it, but so have any number of us. She plays the victim card too easily and too often for my taste. But Thom used to say I was being too hard on her."

I put the package on the counter. It was the packet from the real estate office.

Caroline walked over to the counter and ran her hand along the address label of the package. She fiddled with her wedding ring, rolling it around on her finger.

"You know, Ruth, when I first married your grandfather, I thought I was marrying a clockmaker who owned a shop where he sold and repaired clocks and watches. I expected a quiet life, maybe even a little dull, since Orchard was such a small town. I was so wrong. I didn't realize that your grandfather fixed more than clocks in this town.

"Have you noticed how the walls upstairs are all open now?" she asked.

"I have. I wondered about it. Was that another rehab project?"

"Not exactly. Pat's son, Ryan, needed work this past summer, so Pat hired him to help with some odd jobs. Ryan had the idea of opening up the space."

"That shows some vision. I never saw beyond an apartment."

"Thom wasn't interested and let him know. But nonetheless, a few hours later, the wall between the kitchen and the bedroom was gone. Rather than get angry, which I would have done, Thom said it looked pretty good, may as well finish the job. Which, of course, meant days of prep to close off the upstairs from the shop. Hiring a Dumpster. Getting respirators."

"Wow. I can only imagine."

"The problem was that once the prep was done, Ryan lost interest. In fact, he'd taken another job that paid more. So Pat did the job himself. Happily, Ben Clover helped."

"Ben? Barber Ben?" I asked. "Why did he help?"

"Why not? At that point, the town was blocking his license to open, so he had nothing better to do."

"Why were they blocking it?"

"Who knows why this time? That board is always throwing its weight around. But that was another of Thom's fix-it projects. That one was a success."

"And the Winter family ended up being a project?"

Caroline nodded. "I barely knew Grover's late wife, but I did know Grover fairly well. She was always so stylish, wearing the perfect outfit with the perfect jewelry. Never a hair out of place. Grover and Harriet had some interesting children, that's for sure."

"Jonah called me last night. He asked for the two boxes he'd dropped by to be brought back over to him."

"We took anything of value, but that doesn't stop Jonah from dropping off more collections and anything with the word *clock* on it. That's fine—take them back. They should keep anything sentimental, don't you think?" Caroline shook her head. "What was in the boxes this time?" she asked.

"Small pieces. I opened one to take a look and it was a Seth Thomas miniature. They're in the car."

Caroline shook her head again. "They can't expect us to sell the clocks if they keep adding to what we have to repair and sell."

"But I don't understand. Why did they need cash? Isn't the Winter family rich?" I asked.

"They were rich, but Grover spent a lot of it when Harriet got sick. Aggie took most of her inheritance early, which also strapped the family finances. That house and lifestyle took a lot of cash to maintain. It had been slipping for a while, but really took a dive after Grover died."

I picked up the package Aggie had delivered and went to hand it to Caroline. She shook her head.

"Go ahead and open it," Caroline said.

"Should you open it?" I asked.

"No, the shop is yours. And the meeting was about the shop."

"Would he make a big business decision without checking with you?" I asked. I thought about my ex-husband, who, in retrospect, made a dozen decisions a day that affected me, but I had no say in them. My grandparents had always made decisions together, but perhaps he and Caroline didn't have the same kind of relationship.

"I'm a planner. And I don't make quick decisions. I need a lot of information and I need to ponder. Your grandfather had been percolating a few ideas and was looking forward to talking to me about them when I got back. Then this hearing got called for Thursday and he needed to move forward more quickly."

I opened the package and pulled out three file folders. None of them were labeled. I opened up the first one and read the note attached. *As requested, comps. Here's what the shop is worth, market value.* The number was decent, but not huge. I handed the folder over to Caroline.

I opened the second folder. In it were several stapled

packages of information. I looked at the top one and was surprised to see Ben's Barbershop. I glanced at the sheets and saw the history of the property and its owners over the years. Stephanie had made some notes on purchase prices and the estimated amount due on each property. I wondered if these were facts or educated guesses. Glancing quickly, it looked like all the shops on Washington Street were in the folder. I handed it to Caroline.

The third folder was a stack of forms, peppered with colorful notes with short sentences like *research needed* or *history on deed unclear.* I looked at them more carefully and it seemed to be information about getting buildings marked as historical landmarks, what it meant, and how it varied by town.

I handed that final folder to Caroline. She glanced at it and then handed them all back to me.

"Looks like he was doing a lot more than just proposing this historic landmarking business. He was digging in deep for the long fight," she said, looking up at me.

Oh, G.T., what were you up to? Is that what got you killed?

chapter 31

Caroline and I spent the rest of Monday looking at inventory, looking at the database, and talking through the operations of the store. Midafternoon we agreed on a system. Looking at new inventory was much easier than reading my grandfather's notes on the inventory he'd brought in or was working on.

"I wonder if seeing his handwriting will ever not make me miss him?" I said aloud after we'd broken for a late lunch. We were sitting at the card table in the front of the shop again. I looked out at the Town Hall across the street. I'd never spent much time over here and was sorry that I hadn't. It was a great view of Orchard.

"I was just thinking the same thing," Caroline said. I looked up. She looked tired and ten years older than she had that morning.

"I'm sorry, Caroline. I've kept you too long. You should head home and get some rest."

"We still haven't talked about a service for Thom," she said, shuffling the pile of papers in front of her.

"I've been thinking about this. When my grandmother died, G.T. was completely unhelpful when I was doing the arrangements. He hated the whole thing, made me promise that when it was his time, I'd cremate him, go to a pub, and raise a pint."

The look on Caroline's face was priceless. Her lips trembled as she waffled between horror and laughter. Finally she burst into a surprised giggle.

"That sounds like Thom. Why were you making the arrangements for your grandmother? Where were your parents?"

"My parents were useless. I know that sounds terrible, but it's true. Have you heard from them again this week?"

Caroline shook her head.

"Neither have I. Well, that's not exactly true. I got an e-mail from them this morning, telling me that they were devastated, but were knee-deep in research and wouldn't make it back in time for the services. They both felt that working was the best way to honor Thomas Clagan. An e-mail, no call. I wish I could stop being surprised by them."

"They are your parents. He is Thom's son. Far be it from me to judge anyone. But it does seem that you have had your share of grief, and I am sorry about that."

I wasn't sure what to say. Should I thank her? It was one of the kindest things someone had said to me for quite a while, which wasn't saying much.

The moment passed. "When Grover Winter died, Jonah

asked us to help him with the arrangements. Your grandfather wasn't much help, but I thought it was the grief. It was more than that: the perfect nexus of not belonging to a church per se and his contempt for public displays of emotion. Anyway, he made me promise the same thing. No service, a party instead. So what should we do?"

"I'm not sure," I said. "There are a lot of people who would want to pay their respects."

Caroline mulled that over. "Tammy Dunn. Did you know Tammy?"

I nodded. I didn't know her well, but her face was on the newsletters that the Massachusetts Horological Society e-mailed four times a year.

"She called me this morning. There's a meeting of the society this Saturday. She wondered if perhaps we might want to turn it into a memorial service instead."

"That may be a good idea," I said. The Horological Society was the only organization my grandfather belonged to that I knew of. "Did he still go to all the meetings?"

"Most of them, yes. They were his friends." Caroline was still for a moment and suddenly started to cry quiet tears into her hands. I started to get up, but she waved me off.

"I'd imagine some of the folks here in Orchard would want to see him off as well. Tell you what," I said, "call Tammy and tell her that Saturday sounds like a plan and that we'll be there. And then we can figure out the Orchard piece later. How does that sound?"

"It sounds good. Thank you," Caroline said, smiling even as a few more tears slipped from the corner of her eye. "I always have trouble making these sorts of decisions."

chapter 32

Boom. Boom. Boom. The front door rattled on its hinges. Boom. Boom. Boom. If folks didn't stop pounding on that door, we'd need to replace it.

I jumped up and ran to the front door, pulling the blinds back. Chief Paisley stared at me.

"Open the door, Ms. Clagan," he said.

I did as I was told. The chief walked into the store and I noticed his hand was close to his gun on his belt.

"Is Pat Reed here?" he asked me.

"No, he isn't."

"His car's out front. Don't try and protect him, Ms. Clagan. I need to talk to him," he said, looking past me into the front room.

What in the world would he want with Pat? "He isn't

here," I said. He waited for me to keep talking, but if he was serious he was in for a long wait.

"Mind if I check for myself?" he said, moving around me toward the back of the store.

"Chief Paisley, stop." Caroline walked in. "Chief. Jeff. Please. Pat drove my car over to Marytown to get the brakes checked. He isn't here. I promise. But you are free to look around if you'd like."

The chief stopped and looked at Caroline. "Ladies, it's imperative I speak with Pat Reed as soon as possible. As. Soon. As. Possible. Do you both understand?"

"You want to talk to Pat. Got it," I said flatly.

"He's going to call shortly to give me an estimate on the work. What should I tell him?" said Caroline, crossing her arms and tipping up her chin defensively.

"Nothing," he said. "Just have him call me when he's on his way back into town." With that he turned and left, but had the good grace to close the door softly.

"What was that?" I asked.

Caroline was already picking up the phone and dialing. "I don't know, but I am going to try and find Pat to give him a heads-up. It's what Thom would want me to do," she said.

chapter 33

Caroline and I took turns trying to call Pat's cell phone, to no avail. We talked a little more about the business, but I decided the best way to distract us and deal with some of the challenges for both of us was to appraise the inventory and get it ready for sale. Caroline and I went back to the workroom. I reached over and squeezed Caroline's arm.

"Are you all right?" I asked.

"I am. It just feels so empty in here," she said, resting her hand on the back of Thom's stool.

I nodded, but decided that work was the answer for both of us right now.

"Caroline, let's look at these longcases. I do have a soft spot in my heart for grandfather clocks. Such a statement about clockmaking. So, there are eight all together. Well, seven. This one doesn't count. Pat called it Grover's Folly."

I pointed to the empty case in the middle of the row. Very tall, a steeple top, lovely but plain face. But when you looked inside, it wasn't a clock. There were shelves and wooden doors that opened to reveal places for documents. I hadn't looked at it closely once I realized it was empty.

"That specific case was left to Thom, with all of its contents," said Caroline, stepping toward the clock to inspect it. "It was Grover's, always in his office. It looked like a stopped clock, but, as it turns out, it was really more of a safe. Even the pendulum was an illusion, placed between a mirror and the glass door of the case. Wait. Where's the pendulum?"

"Chief Paisley has a pendulum he is holding as evidence in the death of G.T. That may be the one that is missing."

"A pendulum?" Caroline looked back at me, shocked. "How do they know for sure it's evidence?"

"From what the chief said, they found a pendulum by the river. Well, Blue officially found it. And Ben called it in," I filled her in.

"So it must have been this missing pendulum. Or another one from the shop, I suppose."

"Which means that the killer must have been in the shop with G.T. and picked it up. Otherwise how could they have used it outside, next to the car?"

"Maybe the killer came in later?"

"Not if the weapon was a pendulum," I said, feeling a little sick at the thought. "From what I understand, the shop was locked up that night."

"So Thom knew his killer. Which means I probably do as well. What a horrifying thought." Caroline leaned against the workbench and lowered herself onto a chair.

"It is indeed. Do you have any ideas?"

"No, none." She looked helplessly around the shop as if searching for an answer.

"I wonder if all this is connected to why the chief is looking for Pat," I said.

"Again, no idea." She bit her lip. "None."

Funny, this time I wasn't quite sure I believed her.

"Anyway," Caroline said, "it's an interesting clock case. Thom talked about using it to model the clock tower when he first got it in the shop. He'd been working on some models, but this one looked like the steeple of the tower." She wiped her eyes and then looked away from the clock.

"These three on the end, they're in really good shape," I said, changing the subject. "What do you think? We could get them ready to be sold, let some folks on the Internet know, and see if we can move them? It would help the cash flow a bit."

"Ruth, whatever you want to do . . ."

"No, Caroline," I interrupted her. "We need to agree on these steps. For the next few weeks while we're both dealing with everything, we need to work together to make sure bills are paid and the business keeps running, so that we can make better long-term decisions later. What do you think? These three?" I said, indicating the three clocks closest to us.

"No, those two and this one. Your grandfather said that one there has potential," she said, pointing to a fourth clock. "His words. So I suspect you may want to take more time with it."

I looked more closely at the last one she pointed to. A David Wood? I looked at the clock face with its hand-carved numbers and painted face. What a thrill it would be to find a piece by one of the great masters. I couldn't believe I hadn't noticed it before. The mahogany cabinet had a warm patina and the bonnet was in excellent shape. Caroline had a point.

"You're right. That one needs more time."

I was intrigued, I'll admit it. Most of the time, fixing old clocks was getting it close to what it must have been like new. But there was a fine line that couldn't be crossed between fixing, and restoring, and replacing. Most clocks had had inner workings fixed over the years, so it was already a patchwork. But once in a long while, you found a clock that was close to its original state. The David Wood replica must have been such a find. Surely it couldn't be real, could it? These clocks were copied by many clockmakers, to varying degrees of success. Even today, they were manufactured. But if the David Wood was an original?

If it was an original, the clock would be both a horological and financial treasure. That clock alone would be a big step toward getting the Winter estate into the black—and the Cog & Sprocket, for that matter.

I took a deep breath and resisted the urge to stop everything and open the clock. Instead I inspected the three we'd decided on. Caroline took notes on my observations and then together we came up with a to-do list. The three clocks Caroline chose were excellent candidates for quick turnarounds. I had to wonder how much she knew on her own about horology.

"Pat can work on the cases," Caroline said. "If we hadn't had Pat, Thom never would have brought in all these clocks. They were quite a team."

"It looks like Pat put the weights and pendulums in these three. Let's try to wind them, see how they run," I said. I brought in my cell phone and we set the time. One of the clocks was key wound. The other two were wound by pulling the chains with the weights, getting the weights lined up, and letting gravity and mechanics do their work. I wound the one with the key, and set the time. Then I wrestled with one set of weights while Caroline went to work on the other.

"You're good at this," I said.

Caroline nodded. "Winding clocks is part of the business. Being in this shop has taught me a lot over the years. We have a dozen house calls we make every week, most of them over at Harris University, keeping clocks running."

"Another revenue stream," I said.

"Not huge, but yes, a revenue stream. We also have contracts to wind and maintain some clock towers in the area."

"Pat mentioned that."

"I helped with those, but that was mostly Pat and Thom. Lots of work winding clock towers."

"I haven't done it in a while, but yes, it's an excellent workout," I said, smoothing a wayward curl back into my bun.

Caroline finished prepping her clock before I did. We reset the times to all match, and then stepped back and watched the three clocks.

Nothing happened for three minutes. They kept time. Honestly, we probably could have stood there forever, except for the sharp knock on the back door. We both jumped, and Caroline put her hand over her heart.

I opened the door, chain in place. Nancy Reed stood on the stoop, still wearing her apron and without a coat. I closed the door, slid the chain off, and reopened the door to let her in.

"Nancy, is everything all right?" I asked. "Is Pat all right?" I asked. Suddenly I was ashamed that I hadn't called Moira and Nancy to let them know the chief was looking for him.

Then something happened I never thought I would live long enough to see. Nancy Reed started crying. Big, loud, ugly crying.

chapter 34

Caroline walked over and put her arms around Nancy. Nancy clung on, but then the quarter hour chimes started. We all looked up as one clock chimed, then another, and then the third. Not even close to one another. I looked down at my cell phone. Sigh. They were all at least five minutes off.

Nancy reached into the pocket of her apron and pulled out a dishrag. She noisily blew her nose. Yuck. It wasn't like I had a tissue to offer her, but still, a dishrag?

"It's Pat," she said. "He's in real trouble and I need your help." And then she started crying again.

"What kind of trouble?" I asked. We'd moved into the front part of the shop, and I dragged an office chair in so we could all sit at the card table.

"The chief came by to look for him and then came by again an hour later."

"He came by here as well," I said. "We told him Pat was in Marytown. He dropped Caroline's car off."

"I know, and I told the chief so. I kept trying to call Pat, but it took him forever to pick up the phone. When he finally did, I told him that the chief was looking for him. And that's when he told me."

"What is it, Nancy? It can't be that bad."

"It is that bad. Pat said he was going to tell the chief that he stole the clocks."

What little color Caroline had left drained from her face. Nancy stared at her hands.

"Which clocks?" I asked slowly.

"The five last month," Nancy said between sobs.

"No, that's not possible," Caroline said.

I was uncertain about a few things, but not this. Pat Reed would never steal from my grandfather. Something else was going on here.

"Tell me more about the clocks," I said. "I remember hearing that they were stolen, but I don't remember the specifics."

Caroline looked uncomfortable, but she started to explain nonetheless.

"When we first brought the clocks into the shop, we invited people over to see some of them. Neighbors, a couple of collectors. Anyway, we'd been showing people the clocks off and on for a week or so. Especially these clocks—they were real beauties. Five Seth Thomas mantel clocks. All mid-1800s. Really lovely specimens. We made sure we locked up, but the Cog & Sprocket is hardly Fort Knox. I was looking for a clock I thought might be in one of those crates and I noticed that one crate was empty."

"Could you narrow down the window of time?" I asked. "Maybe there's an alibi for Pat there?"

"It was a broad window. But since we'd shown several people the clocks, we did know what exactly was missing," Caroline said. "I filed a report with the police. And then Thom decided to withdraw it."

"Why?"

"He didn't say." Caroline looked away from me. I'd bet dollars to donuts she knew anyway, but I didn't push it.

"They were all Seth Thomas clocks? They're pretty popular, not terribly rare. But worth a fair amount, if they're in good shape." Both Caroline and Nancy stared at me. "Listen, I know Pat didn't steal any clocks, and no one can convince me otherwise. But look at it from the chief's point of view. These were a good choice for a clock-savvy burglar. And getting them out of here took some moxie. Why would the chief think Pat stole the clocks?" I asked. "Did he have a motive?"

Nancy started to cry again. She shook her head.

"It wasn't Pat," Caroline said, reaching out to put her hand on her friend's heaving shoulders. "Was it, Nancy?"

Nancy looked up at Caroline and shook her head.

"I'm so, so sorry," she said. "It was Ryan. Ever since he lost his scholarship he's been at sea, trying to figure out how to pay for school. His father and I helped as much as we could, and we thought he was all set. But apparently he had to take one class a second time and was a few thousand dollars short.

"I went down to the basement last week to put the summer clothes away. There were boxes I'd never seen. I looked in one and saw a clock. Then I looked in another box and saw another clock. They looked like ones we'd seen at the Cog & Sprocket one night when Thom and Pat were showing us some of the new stock. Same thing with the other three boxes. I didn't know what to do."

"You could have called the police or Caroline," I said. I know it was unkind, but I wasn't feeling terribly charitable at that particular moment.

"He's my son, Ruth," she said, her eyes pleading. "And I wanted to check in with Pat first. When he came home, I went down to the basement with him and showed him the boxes. I swear, he was as surprised as I was. But then he got angry, really angry. He kept saying Ryan's name over and over. He went out looking for him. I thought he was going to kill him, I really did. Oh, I'm so sorry."

"When was this, Nancy?" I asked.

"Last Tuesday. Ryan never came home that night. And then the next morning, Pat found Thom."

Caroline sighed.

I didn't know what to say. While this was a lot to take in, I couldn't help but feel that there were many missing links in the story. How would Ryan know which clocks to steal? They were good choices—old, great craftsmanship, lovely examples. But common enough that only an expert would be able to tell if they were the stolen clocks. And would Ryan really be able to pull off a robbery like this without help?

Nancy's phone began to beep and buzz several times in a row. She hunched over the display and pressed the phone to her ear.

"Moira? Is your father— What? Oh, I'm sorry, I forgot that it's Eddie's afternoon off." Her tone shifted. "No, I'll be right there. Hey, sweetie, you haven't heard from your dad, have you? No, it's nothing. All good. We just got cut off when we were talking earlier."

"I need to get back to the shop," she said as she stuffed the phone back into her apron pocket.

"Does Moira know?" I asked.

"No, of course not. Oh my, I need to pull it together. I'm sorry, I don't know why I came over here. It's just that . . . you know how much Pat thought of Thom, right?"

"Of course," Caroline said. "We'll figure out the mystery of the old clocks, I promise. In the meantime, go back to the shop."

She left by the back door, barely visible in the low light of the late afternoon.

"Ruth, I'm done in. Would you mind giving me a ride home?"

"We need to talk about this," I said.

"We can talk on our way home. Not here. I don't want to talk about it here."

chapter 35

I locked up carefully and left lights on all over the shop. We walked out to the space in the front where I had parked my Scion xB.

"I've always liked these cars," Caroline said. "They look like a London cab, don't they?" she asked.

I made room on the passenger seat while Caroline hovered behind me, rubbing her left arm with her right hand. It took me a minute. My car had been my office lately. This lifestyle led to a lot of clutter, a bit of trash, and a very full passenger seat. I piled up the papers, put them in a shopping bag, and put it all in the backseat.

"There's a lot of room in here, isn't there?" she asked as she climbed in.

"It is perfect for hauling things," I agreed.

"Things like clocks?"

"Yes, of course, clocks. And, well, I actually make some nontraditional clocks as well, and so I tend to haul around things I've picked up."

"Nontraditional clocks? Hauling around 'things'?" she asked, a smile creeping across her face.

I took a deep breath and then reached into the backseat, pulling out my smaller portfolio case. I unzipped it and flipped it open, then laid it on Caroline's lap.

"See that?" I asked, pointing to a large clock that looked like it was rising out of a Lucite table. Caroline took her reading glasses out of her purse and looked at the picture.

"It's a working clock," I said.

"Of course it is. Digital?" she asked.

"No, actually, that one is an eight-day clock, and you wind it up right there." I pointed to a spot on the front of the clock. "I started with digital, but now I use traditional parts. If I can't make a clock work, I make a new design."

"This is beautiful. May I look at the rest of the book?" she asked, her eyes fixed on the pages.

"I guess," I said. A part of me wanted to yank it back. I was always nervous when I showed my own work. These clocks were my passion. I usually did them on commission, and given the hours I spent on each one, they were not a lucrative business model. But they made me happy. Horology captured in an art piece. As much as you can capture time, that is.

"Is this how you make your living?" she asked, flipping the page and taking in the images.

I started the car and pulled out of the space.

"My ex-husband was, is, a professor, and we had on-campus housing. We were housemasters so we had access to storage space, and I had help from students interested in learning about my work. So long story short, I did this for three years, but for the past few months, since the separation, I haven't been able to find the time or space to make anything."

"I can only imagine that has been very difficult."

"It has, though this museum job was an interesting opportunity to expand my career options. I love making big pieces, but I don't want to make them for collectors only. I want anyone who loves the idea of having a clock integrated into a home in a bold, artistic way to have access to my work at some level. At the same time, I wouldn't mind a couple of commissions. That book you have in your hand? I had a dozen printed up. The museum is considering selling them in the gift shop."

"That's very exciting," Caroline said.

"It is." I should have sounded happier. And a month ago, it was the most exciting thing that had happened in a long time. Maybe it was a consolation prize since the funding for my job got cut, but it was a pretty good consolation prize. An opportunity to pitch my work to people who could afford to pay me.

Time to get the conversation back on track. "Caroline, I haven't been around for a while, but I can't imagine Pat Reed helping his son steal clocks, can you?"

She hesitated for a moment. "No, I can't."

"Tell me about what happened when the five clocks were stolen."

"I'm the one who noticed. There were seven clocks all together in one of the crates. The Winters had displayed them all together in one room of their house. It was one of their favorite groupings and we hated to break it up. Really lovely pieces."

"In working order?"

"We hadn't gotten there yet. They were all wonderful examples of mid-nineteenth-century mantel clocks, that's for sure. If they were in working order, we were looking at a thousand dollars apiece, probably more, as is. We were doing the overall inventory and I was gathering information in order to price them. Anyway, I took one home so we could look at it more closely. That meant the top of the crate was loose."

"Which means if this was a robbery, those would have been easily accessible. The robber just lucked out that they were also very valuable."

"The longcases are more valuable but it would take a very motivated robber to steal those. And it would also take time to move them out."

"It's a shame you don't have real pictures of the missing clocks." I waited for Caroline to reply. "Do you have any pictures?"

"We have some pictures from the Winter home. They are at the house."

"Did you give them to the chief?" Another pause.

"Caroline, you're not telling me something. What's going on with the stolen clocks?"

"At first blush, it looked like a straight-up robbery. A customer was looking for a walnut gingerbread clock and I remembered seeing one in one of the crates, so I went to look for it. I found the empty crate. So I called the police and filed a report."

"At first blush?"

"When the chief came over, he started to do a very thorough investigation. Now, don't get me wrong. The old chief was a good man, and he kept the peace. But Jeff Paisley's much more inclined to dig a little deeper. After a thorough assessment, he quickly helped us realize that the robbery had to be an inside job, as it were. The back door wasn't forced. The robber knew exactly what he, or she, was looking for."

"Which meant that the prime suspect was . . ."

"Pat Reed. Thom and I were off the hook, since we weren't making an insurance claim. That and the fact that Jeff Paisley didn't think we did it. The only thing that kept the chief from arresting Pat was the fact that we couldn't pinpoint exactly when the clocks were stolen. And that Thom and I were insistent that he couldn't be responsible."

"So you withdrew the robbery complaint?"

"We tried. Officially, the case was unsolved. Unofficially, the chief wasn't letting it go."

"Why didn't you put a claim in for the clocks?"

"We'd been in the middle of upgrading our policy and decided to take them as a loss rather than put in a claim for them, so they didn't raise our rates. Claiming them was going to cause more problems than it would solve."

"I still can't believe Pat would steal from G.T., or from you."

"Thom couldn't, wouldn't, believe it either."

"What did Pat say?"

"In typical New England fashion, we never talked about it. The chief made it clear what he thought, but we were at an impasse."

"You said there were seven clocks all together in that crate originally?"

"We'd taken one home with us. I'll show it to you. There was another one we'd taken out of the crate, and Thom was working on it. It was a Seth Thomas black Adamantine.

Wood, but painted to look like marble. Gold columns. It should be in the shop."

"I've been taking pictures of everything that's on display with my cell phone as I go. Here, see if you can find it." I fished in my purse without taking my eyes from the road and handed her the phone. I told her the password and waited as she struggled to scroll through the images.

"You took these with your phone?" Caroline asked, squinting at the screen. "They're good."

"They'll do for now. When we want to get these ready for sale, we'll take better photos. I just wanted to get some visuals in the database. I find that easier, since every clock is unique."

"You sound just like your grandfather. No, I don't see it."

"Odd."

"Maybe G.T. brought it home to work on it there?"

"He may have. We'll look in the barn."

"So if we believe Nancy's story, Pat found the clocks at his house last week. I'll bet he went in to tell G.T. right away."

"I'd take that bet."

"That was the night G.T. was killed. So if we tell the chief that part of the story . . ."

"It would point to him as a murder suspect even more."

"Yeesh. I wonder why the chief was looking for Pat today with such urgency? He must have more information. I wonder what it is?"

"He hasn't confided anything in me," Caroline said. "He might answer some questions if I give him a call."

"Since we both know Pat didn't kill G.T."—I looked over

at Caroline, who nodded—"we need to help the chief come up with another idea, another lead to follow. I can't help but think G.T.'s death has something to do with the whole rezoning business."

"I think so too. But I still have trouble imagining which of our neighbors could do such a thing."

"Since I don't know them as well, maybe I could be more objective."

"Well, whatever we do, the clock's ticking. The town meeting is Thursday, and the chief's looking for Pat."

"Did you have any luck trying to get the meeting moved?"

"None. I spoke to Kim Gray herself after our lunch. I meant to tell you. She was very sympathetic, but there were too many wheels in motion to stop now."

"Does she have an alibi?" I asked.

"She was in New York, at a conference."

"You asked her?"

"Not outright, but I got the information. She asked if we'd found the deed yet."

"What did you tell her?"

"I told her you were in town and going through the shop from top to bottom while I looked through the house. If it was going to be found, we'd find it."

"What did she say to that?"

"She said she really hoped we found it soon. Because her lawyer told her that they could make a case for taking the Town Hall over by eminent domain."

"That's pretty drastic," I said.

"This battle has been brewing for over a year. Thom and Grover were determined to stop her. You should have seen her face when Grover took the first step and got the store behind the library declared a historical site. She had planned on flattening it to make a parking lot."

"What store? Not that old shack, the one set back? Isn't that a storage shed?"

"Beneath that awful vinyl siding, it turns out it's the oldest building in Orchard. So they agreed to make it a historical site, and put the parking lot all around it. It's ironic that the ugliest building is the one that was deemed worth saving over all of the others."

"This all sounds like a nightmare," I said.

"Even though the Clagans are one of Orchard's oldest and most respected families, Thom was being portrayed as an obstacle to progress."

"I'm sure that didn't sit well with G.T."

"Of course it didn't. Even our business was being looked at as old-fashioned and out of step with the new Orchard she had in mind. Kim had begun to sway the Clarks to her side by telling them that their store would be featured in the new Orchard plans—it would just need to be relocated into the new mall in Marytown, with a boutique store in Orchard."

"They were buying that?"

"They were listening and they never really respected Thom anyway, what with their family's history. The old store isn't big enough for them to host the sort of lavish wine and cheese tastings they wanted. Plus they were offered a two-year lease, free. And Beckett Green met with her as well. She even gave Ben a few calls.

"Anyway, Grover had started to get the old Town Hall on the register, and Thom continued that fight. Since it was smack in the middle of the block, it was necessary to the overall plan that it be flattened."

"And so the clock tower idea started to take root again."

"Thom had even gotten some drawings done, showing what it could look like with the tower reconstructed. That was getting traction in town—rebuilding the old Orchard instead of building a new one."

"I like that plan better. He did always say 'fix, don't replace.'"

"He is, was, right. I love Orchard just the way it is and would hate to see it change completely. Sure, it's tiny, but it's a great community. It just needs a fresh coat of paint. And we're close enough to other towns to have the benefits of more recent development, and then we can come back here and just be Orchard."

"Was G.T. giving any thought at all to selling the Cog & Sprocket?"

"He was thinking about a lot of things. If Kim Gray's plan had gone through, I think he'd have sold the business. Or moved it out to the house and the barn. But honestly, that didn't seem likely. He sounded more optimistic than he had in months the last few times we'd spoken about it."

chapter 36

We had arrived at the cottage long before our conversation ended, and we both realized at the same moment we were just sitting in the idling car. The light was beginning to dim, but it would be a while before it was dark.

"I should get the mail," Caroline said.

"I'll get it."

I walked down to the end of the driveway and reached into the mailbox, hauling out a large stack of cards and a few bills. I flipped through, checking addresses. Condolence cards.

As I walked back to the cottage, I looked to my left, out at the lake. I walked over to the side yard and stared out. The old dock had been replaced by a wider one, with steps leading down to it from a deck. It wasn't a huge body of water, but it was the site of many happy memories of my childhood. There was enough movement in the water that it wasn't stagnant, and it was perfect for swimming in the summer and skating in the winter. I noted the two Adirondack chairs on the deck, and pictured Caroline and G.T. sitting out there in the evening. That image made me happier than the idea of him sitting alone. Caroline had been good for him.

There was a large grill covered in the corner of the deck. Flower boxes were on each corner, and I noticed the flower beds throughout the yard. The inside of the house may have basically looked the same, but outside Caroline had infused some of her personality into the place with a few changes. Lovely changes. I stood for a minute and took it all in.

When I finally turned back to the house, I saw Caroline's shadow in the kitchen doorway. She held the door open for me as I walked up the side deck and through the doorway.

"The decks are wonderful," I said. "They must be great in the summer."

"My son, Levi, built them," she said. "He made the mistake of saying he was bored one summer day, and so Thom suggested a few projects."

I laughed. "Never admit boredom to G.T. I learned that one the hard way myself. How did he decide to build decks?"

"I'd mentioned that it would be nice to be able to sit outside. So, the first project was this deck, off the kitchen. Levi took it on, poured the foundation footers, and built it. Pat oversaw the work, but Levi did it himself. It was a real turning point for him."

"What do you mean?"

"He'd been lost for so long, but doing a project like this was a tonic for him. It was also good to have two older men mentoring him. He'd missed having a father around, more than I realized. Levi, with Pat's help, came up with the dock and deck project the next summer, and Thom approved it."

"He's good. I never would have thought of the deck by the dock, but it looks like it's been there forever," I said, admiring the solid craftsmanship.

"He is talented." Caroline smiled. "Of course, I'm his mother, so I'm not impartial."

"He lives in Vermont?"

"He's studying to be a landscape architect."

"If this is any indication, he's got a future. I look forward to meeting him. Do you think he can make it down for the memorial service?"

"He won't make it to the one on Saturday. He's been invited to a conference in Oregon this weekend and Thom wouldn't want him to miss the opportunity, especially for his memorial service."

"I can hear G.T. now. He'd definitely want Levi to get back to learning. He made me go back to school right after my grandmother died. He told me the best way to honor her memory was to keep moving forward."

"Once we have plans firmed up, he'll come down. He thought the world of Thom. He was the closest thing to a father Levi ever had. He would have come down with me now, but he's still recovering, and trying to catch up with his schoolwork before he takes some more time off."

"I look forward to meeting him," I said. I handed Caroline the stack of mail. "Did Pat leave any messages on the house phone?"

"No, he didn't," Caroline said. "I'm worried about him,

of course. But I also need my car. I wanted to do some food shopping and pick up a prescription over in Marytown. It can wait until later this week, I suppose."

"Does G.T. still have a bike?"

"In the summer, yes. Getting to town on a bike is actually easier in some ways."

"I remember. I loved biking around Orchard when I was growing up. You could get anywhere. Listen, is the bike in decent shape? How about if I borrow it and ride back to town? You use my car to run your errands. And then once Pat brings back your car, we can switch?"

"I can't ask you to do that," Caroline said.

"I'm offering. You're not asking."

"It would make my life a little easier. I could even go over to Marytown tonight. If you're sure you don't mind?"

"I wouldn't have offered if I didn't mean it," I said.

"Thank you so much. Now, come in and see the clock. I'll find the pictures we took of the Winters' house when all the clocks were in place."

We walked into the living room, then through to the three-season porch. The windows were down, and the sunny day had heated it up nicely. I knew from experience it would cool off quickly in the evening and was useless in the winter months. There was a long window seat under the window, with storage underneath. Caroline walked over, took off one of the cushions, and lifted the seat. She reached in and lifted a bundle gingerly. I still heard a clanking sound. We both winced.

She put it on a side table and unwrapped it carefully. I sucked in my breath when I saw it. A real beauty. Caroline was right—it looked like it was dated from the mid-1800s.

I turned it gently and looked at the back of the clock. The mechanisms were all there, and looked original. I turned it back around and put it on the coffee table. I tried to open the front door. The handle was missing.

"Why is it out here?"

"It's ridiculous, I know. But being here alone, thinking about what happened, just in case it has anything to do with the clocks, I just thought I should hide it when I'm not here." She turned away, embarrassed. "See, I told you it is ridiculous."

"No, it isn't. I'll grab some photos, from all sides, so I can do some research on it. See if we can come up with anything." I took out my phone and snapped a few photographs. "There we go. Why don't you put it back and I'll take a closer look at it tomorrow." I ran my hand along the top of the clock. I looked out at the lake and the setting sun. I ached to take the clock back to the Cog & Sprocket with me, but carrying it on a bicycle wasn't practical. And I'd already offered my car. "Would it be all right if I went out and looked in the barn?"

"Of course. Pat's getting you a set of keys made. Oh my, maybe that's where he is? Never mind that for now. Take mine. The code is 654321."

"Code?"

"Thom had an alarm system put in while I was gone. He was going to have one put in the shop next month. But since Ben was right next door he decided to spend the money here first."

"Then wouldn't it make sense to put the clock out there too?"

"As Jeff Paisley said, the alarm might not stop them from stealing, but it will stop them from stealing as much. I couldn't bear the idea of losing this one."

"I get it. Were all the clocks in this kind of shape?"

"All as stunning."

"Wow. I should be going before it gets too much darker out."

"The bike's in the barn, and there should be a pump nearby. I'll meet you out there. Let me grab the photos of the Winters' house. It's a good thing your purse can go across your body like that. It will be easier to ride with it."

My purse, as she called it, was my usual courier bag that had been made out of oilcloth. At least she didn't call it my hipster Mary Poppins bag. Since riding a bike was my transportation of choice in Boston, the fact that it was bike friendly was not a coincidence.

We always called the workshop out at the cottage the barn, even though the only animal that had ever lived in there was the occasional field mouse, who was usually displaced by a visit from the family cat. But when it was being built, my grandfather got a permit by calling it a barn, a normal home appendage out here in the Berkshires. A place of business wasn't. It was splitting hairs, but since G.T. considered the barn an expansion of the Cog & Sprocket workroom, he was more than willing to split the hair. And Grover Winter, chairman of the board at the time, was willing to let him. The barn was where the woodworking and restoration work was done, and larger pieces were stored. I often dreamed of a space this size to do my own work.

I turned on the lights in the barn. As I looked on the neat and ordered workbench, I wished I'd inherited the organization gene from my grandfather. Horology required order, but my order was often found in chaos. I always knew where everything was, but anyone else would be lost. Not so with

G.T.'s workbench. Visor, lights, tools, parts, all lined up to
be used.

In the middle of the workbench there was a large wooden
box fastened on two sides with brass hooks. I swung them
aside and lifted the lid carefully. The glass dome of the clock
was opaque in the light, so I refocused it to better take a look.
A Harrison sea clock, in skeleton form so the genius of the
design could be fully appreciated. Modern built, but based
on the eighteenth-century clockmaker's original. Gold- and
rhodium-plated parts. Incredibly fine work. Stunning details.
The clock itself almost looked like a little man, feet firmly
planted, accurately telling the time. The glass dome had a
keyhole so it could be wound every week without lifting the
lid, but the fingerprints on the glass indicated a far greater
curiosity of the workings of the clock itself. I put on the visor,
added the extra headlamp to fight the late afternoon gloom,
and looked the clock over.

I looked back at the lid and noticed the note taped inside
at the top. *This is the key to it all. Best, Grover.* I carefully
lifted the note and saw the insignia of a famous English
clockmaker. Well, famous in my circles. I made a mental
note, but didn't have to write the name down. I'd drooled
over their work several times when I was a student in London
and had spent six weeks as an apprentice in their shop. I'd
e-mail them tonight. I'm not sure what I'd ask, but maybe they
had the next clue in whatever scavenger hunt Grover Winter
had put in motion. I put the lid back on the clock, and fastened it. I decided to use the Caroline method of security and
hide it in plain sight. I put it on the shelf underneath the
workbench and covered it with a dusting cloth I found.

I went over to the workbench to put it back in order, and

to turn off the lights. In the corner of the shop, out of the direct light, I saw a building model and walked over to it. I used my cell phone as a flashlight to take a closer look. It was a model of the old Town Hall, with the tower restored. This model was built out of wood, with painted details that made it very identifiable as the current Town Hall, just spruced up a bit. G.T. had gone farther than we had on the paper model, adding the clock in full detail. There were doors and miniatures of figures on the front. I walked over and lifted the roof of the Town Hall. The inner workings were indicated in scale as well. The Clagan clock dream was a 3-D model. I took out my cell phone and snapped several pictures from all different angles and then did a panoramic by walking around it.

I glanced outside. It was getting dark fast and I needed to get back to town. I found the bike right where Caroline said it would be. I checked the tires, which were fine, and rolled it out of the shop. At the last minute I grabbed G.T.'s helmet and put it on. I set the alarm and closed the door, double-checking it was locked behind me. I turned and saw Caroline approaching.

"I was just looking at the model," I said.

"Thom's Folly, that's what your grandfather called it." I smiled, but didn't laugh. One man's folly had become his granddaughter's dream. The Town Hall needed to have its clock tower restored.

"I didn't come across the Seth Thomas black Adamantine that we were talking about earlier, but I couldn't help but take a look at the Harrison sea clock on the bench. I hid it underneath the workbench for now. I'd love to take a closer look at it later."

"You should use it in the shop, Ruth, as a display piece. It's as much fun to watch it work as it is a timepiece."

"Can you imagine how brilliant John Harrison must have been, to be able to invent such an accurate timepiece two hundred and fifty years ago?"

"Of course, it was only when he turned to making watches that the accuracy at sea was truly achieved."

"You know your history," I said, surprised.

Caroline laughed. "No one could help but become fascinated by the history when you spent any time at all with Thom. Anyway, the clock was a posthumous gift to Thom by Grover. I think that Grover bought it specifically for Thom. It didn't really go with any of their other collections. Speaking of which"—Caroline handed me a book—"here are the clock collections from the Winters' house."

"You made them into a book?"

"I took the photos to help us remember the groupings, since they are part of the history of the clocks. I thought the Winter children might enjoy having the book as a remembrance, so I had a couple of books made."

I flipped through the pages. "You take wonderful pictures. These are really great. And you're right, they help me understand some more about the collectors. Very interesting groupings." I noticed one wall of clocks that had little to do with one another at first glance, but the up-close pictures of each clock showed that they all had grapes as part of a painting on the clock face or as a detail on the clock itself.

"Are the grape clocks in the shop?" I asked, showing her the page.

"Yes, they are. They are listed on the inventory sheets as the grape collection."

"Clever naming," I said, teasing.

"It only had to make sense to me at this point. I wanted to try and honor the Winters' collecting habits as much as possible."

"Are the ones that were stolen in here?"

Caroline turned to a page and held it open for me to look at. I recognized the clock in the bench. "These five here—they are the ones that were stolen. The Winters grouped clocks by collections of their own making, as you can tell. There were a couple of groupings like the grape collection. But others were more standard, by manufacturer and type, which made sense. Clocks made by the Seth Thomas factory in Connecticut were particular favorites. The clocks that were stolen were all from the same decade, and they were roughly the same size."

"Interesting." I took my keys out of the front of the bag and took the car key off the ring. I double-checked that the car was locked, and handed the key to Caroline. She smiled at me.

"You sounded like your grandfather again. 'Interesting.' I'd come to understand that *interesting* meant he had an idea, but wasn't ready to share it yet."

I laughed. "Trust me, I have no ideas right now. But I feel like the cogs are moving. I look forward to looking at these pictures. We'll check in tomorrow."

"You're sure you'll be all right riding home?" she asked.

"More than all right, thanks."

"Please call me when you get back to town. Would you do that?"

"Of course," I said. No one had asked me to check in with them for a long time. I didn't mind the feeling.

"Here's a flash drive with my computer records," she said. "And here are some of the clock cards that Thom had brought home. We should make sure everything is in one place, don't you think?"

"It makes sense. We can figure out a way to get all the information in one place and get a work plan set up." I swung my leg over the bike. It was a little tall for me, so I had to bend it to the side a bit. "I'll call you when I get home. But don't worry if it takes a while. I'm going for a ride."

And with that I was ten years old again. I pushed off and rode down the driveway, heading back to the Cog & Sprocket, the wind in my hair.

chapter 37

I rode back to town using back roads and shortcuts I'd internalized from childhood. Most of the roads were the same, with a few more paved roads and a new house here and there.

Though I wanted to avoid Washington Street, I couldn't bring myself to pedal up the back alley to the shop. The alley, as it were, ran parallel to the river and was more of a shared access road for the Sleeping Latte, Ben's Barbershop, and the Cog & Sprocket. There were parking spaces for employees and room enough for delivery trucks to park. There were two ways of accessing the alley: one via Maple Street and the other a little farther up, on Pine Street. Rumor had it that during Prohibition, the river and back entrances of the buildings were also used for rum running, perhaps by G.T.'s own father. I'd tried several times to confirm that

part of the family history, much to my grandmother's cha-
grin. She didn't like discussing family skeletons, and in the
Clagan family, the closets were full of them. Of course, I
loved that.

I came up around to the front of the Cog & Sprocket and
hefted the bike upstairs onto the porch. I opened the door
and wrestled the bike into the shop. It was a tight fit, but I
got it in. I went back outside, calling Caroline on my cell to
let her know that I was back in town.

"I'm going to head over to the Sleeping Latte and see if
Moira's still there," I said. "If not, I'm going to the Corner
Market to get some food." It's not that I wanted food; I
wanted to know if Pat had shown up or if the chief had
tracked him down. I couldn't get the image of how upset
Nancy was out of my mind.

"I'll see you tomorrow," she said, and hung up. I put the
phone back in my bag, first checking the power. I'd missed a
call from Anita at the museum. I thought about calling her
back, but decided she could wait. Besides, the phone was
almost out of juice again. I needed to recharge it soon. I
started to walk to the Sleeping Latte, but heard someone calling out my name in a very loud whisper. I whipped around
and saw Ben gesturing to me from the back of his shop.

"Yeesh," I said, starting a bit. "You scared me."

"Sorry about that. Could you come here for a second?"

"On my way back. I'm heading over to the Sleeping Latte
to beg for food. Unless Moira is still in your shop getting her
hair done? In my search for food I almost forgot about your
offer to do something about this," I said, gesturing to my
windblown curls.

"I had Moira reschedule her appointment. Something

came up. Could we talk? Now, please?" Ben said, but he wasn't really asking. I walked into the shop and saw Pat Reed sitting at one of the washing stations at the back of the shop, looking down at his hands.

"Pat called me and asked me to pick him up from Mary-town this afternoon," Ben explained quickly, his hands on his hips.

"Pat!" I said, rushing toward him. "Nancy's worried sick. You were at the garage all that time? Why didn't you call us back?"

"I wasn't at the garage," Pat said, still refusing to meet my eyes. "I dropped off Caroline's car and then borrowed another one to go and run some errands." He stopped.

"Pat, tell her what you told me. She has a right to know."

"It can't be that bad," I said, taking a step toward the light switch on the wall. "Here, why don't we turn on a light."

"No," they both said in very loud whispers, stopping me in my tracks.

"You're freaking me out. What's going on?"

"A few weeks back, there was a robbery at the shop," Pat said, looking up at me for the first time, a pained expression on his face. "I stole five clocks."

"Nancy told me this earlier. But I didn't believe it. Ryan stole the clocks and you're covering for him. At least that's what I think," I said. "I'm right, aren't I?" I demanded.

Pat nodded and looked back down at his hands.

"Where'd you go today, Pat?" I asked, sighing.

"I went to find Ryan," he said softly. "Last week I found five boxes in our basement. The clocks were in them. I'd sworn to Thom I didn't know where they were, and until that night I didn't."

"But you knew who'd taken them?" I said, looking over to Ben, who was pacing back and forth. "Stop that, Ben, you're making me nervous!"

"I knew the chief was right—it had to be someone who could get in the shop easily and could have an idea of which clocks were good ones to steal."

"How did Ryan know which ones to take?"

"I practically told him myself," he said, shaking his head. "He came by one night to see all of the clocks, and I was showing him around. Showing off what I knew, I guess. The next night, someone broke into the shop. I told Thom the next day that I was afraid it was Ryan."

"Why? Why would you suspect him?"

"Ryan's trying to stay in school. He lost his football scholarship. We were able to pick up the slack on that. But then his grades slipped and he lost his academic scholarship too. Rather than letting his mother and me know about that, he was trying to make ends meet himself. He was coming up short, so I'm afraid he got a little desperate."

"Nancy told me earlier today about when you found the clocks last week," I said.

"I stopped by the shop that night and told Thom that we found them. The plan was to make Ryan bring them back, and to apologize in person. We both thought that would be a good first step. And Thom wanted to talk to Ryan, see about helping him with a loan once we sold a couple of clocks."

"That sounds like Thom," Ben said. "Tell her what happened this morning."

"After Thom died, I wanted to wait to return the clocks to the shop until you and I could talk, and I could explain about Ryan. Ruthie, you have to know, I was going to bring them back to you. I promise. But they couldn't just show up, because then the chief would have to know."

"And that would be a problem because?"

"Because I'm not sure Jeff Paisley would see beyond the robbery. Beyond the letter of the law."

"Okay, I understand that. So then what happened this morning? What changed and made you start switching cars and hiding in the dark?"

"The clocks Ryan stole were gone. I'd moved them up to our attic at the house a few days ago. They were there on Saturday when I checked on them. They were gone, Ruth. And I panicked. I knew this was all about to come crashing down."

"And you think Ryan took them?"

"I don't know who else could have. I haven't seen him for over a week. He's been staying with his girlfriend, Helen."

I mulled all of this information over and didn't like the conclusions I was drawing. I looked Pat in the eye. "Pat, do you think Ryan had something to do with G.T.'s death?" I hadn't seen Ryan for a long time, but I just couldn't believe it. I didn't want to believe it.

Before Pat could answer, someone pounded on the back door of Ben's shop. Ben walked over and opened it. Chief Paisley stood there with his arm raised, about to pound on the door again.

"Clover," he said, walking into the shop. "Ms. Clagan."

"Chief," Ben replied, stepping back and avoiding his gaze.

"Pat, we've been looking all over for you," the chief said.

"I've been here for a while," Pat said, shrinking a bit in his chair.

"I know. It took us a while to pinpoint the GPS on your phone. I've spent the afternoon searching the historic district. Funny, this is the last place I thought I'd find you. Hiding in the shadows of a closed shop with the lights off."

"Catching up with a couple of friends," Ben said not too convincingly.

"Pat, I'd like to ask you some questions, down at the station."

"What kind of questions?" Pat asked, not standing up.

"Questions about five clocks that showed up on eBay this morning. The five clocks that were stolen from Thom Clagan."

I gasped and put my hand over my mouth. eBay? Surely Ryan didn't think the chief wouldn't be able to track these clocks on the Internet?

"Chief, I thought that the complaint was rescinded by G.T.?"

"He did. But when he died, I reopened the investigation. I figured one had something to do with the other, and it seems like I was right. I had several alerts in place in case someone was stupid. The alerts worked. I'm hoping Pat can help me understand how they ended up on eBay."

"I have no idea how they ended up on eBay," Pat said, hanging his head.

"Pat Reed, I'm arresting you on suspicion of five counts of grand larceny, and the murder of Thomas Clagan."

"What are you doing?" I asked, stepping forward. "Arresting Pat Reed for my grandfather's murder? That's just plain crazy."

"Ms. Clagan, I have very little choice in the matter. I believe he's responsible for the theft of the clocks. After you get through the false identities, the online auction lists him as the owner. So we aren't even going to pretend that Pat had nothing to do with the clocks."

"Chief, Pat's like family. Which makes the idea, the very idea, that he killed G.T. preposterous."

I choked out the last part of this speech. I was fluctuating between spitting mad and heartbroken. I knew Pat didn't hurt, wouldn't hurt, G.T. But was a Reed involved? Did the clocks have something to do with G.T.'s murder after all? The thought horrified me.

"I'll go with the chief," Pat said, heaving himself up out of his chair. "Ben, would you call Nancy?"

"Sure," Ben said. "I'll find you a lawyer too. Don't say anything without a lawyer in the room."

Pat held out his hands. "Don't you want to cuff me, Chief?"

"Pat, I don't want to do any of this, but I have to. It's my job." Chief Paisley ignored the outstretched hands and took Pat by the elbow. "I'm going to trust you to walk out to the car with me."

Pat stopped for a moment and looked right at me. "Your grandfather was the best friend I've ever had. I would never hurt him. You know that, don't you?"

"I do," I said as the chief led him out the door. "Hang in there, Pat."

chapter 38

B en and I decided to drive over to the station. I called Moira from the car and let her know what was going on. I put my phone on speaker so Ben could help me break the news. But before I had said much of anything Moira had her own question.

"What has he done?"

"Chief Paisley was doing his job. He's wrong, and we both know that, but . . ."

"Not him. Though I'm going to give him a piece of my mind. Ryan. What has Ryan done?" Moira demanded.

"Why do you think Ryan had anything to do with it?" I asked. We hadn't had a chance to talk about Ryan, and I wanted to hear her thoughts.

"Listen, my parents have had money troubles my whole life, but we get by. Ryan doesn't have the same coping skills.

He asked me for a loan a few weeks ago, but I couldn't help him. I'm barely keeping myself afloat these days. I looked into getting a short-term loan, but when I told Ryan about it, he told me he was all set and I shouldn't worry. So, being an idiot, I didn't. I'm worried now though."

"The chief brought your dad in about the clocks. They've shown up on an auction site, and your father is listed as the person selling them. But he also brought him in on suspicion of murder," I said.

"Of G.T.?" Moira asked. "How could Jeff think that my dad was capable of that?"

"Moira, he's just bringing him in. I know your father's innocent. We all do. But the chief is following the clues he's got to support the story he's decided on. We just need to get him another story that fits better. We need to figure out what really happened."

"How are we going to do that?" Moira asked.

"I'm working on that," I said. I hoped I sounded more confident than I felt.

"Moira, could you call your mother?" Ben asked. "And you're going to need a lawyer. Do you have one?"

"A lawyer? No, we don't. Well, just Kristen Gauger. She helped us with the contracts for the Sleeping Latte. Should I call her?"

"She was G.T.'s lawyer as well," I said. "Call her. If she can't help, she'll know someone who can. And at this point, let's hope she can keep Pat out of jail. Or that she can get bail posted if worse comes to worst."

"Jail? Oh, Dad . . ."

"Moira, I'm so sorry." I hated hearing the tremble in her

voice as she tried to stay strong. This family helped save me when I was a little girl. It was my turn to save them.

We got to the station in good time, but I had one more call to make. Caroline sighed as I told her the story.

"I'm sure Kristen can keep him out of jail. In the meantime, I'll try and raise some cash, just in case."

"Thanks, Caroline," I said. I shut down the call and looked out the window. "Caroline's going to raise bail, just in case. She's a very strong woman."

"You sound surprised."

"She isn't what I expected. She cares about Orchard."

"As much as you do. Yes, she does. And she cared about Thom. She's good people." Ben pulled into the station parking lot. "Moira's not here yet. She's probably calling the lawyer and going to get her mother. I'd imagine they'd want to talk things through a little first."

"Ben, you seem pretty comfortable covering for Pat."

Ben took his phone from me and flipped it over in his hand. "Pat Reed's a good guy. He wouldn't hurt Thom for the world. He'd do anything to protect his family, but I know he didn't do anything wrong. And even if Ryan's gotten off the straight and narrow, I can't see him murdering Thom."

"Maybe it was an accident."

"Ruth, Thom was attacked while he was getting into his car, and hit over the head. I don't know—maybe Ryan is capable of that. But I doubt it."

We got out of the car when Moira and Nancy pulled into the parking lot in Nancy's car. Nancy sped ahead into the station, but Moira hung back. I grabbed her hand and gave it a squeeze. When we walked in, Nancy was yelling at Chief

Paisley. Ben walked over and put his arm around her, lovingly, but firmly, pulling her toward him.

"Nance, the man's just doing his job," he said. "Did you call Kristen?"

"She's on her way," Nancy said, breathing heavily.

"So we wait."

We all sat down. The molded plastic chairs had seen better days. I suspected the orange linoleum was the 1970s original, rather than a retro throwback. I held Moira's hand. And Ben kept his arm around Nancy. She leaned on his chest, and he kept telling her it was going to be fine. When he caught me staring, he gave me a smile, which I returned.

Kristen arrived a short time later. She went back into the station. About twenty minutes later she and Pat walked out to the waiting room. The chief followed them.

"Let's all go home," was all Pat said.

"Dad, what's going on?"

"What's going on is that they don't have enough to arrest your father, so they have to let him go. They could hold him, but we've agreed to come back tomorrow morning to answer any and all questions. We've offered to bring Nancy with us tomorrow. So tonight Pat is going home. He's not to have any contact with his son, nor are the rest of you. If anyone hears from Ryan, we are to report back to Chief Paisley immediately. Is that clear?" Kristen said.

"Why should we turn our back on our son?" Nancy asked, her voice trembling. "I'll never believe that he had anything to do with Thom's death."

"Of course he didn't, Nancy. But this isn't the best place to have this conversation," Pat said, taking Ben's place at his wife's side. "Let's go home. We'll both see you in the morning, Chief. And thank you. We won't let you down."

As we all walked out of the station, Moira suggested we go back to the Sleeping Latte to talk. Pat turned her down.

"No, Moira, I need to go home and get some rest. The chief asked me not to talk to anyone, and I'm not going to. You'll need some help at the shop tomorrow, sweetheart. Your mother's coming with me."

"Patrick Reed, we are not turning on our son."

"Nancy, in the car. Please. We aren't turning on our son. We are going to help him."

The four of us watched as they drove away.

"Moira, why don't I come by the Latte tomorrow and help you open?" Ben said.

"You have your own shop to run," Moira said, her eyes still fixed on the taillights of her mother's car as it vanished into the darkness.

"Aunt Flo just got back in town. I bet if I call her, she'll be thrilled to come in and run the shop for a day or two."

"I can't ask you to do that," Moira said.

"You didn't ask. I offered. See you in the morning?"

"Yes, thanks. I am going to hitch a ride home with Kristen, and talk. Thanks again. Your faith in my father means the world."

Ben and I walked over to his car and climbed in. He started the car and pulled out of the lot. I stared out the window.

"Do you want to tell me what you're thinking?" Ben asked.

"Just thinking that I don't know what to think."

"Ruth, I don't know you that well, but I have complete faith that if anyone is going to figure this all out, it's you."

"That's very nice," I said, taking a deep breath. "And probably wrong."

"I'm never wrong." He smiled as he shifted Betty into drive. "Let me get you home. We have an early day tomorrow."

"We?"

"You don't think I'm slinging hash first thing in the morning by myself, do you? First of all, I'm a lousy cook."

"Hey, I have my own shop to run. Besides, what makes you think I'm a good one?" I couldn't help but laugh.

"We'll get you back to your shop by ten o'clock, I promise. I'm heading home to read a cookbook. I just hope a day of bad food doesn't sink Moira's business."

chapter 39

I'd barely fallen asleep when I felt Bezel standing on my chest and batting my head. Her claws weren't out, but her intent was clear. Wake up, human.

"What?" I opened my eyes and saw her staring at me. Bezel and I had adopted each other, but up until now she was very good about letting me sleep, mostly. I hated to think this was a new phase of our relationship. Because sleep and I were elusive enough friends without my cat scaring it off. My cat.

She batted me again.

"Bezel, I just got to sleep. It's past midnight. I have to wake up early to help Ben at the Sleeping Latte. So stop." I rolled back over, flipping Bezel on her side. She retaliated by jumping back on my side and kneading up and down from my hip to my shoulder like a rotund tightrope walker. It was not a pleasant sensation.

One of the challenges with an open floor plan was there was nowhere to separate me from the cat. When she added a chorus of meows, I finally gave up.

"What is wrong with you, beast? Are you hungry?" I asked. I didn't think that was possible. I'd been a little over-generous with my food portions. I assumed that losing my grandfather had been a trauma for Bezel as well, and just in case she fed her feelings, I wanted her to have that option.

I started to get out of bed, but I heard a noise. I heard boxes being moved, and a crash. I couldn't tell where it was coming from. Maybe the shop? I listened carefully, but didn't hear anything else.

I swallowed hard, trying not to panic. I looked at my nightstand, but my phone wasn't there. I'd forgotten to plug it in. My bag was on the chair next to the bed. I rummaged around the front pocket for my cell phone, and found it. I called 911 and breathlessly whispered my address and that I was fairly sure that someone had broken in downstairs.

"We'll send someone over as soon as possible. It may be twenty minutes or so. Are you safe?" said the formal voice on the other end of the line.

"Twenty minutes? Aren't you at the station?" I whisper-shouted.

"Ma'am. You've reached the barracks in Lee. We field the after-hours calls for Orchard. We'll get someone there as soon as possible. Just lock yourself in and don't confront the intruder. Do you want me to stay on the line?"

"No." I hung up the phone. I heard another muffled noise. This one sounded closer. I called Chief Paisley on his cell.

"Paisley," he said. He sounded really groggy, and I was

oddly thrilled that I woke him up. After the party at the station, he sort of deserved it. Sort of.

"Chief, it's Ruth Clagan. Someone's in the shop. I called the barracks, but wanted to call you too."

"They should have called me right away." He was suddenly very awake. "I'll be there in a few. Make sure the door's locked. And don't go downstairs—do you hear me?"

"I do." And I did. I was no hero. Let the police do their job, at least this part of their job. I got up out of bed, using my cell phone as a flashlight. Bezel meowed at me.

"I'm just going to check on the door to downstairs. I want to make sure I locked it," I whispered to my disgruntled guard cat. And to move the kitchen table in front of it, but Bezel didn't need to know I was such a chicken. I didn't want her to lose respect for me this early in our relationship.

I tiptoed toward the kitchen area, tugging my oversized T-shirt down over my sleeping shorts. Leave it to me to risk confronting a robber without any pants on. The door to the shop was open. Wide open. Hadn't I closed it when I came in last night? Of course I had. I slapped my hand over my mouth to keep in a scream. I'd never go to sleep here without triple-checking the locks on all the doors. So who'd opened the door? What was that over there? I swung the flashlight beam to something beside the door. It was a black sack of some kind. My breath came in short pants. Where was the chief?

I took two steps back, my feet cold on the hard wooden floor. An arm looped around my waist. As I screamed I was flung into the wall of boxes. I lost my footing, and my cell phone, and fell backward. My back smacked the floor and knocked the wind out of me. The intruder, a blurred shadow in dark pants and a hoodie, flew at me. I rolled away, and the shadow stumbled. I gasped in gulps of air. Jumping up, the shadow ran back to the side of the room, grabbing a box. I tried to stand up, and grabbed one of the kitchen chairs to steady myself. When I'd finally pulled myself upright, I couldn't see anyone else.

A siren sounded, coming steadily closer. I looked over toward the door, moving in front of it as best I could without getting directly in the path of the robber. I couldn't just let him, or her, leave. If I could just stall for another minute or two.

I put my hands on a chair back and picked it up. I heard Bezel yowl from my left. I turned to look just as the shadow ran at me with a brass carriage clock raised overhead. I darted to the left, but the shadow kept coming, hurtling toward the door . . . and me. I tossed the chair in its path. The figure stumbled and turned to throw the brass box toward me. I saw the gold blur coming right at me and felt it hit my shoulder as I turned around. I fell again, catching a final glimpse of the shadow hurtling down the stairs as it snatched up the sack by the door, carrying a box under its arm. Then it all went black.

chapter 40

"You really should go to the hospital and get checked out," the EMT said. Again.

I moved around on the kitchen chair they'd deposited me on and tried to move away from her poking and prodding. Yet again, I declined.

"I'm fine," I said.

"You weren't fine when I got here," Chief Paisley said. "You were on the floor, clutching your shoulder." He'd beaten the state police here by a few minutes and had taken control of the crime scene. Otherwise known as my home.

"You try getting clipped by a carriage clock and see how you do. Really, I'm fine. Just bruised. And shaken up. Where's Bezel? Is she okay?"

"She's fine. Hiding out under the bed. I moved her food nearby."

The EMT reached over and tried to poke my shoulder. Again.

"Stop fussing," I said. "I'm not going to go to the hospital. Do you need me to sign something that lets you off the hook if I keel over?"

"She's just doing her job," the chief said. "We're all just doing our job."

"I know. I'm sorry." I looked around the apartment. Piles of boxes had been pushed over. The kitchen chair lay broken by the door to the stairs. "I hate that all of my hard work bringing some order to the chaos of this shop has been undone."

"Downstairs looks a little better," he said. "It's been searched, but you'd barely notice unless you happened to have photos of the space from earlier in the week. Tell me again what happened up here."

"A noise woke me up. Well, actually, Bezel woke me up, but then I heard the noise. I thought it was coming from the shop, but it must have been up here." I shivered. "I called you, went to make sure the door was closed, and then met the shadow. He . . ."

"Are you sure it was a man?" the chief asked.

I thought about it. "No, I'm not sure. But I'll call it 'he' for now. Is that okay?" The chief nodded. "He pushed me into a stack of boxes, but then didn't leave right away. Went back to the side table, over there, and grabbed something. I tried to stop him. I threw a chair, but then he threw a carriage clock at me. He grabbed the sack and left. Poor old clock. Where are the parts?"

"All over the place. Lots of glass. Do you recognize it?"

"Specifically, no. But it was a brass carriage clock. Please don't throw anything away. I might be able to restore it. Or save some of the parts."

The chief shook his head. "Always on duty, aren't you?"

"Look who's talking. Do you sleep in your uniform?" I asked. He looked less crisp, but fully dressed.

"I fell asleep reading. And at the moment, you are in no position to critique anyone's clothing." The chief ran his hand over the stubble on his chin and I thought I almost saw him smile. "Did you get a good look at the robber?"

I swallowed my instinct to make a smart comeback and said, "I didn't. He, or she, had a hood pulled up over his or her face. And just a black, or maybe dark blue, sweatshirt, no logos. Dark pants. Black boots. Not very tall, but it's hard to tell, since I was on the floor looking up most of the time. Strong. He threw me to the side like I was a sack of potatoes. I think he wore gloves, since I don't remember seeing a hand. Beyond that, I've got nothing. Sorry about that."

"You did fine. Do you think you feel up to looking around and seeing what he might have taken?"

"Um, sure." Someone had wrapped the quilt from the end of my bed around my shoulders, and I pulled it tighter. Somehow I didn't think that my oversized T-shirt featuring cats drinking tea and white sleeping shorts were the normal crime scene uniform. I reached for the yoga pants I'd tossed on the footboard, and the chief had the good manners to look away while I pulled them up, trying not to flash anyone. The chief handed me my flats and I put them on. I wobbled a bit when I stood up, and the chief put his hand under my elbow. I let him keep it there. We walked around to the card tables. There were piles of clocks, parts, and books all intertwined together. Four empty boxes were cast aside. I shook my head.

"I really hadn't gotten to this area," I said. "So I don't have a sense of what exactly is missing. I can tell you that there were three—no, four—mantel clocks over there. I don't see them."

"Mantel clocks? Like the ones that were stolen last month?"

"Those were valuable antiques. The ones up here were modern replicas, or so I thought. Not without value, mind you, but not nearly as valuable as some of the other clocks."

"Would I be able to tell the difference?"

"Probably, after I gave you a lesson." I looked around the room.

"What's that?" I asked, bending over the smashed remains of the carriage clock. "See that? There?"

The chief grabbed his flashlight and shined it where I pointed. The beveled glass glistened in the light. Brass clock parts were mixed in, surrounded by the battered body of the clock itself. But sitting amongst the ruins was a small gold pin.

"Did you grab photos of this area already?" Chief Paisley asked Officer Troisi.

"Yes, Chief," she replied.

He reached down with his gloved hand and pulled a piece of metal from the wreckage of the old clock. At first it looked like a piece of the clock itself, but the shape gave it away. He held up the white gold wreath pin.

"Does one of these come with every clock?"

"It doesn't."

"Not yours?"

"No. I have no idea where it came from. It looks familiar, but that's a pretty common style of pin. I think my grand-mother had one."

Chief Paisley put it in a plastic evidence bag and handed it to the officer.

"Should we take a look downstairs?" I asked.

"Sure, why don't we do that. But before that, why don't you pack a few things. I'm going to drive you over to Caroline's."

"Caroline's? I don't want to wake her up in the middle of the night."

"I already did. She's expecting you. You can't stay here. The back door is wide open and this place is a crime scene. Ben came by to see what happened. Apparently Blue was barking and howling to wake the dead. According to Officer Troisi, he has offered to take care of Bezel and to let the locksmith in tomorrow. I assume you trust him?"

"I do. Do you?"

Chief Paisley looked surprised by my question, but recovered quickly.

"I do. So pack your toothbrush and some clothes. We need to get you over to Caroline's. I'll call and let her know we're on our way." He took a few steps toward the front kitchen to give me at least the illusion of privacy.

I sighed. I fished out another pair of leggings and a plaid shirt dress, rolled them up, and shoved them into my bag. I laid the quilt back on the bed and pulled a sweatshirt over my head. I exchanged my flats for my boots to complete the ensemble, and was ready to go.

The chief took a look at me and his lips twitched.

"What? This isn't high fashion enough for you?" I said, looking down at my outfit.

"It's a look. Is this all you need?"

"Yes, everything else is in my bag. Oh, can you throw

the charger in? I want to charge my phone. Where's my phone?"

"We found it over by the pile of boxes. You might as well take it."

"Thanks." I pointed to the table.

The chief picked up my bag and made an exaggerated show of almost falling over. I appreciated the effort to make me smile. It worked, and helped get my mind off the robbery and being attacked in my own apartment in the middle of the night.

"Watch out, it's a little heavy," I said, smiling and wincing at the same time. "Are you sure that Bezel will be all right?"

"She'll be fine. Now let's go downstairs. I have more bad news for you. Your car isn't parked out back, or out front."

"It's at the cottage. Caroline's car is in the shop—Pat drove it over to Marytown today. What time is it? Yesterday. He must have told you that."

"So it looked like you weren't home tonight. Interesting. Do you know what time he drove it over?"

"Late morning? Not sure. Why? Is that important?"

"It may be. We're piecing the day together. There are a lot of holes in Pat's timeline, which aren't helping anyone. You wouldn't know more about that, would you?"

"Chief, I may have a concussion after all, so anything I say is suspect. When I know something, you'll know something."

"I'm counting on that. Sure you have everything?"

"Oh, wait. One more thing. I want to bring the clock tower notebook over with me. G.T. had built a model, and I'd love to compare it with his notes."

"I'll get it for you. Where is it?"

"Maybe it's still locked up in the wardrobe? Oh, wait, no. It's right there. On the floor, next to the chair. I don't think I left it on the floor though."

"Maybe the robber moved it? Looking for something?"

"You would have thought I would have woken up. Yeesh."

"Or maybe Bezel knocked it over." The chief didn't sound convinced, but we both let it go. "Have you had any luck finding his current notebook?"

"None. And no luck finding the elusive deed. Though I did find the clue Grover Winter left for my grandfather. A lovely old Harrison. Whoa."

"Whoa? What are you doing, Ruth? Be careful."

I'd rushed back to the wardrobe and found the key on the back, just where I'd left it. I unlocked the door and searched through the top box of notebooks.

"Grover Winter left my grandfather a clock, a Harrison sea clock. There was a note inside, telling him that the clock would lead him to what he needed, or something like that."

"I know all about it. Thom told me."

"The other day, I found an envelope addressed to G.T. Here it is. The return address was John Harrison. I looked in it, but all I saw were old files. But maybe, just maybe."

The chief had put on some gloves and gently took the envelope from me. He pulled out the contents and laid them out on the bed. I leaned over and put my hand on his shoulder to see better. And to stop me from toppling over.

There were articles and pictures and a treasure trove of information about the old Town Hall. There was also a commemorative booklet that had been published on its centennial in 1965. The chief picked it up and gently fanned the pages. Something was stuck in the middle. With far more patience than I felt, he opened the book to the page and pulled out an oversized envelope. It looked fairly new, and was addressed to Thomas Clagan. The chief looked inside and pulled out another envelope. He looked inside that one and made a slow whistling sound.

"Is that?"

"The deed to the old Town Hall. Signed over to your grandfather. You found it, Ms. Clagan."

"More importantly, the robber didn't," I said.

chapter 41

I woke up in my old room at the cottage. It was a little different now, since it was the guest room, but the bed was the same, the quilt was the one my grandmother made me when I was ten, and the rocking chair was in the exact same place. I thought for a minute that I was refreshed, but then I tried moving and my back ached. Every shift hurt, but I tried to stretch, hoping to work out some of the kinks.

I remembered last night. Caroline hadn't fussed over me when I arrived, but I could tell she was concerned. The chief stayed and had a cup of tea with us, and we told her about finding the deed.

"That's wonderful news. It's wonderful news, isn't it, Jeff?" she asked.

"I'd think so."

"He's going to bring it by Kristen's in the morning," I said.

"Unless you'd like to take custody of it?" the chief asked.

"Since it was in the shop, I think it technically belongs to Ruth. It's probably safer with you for now," Caroline said as she put down her teacup. "This piece of paper has caused enough grief already. First Thom, then Ruth."

"So you think that both incidents had something to do with the deed?" the chief asked.

"Of course I do, Jeff. This piece of paper could cost folks thousands of dollars. Look for the person who attacked Ruth tonight. That's who you are looking for," Caroline said.

"You may be right, Caroline. But there are still the five stolen clocks."

"A gift to the Reed family, from Thom and me. No stolen clocks, aside from the ones that were taken tonight. Tell me, Ruth, was it Pat Reed who attacked you?" Caroline asked.

"No, of course not. This person was not big enough to be Pat, anyway."

"How about Ryan Reed?" the chief asked, staring right at me.

I couldn't help but look away. "I don't know."

"All right, that's enough. Ruth needs some rest. You can talk to her again in the morning." With that, Caroline shooed Chief Paisley out of the room. We followed him out and she locked the door behind him.

"Thank you, Caroline. I'm so sorry to impose like this," I said, shifting gingerly in my chair.

"Please, it isn't an imposition. How are you feeling?"

"I feel like a truck ran over me and then backed up and parked."

"The adrenaline is wearing off. Go ahead upstairs. I'll bring you up some water and ibuprofen. Maybe we can get ahead of some of those aches and pains. A hot bath would also be good."

"I don't have it in me to take a bath. I think I just want to go to sleep."

"I'll be right up."

The second my head hit the pillow, I had fallen into a deep, deep sleep.

Now I looked at the bedside table and saw the three tablets laid out beside a glass of water. I could either lie in bed and wait for the pills to kick in or I could get moving and try to go to the Sleeping Latte to help Moira and Ben. I sat up gingerly, regretting throwing off the warm covers almost immediately.

My bag rested on the rocking chair, and I reached in for my cell phone to check the time. Dead battery. I found the charger and plugged it in. It was so dead that it wasn't coming right back to life, so I shuffled down the hall toward the bathroom to get ready for the day. Caroline was just coming out of her room, dressed in running tights and a fleece.

"You're up," she said. "I was going out for a quick run, but let me make some coffee."

"You run?" I asked.

Caroline laughed. "I do. I used to race, but my knees won't tolerate that anymore."

"Did you get G.T. to run with you?" I asked, enjoying the mental image.

"Heavens no. I barely got him to take walks with me. But I find that when life gets a little overwhelming, a run helps clear my mind."

"Maybe I should try that," I said. "But not today. Do you mind if I take a shower?"

"Of course not. I left a towel for you and there's shampoo in the shower. Take all the time you need. I'll be back shortly."

I expected another trip down memory lane when I stepped in the bathroom, but I was happily surprised to see the update. The old vanity was gone and replaced by an off-white solid-surface sink and countertop on top of a cherry cabinet. The old, metal medicine cabinet had been replaced by a larger cabinet and the tiles were all in shades of white and beige, simple but elegant. I wondered what, if any, other modifications Caroline had planned for the rest of the house.

The hot water streamed down on me from the tall, rain showerhead, pounding on my aching body, and I offered up a silent prayer of thanks that I was not crouched in the torture device that passed for a shower back at the apartment. I could have stayed there all day, but after a few minutes of steaming, I climbed out. I toweled myself off and borrowed some of the lotion on the edge of the tub, slathering my body and pulling some of it through my hair. I didn't have any hair product with me, and knew that I would have a frizz attack very shortly. I wove my hair into a quick braid and finished getting dressed.

I was hobbling like an old woman, but that couldn't be helped. The few bruises I could see in the mirror were impressive. I forced myself to think back to what had happened last night. There was something that seemed familiar about the shadow, but I couldn't put my finger on it. The whole thing felt like a nightmare, but each time I moved or breathed too heavily it became all too real again.

I went back to the bedroom and made the bed. The phone

responded when I turned it on, and I was surprised that I had four messages waiting for me. The first and third were both from Jonah, asking me to bring the files and box over to the house. Shoot. In all the hustle and bustle yesterday I'd forgotten to drop off the boxes, but they were still in the back of the car.

The middle message was from Ben Clover.

"Ruth, just checking in with you. Don't even think of coming in to the diner this morning. Aunt Flo is going to keep her eye out for the locksmith. I went by this morning and did what I could to fix the door, but I think you'll need a new one sooner rather than later. We can talk about that this afternoon."

The last message was from Chief Paisley.

"This is Jeff Paisley. I hope you've recovered a bit from last night. I want to make sure we've crossed all the t's and dotted all the i's regarding the deed. I'd like you to come by the station so I can take an official statement. Could you do that this morning so we can get the paperwork filed today? I'll see you by ten o'clock, all right?"

I checked the time on my cell phone. The chief wanted to see me in an hour. I suspected dealing with the deed would take the better part of the day, so I needed to make two quick stops first. A stop by Jonah Winter's house, and then the Sleeping Latte for breakfast. Maybe I'd bring the chief a breakfast sandwich, if Ben had figured out how to make them.

I went down to the kitchen and grabbed a cup of the coffee Caroline had made before she set out for her run. I didn't properly enjoy it, but it was useful in both warming and waking me. I wrote her a short note, explaining that I was heading into town per the request of Chief Paisley. I'd get the car back out to her as soon as I could. I rinsed my mug and left it on the draining board as I headed back toward town.

chapter 42

On my way to Jonah's, I called Ben. I didn't reach him so I left a message.

"Hi, Ben. Thanks for the call. I'm feeling okay. I need to drop something off at the Winters' house that I just keep forgetting about, but I'm hoping I'll be able to grab a quick bite at the Latte. I'm meeting with Chief Paisley at ten o'clock, so I won't be able to help out this morning. Sorry about that, but I have some good news to share so I'll be by later. And I know seeing you sweating behind that counter in a hairnet will make me feel better. See you soon."

I plugged my phone back in my lighter and stored it on the dash. I liked the voice of the woman who left that message. She was bright and cheerful, despite having been beaten up a few hours prior and being in the middle of a challenging, to put it mildly, week. Dare I say it, I might have even been flirting with Ben. Just a little bit. The air of Orchard was changing me.

I hadn't been to the Winters' house for years, and even then, only a couple of times as a visitor when G.T. took me along while he talked to Grover. But as a citizen of Orchard, I'd been there three times a year, every year, once I moved to Orchard full-time. Besides the Fourth of July picnic, there was the Halloween Haunted House, held the Saturday before Halloween for all the kids in town, and the Holiday Open House, held the weekend between Christmas and New Year's. The picnic and Halloween parties were open to the entire town, but the Holiday Open House was invite only, and my grandparents were always on the list.

I loved all these events, but especially the Holiday Open House. The entire first floor was open, decorated from floor to ceiling with garlands, twinkle lights, and at least one tree per room. The food was plentiful and there were games, music, and even folk dancing to keep everyone laughing late into the night. But I, of course, always took a tour of the clocks. Perhaps it was because of the size of the house, but there didn't seem to be too many clocks, just enough. I'd looked through Caroline's book that was a clock tour of the Winters' house last night, and I recalled a lot of them. I remember trying to be in a different room each quarter hour to hear the chimes and to see if I could identify the clocks. My grandmother was oblivious to the effort, but my grandfather had caught on and joined me a few times. On the way back home, we'd talk about the collections, my grandfather quizzing me on the characteristics of the longcase in the parlor or the shelf clock in the music room. My visits to the Winters' home had been an important part of my clock-appreciation development.

I came around a corner and there sat the Winters' house
on top of a hill. As I approached the house I realized the
current Winter estate paled in comparison to my nostalgia-
tinted memories, but I suppose that was to be expected. Sure,
the lawns weren't as manicured as they always had been and
the gardens were in need of tending. It was a lot of house
for one family to keep up with, and I suspected that it would
return to its former glory under the care of Harris University.
The empty flower urns on the front stoop just looked sad.

I pulled around the horseshoe-shaped driveway to the
front of the house and parked. I was tempted to tap on the
horn, but I didn't think it was appropriate. Instead I climbed
up the front steps, gritting my teeth as my muscles ached,
and rang the bell. It made a satisfying chiming sound that
bounced around the front hall. I looked down at the battered
garden and noticed several concrete animals lined up. Each
one was missing a limb or an ear. The carnage looked inten-
tional, and I shuddered a bit at the sight.

No one came to the door, so I went back to the car and
opened the back hatch. I put the keys in the front pocket of
my dress. I loved pockets and was so relieved when I found
clothes with them. I felt something small and sharp in there
with the keys and pulled it out. The earring I'd found that
first day in the shop. I needed to remember to ask Caroline
about it. And I probably should ask her if I could do a load
of laundry at her house.

I dragged one of the boxes out of the trunk. Fortunately,
it was more cumbersome than heavy, but still, my battered
body felt the half-dozen steps to the front porch. I went back
and took out the second box, and was almost to the first step
when the front door opened.

Jonah Winter stood with the door half opened, making no move toward helping me with the box.

"Jonah, I could use some help with these."

"Just leave the boxes there. I'll get them. Very kind of you to bring them. Thanks so much. Family history, missing bits and pieces. Sorry I can't invite you in, but I'm in the middle of something."

"Are you all right?" I asked. Not only was he acting odd, but I could swear he was wearing the same clothes he wore when we first met. He hadn't shaved since, and his eyes were rimmed with red, with dark circles underneath.

"I'm fine, really. Thanks again. I'll be seeing you." Jonah went to close the door, but it suddenly swung open. Aggie Kurt, wearing black jeans and the top of her delivery uniform, stepped out from behind her brother. She held a gun in her hand and moved it toward me.

"Jonah, what would Dad say about your hospitality? Invite her in." She pushed him forward a bit. "Let's make sure she really brought us our clocks, shall we? You, bring that box in here. Jonah, grab the other one. And neither of you try anything. I've got plenty of bullets."

I could have dropped the box and run, but I had no doubt that Aggie would shoot. And even if she missed, she'd probably catch me. If the angels were on my side, maybe I could get the car started and leave, but it was a big maybe.

And then there was Jonah. He looked terrible, and from the way Aggie was grabbing his shirt and moving him around like a tall puppet, I didn't think he'd survive if I ran. Not that I knew Jonah very well, but still. I couldn't leave him to fend for himself.

I followed Aggie's directions and brought the box into

the front hallway. I was shocked by the change in the house. The old-money elegance had been completely replaced by a postapocalyptic nightmare. Frequently a house lost its personality when it was emptied out, but this time the markings weren't just normal wear and tear; they were vandalism. The corners of wallpaper were torn and the bare walls adorned with hooks and bright boxes the only indication of where the magnificent artwork had hung. The floors were naked, with long drag marks marring the parquet.

"Go get the other box," Aggie said bitterly. "Baby brother isn't up to it after all."

I almost refused, claiming a bad back, but I didn't want to let Aggie know I was hurt. I suspected that if she decided I wasn't of use, I'd be deemed expendable. I had to step down to ground level to pull the box toward me, rather than bend over and pick it up. But I did it, trying to ignore the twinge I felt in my lower back. I breathed through it and held my stomach muscles as tightly as I could.

I walked back up the stairs and into the foyer. Aggie slammed the door shut behind me, throwing the locks, including the huge bolt at the bottom of the door.

"Make yourself useful, little brother, and grab that other box. Bring it in here." She pointed to the room to the right of the foyer. A front parlor, if my memory served. I focused on my breath and tried to remember what I'd learned at the yoga retreat last week. Was that only last week? I shook my head and focused on what was happening right now, trying to keep the fear that kept rising in my throat at bay.

Jonah struggled with the box, but finally got it up. He barely made it through the doorway before he dropped the box on the floor and then crawled to the sofa, where he lay down. Sweat soaked the back of his shirt, and I noticed he was shaking.

"Your sports drink is right there, Jonah. The red one, the one you like so much. Drink up, little brother."

I put my box down on the seat of a wing-back chair and stood up carefully. If there were signs of damage in the hallway, this room had become the symbol of a new reality for the Winter family. The couch that Jonah was lying on was ripped open, with horsehair and springs forcing their way out. The fireplace to my left was full of books and mangled picture frames. Singe marks indicated that some-one had tried to start a fire. The leather club chairs were both gashed open, and the stuffing had been pulled out. I recalled this room from the open houses of years past. I remembered the wonderful cacophony of chimes on the hour, and I was immediately grateful that the clocks were all safe, back at our shop.

"Open the box and take out the clocks. All of them," Aggie said, turning the gun on me.

I did as she asked, laying them all out on top of the otto-man carefully. She picked up the first one, the lovely Seth Thomas miniature I'd looked at the other day. She dropped it in front of her and stomped on it. I couldn't help it—I cried out. Still keeping the gun trained on me, she bent over and rifled through the debris left over.

"Gotcha!" she said, holding up what looked like a ring. "I told you, Jonah. These old clocks are worth more than you thought."

She picked up another clock, a porcelain carriage clock. I suspected it might be a replica, but I couldn't tell from here.

"Stop, please!" I said. "What are you doing? That clock you just killed—it was worth at least five hundred dollars, probably much more!"

"And this ring is worth ten times that, and a lot easier to hock."

She hurled the clock against the fireplace. This one, made of porcelain, shattered into dozens of pieces. That didn't stop Aggie from rifling through them. Cutting her finger on a shard didn't seem to bother her at all, especially after she found another treasure, this time an earring.

"Where's the other one. Do you see it?" she asked me. "You, find the other earring. Now."

She stood up and grabbed a sweatshirt from the side table, wiping the blood on the dark fabric. The black hoodie looked awfully familiar, as did her heavy boots.

"What does it look like?" I asked. She held up a pearl and diamond earring, but didn't hand it to me. It matched the earring in my pocket. I swallowed hard, hoping to contain the panic that was rising in my chest.

"Aggie, was it you in the shop last night?" I asked, fighting to keep my voice calm. The rest of me was terrified. I crouched down, trying to avoid cutting my shaking hands on the shards. I started to pile the pieces of the clock up. I cleared a space and knelt down gingerly.

"You're a real pain, you know that?" Aggie said. "Your car wasn't there. You were supposed to be gone by now, back to Boston, away from here. Why do you all make me hurt you? Why don't you just do what you are supposed to?"

I sat back on my heels and looked up at the barrel of the gun. I wished I knew more about guns. I had no idea if it had a safety, if the safety was on or off, or even how to tell if it was loaded.

I turned and pretended to search while I reached into my pocket and pulled out the matching earring.

"Is this what you are looking for?" I said, holding it up.

"Yes, that's it." She snatched the earring and reached for another clock, but I put my hands out.

"Stop. Please, don't destroy another clock. Let me take it apart."

She looked at me for a few seconds, then let go. "Have at it," she said. "Might as well make your last few minutes happy ones. Don't ever let it be said that Agatha Winter-Kurt didn't have a heart."

"Yeah, Aggie, that's you. All heart." Jonah half laughed, half coughed. He'd rolled himself up to a sitting position. "All heart. Let's just ask Dad about that, shall we? Oh, wait, we can't. Because you killed him. Just like you're killing me."

"Shut. Up. Jonah."

"But Ruth probably knows that already, don't you Ruth? She figured it out, just like Thom figured it out," Jonah said, looking at me desperately.

Aggie let out a howl and threw one of the clocks at Jonah. He couldn't even try to duck it, but happily for him her aim was wide. The clock crashed against the wall and pieces flew across the floor.

"Go get it," she hissed at me. "Crawl over and get it."

I did as I was told, maneuvering my way over to the side of the room. I tried to catch Jonah's eye, but he was too dazed. Had Grover been murdered? By his daughter? How had my grandfather known?

I remembered the training I got as a housemaster at school on ways to deal with out-of-control students and threatening situations. Keep your tone light, don't accuse, make them think you are on their side. Don't show fear. It had all seemed so simple in a dining hall, practicing with the history tutor. Not so easy today.

"So, Aggie, there's a lot going on here," I said, carefully collecting the broken glass and putting it in the front pocket of my dress along with the porcelain shards. A glint of light caught my eye, and I crawled over and picked it up.

"Is this what you're looking for?" I got up on my knees, but didn't stand up.

"What is it?"

"A pin, silver, with diamonds that look like dew. It's lovely. I'll bet your mother looked beautiful wearing it. Am I right?"

"Give it to me!"

"So what did you do, Aggie? Hide bits and pieces of jewelry in the clocks? Didn't your father notice that they were missing?" I reassembled the pieces of this story like the machinery of a broken clock, one at a time. I was waiting for the final cog that would help it all make sense.

"He did, but I just blamed Delia. The black sheep sister. Dad never suspected me, poor miserable Aggie. The quiet daughter. No one ever suspects the quiet daughter. You know what my father used to call me? Mouse." The lack of warmth in Aggie's smile was more than chilling. I understood now that Aggie had moved into another reality. I needed to meet her there if I was going to get out of this.

"Your father was probably going to give you the jewelry

someday. Why did you hide it?" I tried to keep my voice even and gentle. Maybe if I kept her talking . . .

"He wasn't going to give it to me. He was going to put it in a trust for Jonah's future wife and children. In a trust. Dad loved his trusts. He was all about making us wait for what was rightfully ours."

"You didn't wait," Jonah said, his breathing ragged. "You borrowed thousands and thousands of dollars from Mother and Dad over the years, with no intention of paying them back. Ever. You spent your inheritance ten times over. Don't you understand that? It was all Dad could do to hold on to this house at the end."

"And whose fault was that? All he had to do was to roll over and talk everyone into the rezoning downtown. He could have made a fortune. But no, the integrity of Orchard was more important. Blah, blah, blah. I'm so sick of his games. All Dad had to do was stop with the games. That's all," Aggie said.

"And when he didn't?" I said.

"She didn't give him a chance. She poisoned him. Just like she's been poisoning me. I thought it was the flu, but yesterday I made a doctor's appointment, and she flipped. She's been poisoning my sports drink for weeks. And I never knew." Jonah threw the sports drink bottle at her, spreading the red drink all over the room. She didn't even flinch. She just smiled.

"You know what? Thom was going to see if he could get Dad's body exhumed, so they could run some tests. But do you want to hear the funny part, brother dear? He thought it was you, or maybe Delia. It took some doing, but I finally got him to believe my story. He never even suspected it was me. Of course, I had to be sure. That's why I went back to get the notebook that night."

"That night? Aggie, did you kill my grandfather?"

"I didn't mean to, I really didn't." Aggie turned to me. I heard her words, but saw little remorse on her face. "You believe me, don't you? It's just that he wouldn't listen. I had to make him listen. You see that, don't you? He found a couple of pieces of jewelry and gave them to me. But he told me he'd have to tell Delia and Jonah, just to be fair. To be fair. Even though I'd convinced him they'd killed Dad? When I asked him if he really had to, he started to act a little odd, so I was worried that he'd guessed. I always saw him writing stuff down. All of a sudden I wondered, what was he writing? I had to find out. I tried to pretend I was a robber, and waited for him outside the shop. But he knew it was me. I guess the pendulum I'd swiped when I left the shop earlier was a bad idea. Anyway, when I started toward him, he told me to stop. Why do people always think they can boss me around? Did he really think the car alarm would help him? I gave him a chance to give it all to me. It was his own fault, really it was. He should have just given me the jewelry and left well enough alone."

"Now give me that pin," she said.

Aggie aimed her gun at me and shot it. I jumped up and cried out. The shot was louder than I expected. I heard a pane of glass shatter behind me, and turned to look. It was a few inches over my head. I couldn't tell if she was a bad shot, or just trying to warn me.

"I'm going to bring it to you, and then we're going to find the rest of the jewelry in the rest of the clocks. How many are there all together? Do you know?" I stood up as best I could and walked slowly toward her. My back seized a bit with every step, but I pushed forward.

I handed her the pin, making sure to catch it in the light so it sparkled. As she looked down, I hit the button to my car's key fob. The alarm screeched, and Aggie turned toward the sound. I reached in my pocket, grasped the broken bits of glass and porcelain. Aggie turned back toward me and I threw the glass at her face, aiming for her eyes.

I grabbed her arm with the gun, pushing her backward toward the fireplace. She screamed with frustration as she tripped on the side table and her back hit the brick, hard. But she didn't let go of the gun. She pushed her weight forward and we both fell over, with her landing on top of me. I tried to catch my breath, but she was heavy. She tried to turn the gun toward me, but I pushed back with everything I had left. Another shot rang out, and I heard a moan from Jonah. Aggie's weight crushed my chest; my breath came in shorter and shorter pants. I felt my grip loosening on the gun. I was losing this battle.

My vision was a swirling purple haze with sparkles. I saw Jonah out of the corner of my eye, holding a clock over his head. Aggie cried out as the clock crashed into her forearm and the gun dropped from her grip. She launched herself toward Jonah in a rage, but I grabbed the back of her hair.

"Hold her down," I said.

"How?" Jonah asked. He had a point—she was flailing around. I held on to her hair with both hands.

"Sit on her," I said.

He leaned down and grabbed both of her wrists, holding

them down against the floor. I pulled myself up and sat on her legs. Aggie kept screaming, but she'd stopped moving.

"We need to call the police," I said. "Can you hold her down, Jonah? Jonah?" All of a sudden Aggie's hands got free and she clawed at me. Jonah's limp body was stopping her from sitting up, but not for long.

I heard a huge crash and saw an object fly through the front window. One of the concrete turtles skidded across the room. Another crash and another piece of concrete flew in. The bunny landed nearby. Aggie stopped moving, and finally stopped screaming.

I looked over and saw Chief Paisley's face appear through the window.

"Don't make me shoot! Because you know I will, Aggie," he shouted.

chapter 43

It was a beautiful memorial service. G.T. would have approved. We had it on Saturday, concurrently with the service the National Horological Society was holding. Caroline and I'd decided to go ahead with it, even though it was very short notice and I was still in pretty tough shape. People wanted to pay their respects, and Orchard needed to turn the page and move on.

The Town Hall was full. Some press had tried to come in after catching wind of Aggie's crimes, but the good people of Orchard made sure they weren't welcome. Caroline's son, Levi, wanted to be there, but she'd finally been able to talk him into staying at his conference. There'd be plenty of chances to celebrate Thom Clagan. Caroline made Levi promise to come up with a wonderful memorial garden as a start.

My friends Steve and Rick came out from Boston and sat with me, each holding a hand and helping me navigate stairs, chairs, and people. Ben sat with Caroline and performed the same function for her.

I slowly made my way to the front of the Town Hall and took in the sight of the townspeople who'd shown up. My voice shook as I started to read.

A Reminiscence
by Anne Brontë

YES, thou art gone! and never more
Thy sunny smile shall gladden me;
But I may pass the old church door,
And pace the floor that covers thee.

May stand upon the cold, damp stone,
And think that, frozen, lies below
The lightest heart that I have known,
The kindest I shall ever know.

Yet, though I cannot see thee more,
'Tis still a comfort to have seen;
And though thy transient life is o'er,
'Tis sweet to think that thou hast been;

To think a soul so near divine,
Within a form so angel fair,
United to a heart like thine,
Has gladdened once our humble sphere.

"As some of you know, that last stanza is etched on my grandmother's tombstone. She always loved the Brontë sisters. The quote is perfect for them both. How lucky was I that they had gladdened my own humble sphere? Immeasurably. Thank you, G.T. I love you." I looked around and smiled. I took my seat.

Pat Reed got up and gave his eulogy. A great testament to his friend; he didn't leave a dry eye in the house. And he made it clear that saving this Town Hall was Thom Clagan's final wish, and it was going to happen. There was a huge round of applause for that. I turned and looked at everyone in the hall. I noted that some of the members of the Board of Selectmen were slow to join in, but by the end the only person not clapping was Kim Gray. I smiled sweetly at her and clapped even louder.

There was a reception downstairs in the community room afterward, and I shook every hand that was offered. To say that I was exhausted by the end was an understatement, but the entire day helped me make up my mind.

I brought my Boston friends over to the Cog & Sprocket and showed them around. Ben and Moira came with us and offered their opinions on what could be done to make the upstairs apartment a workable space.

"What a great space. A little cramped, but you will be selling most of these clocks, won't you?" Steve said.

"That's the idea," I said. I knew he'd love the shop. What wasn't there to love?

"Well, that will help with the flow of the space. What about this wall that splits the front of the shop?" he asked.

"Caroline and I talked about it. G.T. was always adamant about keeping it, so maybe it's structural?"

Steve looked around. "No, I don't think so. It does have outlets on it, but they can be moved."

"Then I think we should get rid of it."

Steve grabbed a hammer from the workshop and to my surprise, knocked right through the wallboard. "Excellent choice," he said, grinning. "Now, what we do upstairs depends on what you want it to be. An apartment or a showroom?"

chapter 44

Caroline invited a few people over to her house Sunday afternoon. We decided to use the barn for the party. I'd come to think of the space as a satellite of the Cog & Sprocket. Fortunately Caroline agreed. Nancy and Moira came over early to set up the food, which they'd provided.

"Pat tells me your friends are at the shop, tearing out a wall. Does this mean what I hope it means?" Nancy asked, rubbing her hands together.

"You'll have to wait to hear what it means until everyone else gets here," I said with a wink. "Thank you both for bringing the food."

"Thank us? Thank us? If it weren't for you, Ryan would be rotting in jail right now. As it is, he is free from any legal trouble. Again, thanks to you," Nancy said.

"And thanks to Chief Paisley, who was willing to bend

the rules a bit," I said. "And Caroline, who convinced him that G.T. had given Ryan the clocks as a gift."

"Jeff drove a hard bargain," Nancy said.

"How? By making Ryan do some community service, off the books? Honestly, Mum, he did us a favor. Ryan needed to learn a lesson, but not let it ruin his life," Moira said, raising her eyebrows.

"Well, I'll let you settle that debt," Nancy said. "Free coffee for life? Or something a little more? If you aren't already giving him more than that."

Moira blushed a bit and threw a napkin at her mother.

"What's that?" Moira pointed to the model I'd set on the table.

"It's G.T.'s model of the Town Hall, with the clock tower restored."

"I still can't believe you own the Town Hall now," Moira said.

"I'm relieved I found the deed. Caroline and I talked it over. Since it was in the shop and was in a clock, we are considering it part of the shop itself. So, officially, I own it, but I am going to deed it back to the town with some conditions that G.T. would have wanted. Kristen is working on the details now. The envelope must have been in a pile of documents that G.T. hadn't gone through yet. Grover knew that G.T. would make the connection about John Harrison. Eventually. And that no one else would."

"Grover and Harriet Winter were wonderful people. How could they have raised such a monster?" Caroline said.

I shook my head. "I don't know. Aggie had everyone fooled. She had herself convinced that she lived in a world where getting rid of obstacles that stood in her way was her right. That included her own father, her husband, Jonah. And G.T. It's just so awful."

"How is Jonah?"

"He's getting better," Caroline said. "It will take a while, but they think he'll make a full recovery. At least physically. Mentally, it may take him a while longer. He's going to stay with his sister Delia while he gets better."

"Ruth, what's under the sheet?" Moira asked, pointing to the large wall piece I'd installed that morning on one of the walls in the barn. "Another model?"

"All in good time. Now get something to eat. Nancy, we could feed the entire town with this spread."

"You don't have to offer me Nancy's lasagna twice," Ben Clover said from the doorway, where he was leaning. It was a good lean. "I think they serve it at the pearly gates. Aunt Flo, do you know everyone here?"

"Do I know everyone?" Flo said, joining him. "Of course I do. Or at least I'm going to soon enough. Nancy, it's great to see you!"

The two women hugged and walked to the side of the barn, pouring themselves glasses of wine. Caroline joined them and soon the three of them were laughing.

Pat Reed came in from the storage room, where he'd been moving more inventory around.

"Everything's settled in," he said to me. "Including Bezel."

"Where is she?"

"I told her she needed to lay low since Caroline is here, so she's settled into the guest room here at the barn. She's fine. There's a nice chair in there, and I gave her some extra food."

"You are going to spoil her. And me," I said, putting my

hand on his arm. Pat had been tireless these past few days. I couldn't have even thought about working on the Cog & Sprocket without him, and was grateful that I didn't have to.

"I'm glad you're letting me spoil you, a little bit. You need to take care of yourself." He looked around the barn, now full of crates and clocks. It didn't feel nearly as cramped as the Cog & Sprocket. "It was a good idea, moving things out here while the shop is getting worked on."

"You and Ben didn't have to do it today," I said.

"Sure we did. We're on a deadline. Need to get some of these clocks sold if we're going to stay in business. Am I right?"

"We're going to have to get a lot of the clocks sold. But not today. Grab yourself a glass of wine," I said.

Pat walked over and gave Flo a hug, then he took the glass his wife offered him.

Ben walked over. "Where's Blue?" I asked.

"Back in the guest room, keeping Bezel company. She pretends to hate Blue, but it's all a façade."

I laughed, and just then Mac and Ada Clark walked through the door, carrying two brimming Corner Market bags. Beckett Green followed behind, carrying a covered tray.

"Thank you for the invitation," he said to me. "I know that Caroline is fond of figs, so I brought some over."

"She's right over there, talking to Flo." Beckett walked over, balancing his tray so that he could meet Flo.

I walked over to the Clarks and shook their hands.

"Thank you so much for coming out here," I said.

"Thank you for inviting us," Mac said, and I could see he meant it. "We really appreciate it."

"Listen, our families have had some misunderstandings

over the years, but they don't make sense anymore. I've heard such great things about the way you've been running the Corner Market and the way you treat local vendors."

"We've been trying. I know now that Thom was trying to protect what we were trying to do, and to be. I'm so sorry that the last words we had were cross ones," Mac said, looking down and adjusting his grip on his bag.

"We can't change the past, but we also can't let it predict the future. How about if we all start again, as of today?"

"Sounds wonderful," Ada said. "I hope you don't mind, but we brought over some wine, chocolate, and local cheeses."

"I don't mind at all. Let's pull out another card table. They're over there, by the bathroom. Ben, can you help with that?"

"For wine and chocolate? You bet!" he said. He winked at me and went to work setting up the new table.

"Ruthie, you remind me of your grandmother," Aunt Flo said, coming up behind me and giving me a side squeeze that was only a little painful. "Just set up another card table. Being a gracious host."

"Aunt Flo, that's the nicest thing you could ever say to me. I'm so glad you're back."

"Ben doesn't really need me, but he pretends he does. And after the first few months of traveling, I got bored. I'm back, but only a couple of days a week."

"And, coincidentally, those two days are booked solid with appointments," said Ben as he put his arm around his aunt's shoulders and kissed her on top of her head.

"We'll get this business turned around. You just need to learn how to gossip, nephew."

Chief Paisley came in, and everyone stopped talking. He looked handsome out of uniform. Still formal, with creased chinos and a tucked-in blue checkered shirt. His jean jacket was the only thing that looked fairly worn, and it tipped him into handsome territory.

"Here's my hero," I said, only half joking. "Without his quick thinking, I literally would not be here."

I tried to laugh it off, but I knew it was true. I walked up and gave him a big hug and a peck on the cheek.

"Just doing my job, ma'am," he said, standing up even straighter, if that was possible.

"Thank you for that," Caroline said. "Though I still don't know what would have made you go out to the Winters'."

"Thom had shared his concerns about the Chairman's death with me, but I didn't have enough evidence to get the body exhumed. And to be honest, I wasn't sure that Thom wasn't grasping at straws, trying to explain his friend's death."

"Grover's death did change Thom," Caroline said. "We all thought he was making crazy decisions. But now we all know that he was right."

"We found Thom's notebook at the Winters' house. Aggie had taken that, and a box of clocks Thom was bringing back to the house, on the night he died. I read over the notebook," the chief said. "I'll get it back to you both as soon as I can. He lays out his concerns, but he really thought that Delia was responsible. I just wish he'd talked it through with me. Parts of his notebook are direct letters to Grover. He really missed his old friend."

"Okay, but that still doesn't explain why you went looking for Ruth."

"I knew she wanted to honor Thom, and getting the deed settled was part of that. I was holding off talking to Kristen until she got there, and when she was late, I went by the

Sleeping Latte, fully expecting to see Ruth sitting at the counter or behind it, helping out. But Ben told me she stopped by the Winters' and was on her way. It didn't sit right that she wasn't there."

"Even though I'm late for everything?" I asked.

"I didn't think you'd be late for our meeting. Plus, I started to wonder if the Winters' heirs would be happy about the deed being found, or if the town taking it over would benefit them in some way. As I said, it just didn't sit right, so I thought I should make sure everything was all right. I drove up and heard her car alarm blasting. I looked through the front window. Well, the rest you know."

"Do they teach you how to throw lawn ornaments in the police academy?" I asked, poking him in the ribs.

"If I'd taken a shot, I might have hit you or Jonah. It was a calculated risk," he said, half smiling.

"That paid off. Thank you, Chief."

"Call me Jeff. And you're welcome, Ruth."

"Well, Ruth, I think everyone's here now," Caroline said, looking around.

I walked over and stood next to the Town Hall model and cleared my throat.

"Thank you all for coming this afternoon. I feel like this is a meeting of the Orchard historical district," I said. Everyone laughed. "I wanted to let you all know that I'm going back to Boston tomorrow morning." The long faces got to me, and I couldn't hold back my smile. "I need to go by the museum and thank them for finding money to rehire me, but I need to turn them down.

"Pat, Caroline, and I talked it over last night. The shop is going to be closed for a few more weeks. Pat's going to oversee some renovations in the shop. Upstairs will take a little more work, but he tells me it won't take too long. He did a wonderful job for Caroline at the cottage, and I need the apartment to be modernized if I am going to live there. Plus there are a few other changes we want to make to the shop, opening it up a little more. We'll have a bit more of a showroom, displaying some of the clocks on sale and some of my own work."

With that, I took the sheet off the piece that Pat had helped me install last night on the wall of the barn. It was a working clock, six feet wide and three feet tall. Oversized cogs and gears were made of different types of metal. I'd soldered some frames onto the cogs. They stood out from the clock about six inches. Each frame contained a small art piece I'd created, and they moved with the clock. A replica of the cottage. A clock tower. An apple. Last night I'd added a large bezel with a gray cat face peering through the lens. Toward the center of the piece there were three words made of sculpted metal. They spelled out COG & SPROCKET and lined up every hour. If I had been able to orchestrate the moment better, we all would have seen it, but for now, I just needed to explain it.

"I call it the Cog & Sprocket. I designed it in memory of this place, of Orchard, and in honor of my grandparents. I finished it last year, during one of the most difficult times of my life. Even though I never got to say good-bye to G.T., I felt as if he was with me while I built this. And now I am so pleased that I can hang it where it belongs. Here, in Orchard."

"To the Cog & Sprocket and to Ruth Clagan." Ben raised his glass. "Welcome home."

M2G0610